# RETURN TO
# TWO TOWN

William D. Cornwell III

This book is dedicated to John Bellman, who died from Covid in December of 2021. He was my best and greatest friend, and one of the keenest literary minds I'd ever met. I miss him dearly.

# RETURN TO
# TWO TOWN

ISBN-13: 979-8-9882896-0-9

Cover design by: Design by Rosco
Printed in the United States of America

# Chapter One

Missy hated marshmallows, but she was glad to see them on the table.

It always started with food when she saw Dr. Chadwick. It didn't used to be this way. It used to be that an army of orderlies was sent to fetch Missy from her cell. They used to grab her by the arms and drag her, screaming and cursing, down the hall to the interview room. Nowadays, it was a much calmer affair. Now she'd sit down, see the food, and brace herself for unreality.

Missy never noticed when the doctor entered. Even if she heard the door, even if the doctor was right in front of her, it wouldn't feel like Dr. Chadwick was there. It was like her whole person was an image on a screen: flat and artificial.

Then the food or drink she brought would hit the table, and Missy would know she was real, she was there. Today it was marshmallows. At least it wasn't tea. Tea always heralded the worst things, especially with a little pile of pills that came with it. Missy hated those most of all. She knew she'd end up taking them by the end of the session, whether she wanted to or not.

Dr. Chadwick would make her.

Missy twitched in the doctor's presence. It wasn't because of the large scar that ran along the side of the doctor's face, one that cut a jagged line between silvery blonde hair and empty skin. It also wasn't the piercing blue eyes, and it wasn't because this woman made every decision about Missy's life inside the institute.

No, what truly scared her was that she couldn't *read*

the good doctor.

Whatever had given Dr. Chadwick that scar had perhaps changed the architecture of her nervous system, changed it enough that Missy couldn't pry it open. She couldn't feel the thoughts. She couldn't dig through memories or ferret out deceptions. She couldn't wrap the little mind around her own and push and pull on it until it surrendered to her will.

In a world of open books, Dr. Marie Chadwick wasn't even a book. She was an empty gap in the shelf.

Each week Missy sat across from the doctor, in a cold metal chair, before a cold metal table covered in the scratches and dents of their shared history. She had to look into a face that seemed like it was just an image with no substance, all while fluorescent lighting flickered on and off above her in a pattern she could never predict.

Together with the marshmallows, sitting on the table between them, packaged in bright pink plastic.

The relationship between them had evolved over the last six years. To the doctor's credit, she had eventually realized the effect she had on her patient and made adjustments to compensate. Now it was expected of her to bring different items, each one signaling what they were going to talk about. It gave Missy a guidepost in the sudden, mindless dark.

So at least it wasn't tea. Tea was the worst.

The last few times she'd gotten bad news it was only tea. She'd managed to make it through, but some days she missed the pills. She wanted to know where they'd gone.

If she could just read the damn doctor then she'd know everything.

Still, there was something to be said about having actual conversations. It was a novelty, a new experience: to talk to someone and not feel all the initial responses bubble up from within. It was a trial to listen to the words and have to guess if they were true or not. Every other person around her was a known entity. They were boring, the same fears, the same worries, the same awe for what she was.

Although the fear wasn't as strong as it used to be. Now the orderlies came to her for advice. She'd laughed at the first one to ask, but on days like today she'd hold little briefings for the staff. After all, she was the only one who could tell them what the catatonic and the irrational were thinking and feeling. Having people listen to her made her feel something different.

It wasn't like the roaring, towering pride she'd had when she'd enslaved the minds of a crowd, bending them and pushing them to obey, but it was... something.

"Good evening, Missy."

She jumped. She always did. The words stuck in her senses, seeming to come from nowhere.

"Hi." She managed.

She watched as Dr. Chadwick leaned back and crossed her legs at the ankles with perfect poise. The doctor was all elegance and class. She was tall, with classically refined features. She had the high cheekbones, and bright blue eyes, as well as the blonde hair that was unerringly straight and shimmered in the dim fluorescent lighting.

Missy, in comparison, was short and prone to slouching. She'd never grown much beyond five feet. She was thin, maybe from anxiety, maybe from genetics, but probably from having her diet strictly controlled since her incarceration. Her hair was dark and currently cut a bit longer than she was used to. It was almost below her ears now and that was both comforting and slightly annoying.     They used to shave her head. They'd done so for so long that she'd grown used to the simplicity of it. She was constantly debating with herself if she should keep it long or go back to how it was.

Debates with the voices inside her head were always a long and drawn-out affair. So while they had been fighting, her hair just kept growing.

She did feel more like a woman. That was nice.

She had something to run her fingers through, which became a strangely nostalgic feeling. The last time she'd had long hair…

"They're strawberry flavored." Dr. Chadwick smiled and slid the bag across the table. "You might like them."

Missy didn't jump this time. She forced a smile, hesitating only a moment before using her fingers to tear into the soft plastic.

"Thanks." She locked eyes with the doctor, then turned her attention back to the bag. "Something good?"

"That depends on you."

Missy's hands stopped. She felt the Others stir inside. They didn't like mysteries, and when they didn't like something, Missy wouldn't like it either. She kept them in check by feeling safe and in control. The more helpless she felt, the stronger they got.

"You need to explain." It wasn't a threat. She didn't threaten people. That wasn't her, that was something the Others did.

Some of the Others whispered that it'd been her, too.

That was a long time ago. She was better now.

The whispers questioned that as well.

"Your release has been approved." Dr. Chadwick's words silenced all.

Missy's fingers fumbled, spilling marshmallows onto the table.

"The third application for review was… accepted." The doctor's tone pretended to be light and happy, but she wasn't very good at it. Even Missy could tell she was faking, "The board examined your behavior and demanded a ninety-day trial without medication. It's been twice that long."

Missy tried to count the weeks and failed. Days blended together inside. She only knew a week had passed when they had peanut butter pudding for lunch. That was on Sundays.

"The board is…" Dr. Chadwick turned and regarded

the padded wall beside her for a moment. "...satisfied."

Missy's heart pounded against flesh and bone. She had no read on the doctor. She had no idea what words were coming next. She wanted to know as much as she didn't. The sound of blood pumping in her ears grew louder, but she didn't know if it was from fear, anticipation, or if it was just a heralding of the Others about to rise.

The doctor continued. "They unanimously gave the go-ahead, if you were curious. Now it's all just paperwork to handle. By the end of next week, you may well be on the outside again."

Missy felt her hands shake as the Others stirred. Their excitement rose like bubbles in a boiling cauldron. They thought she would let them escape, that she'd let them take over. She wouldn't. She was strong enough now. Dr. Chadwick said so.

Yet that didn't stop them from making it seem impossible. She opened her mouth and said, "I... I'm not sure I'm ready."

The doctor smiled, an empty smile. There was nothing behind it. Empty, it was *empty!* Still, the smile was there and a hand was there and it reached across the table. The arm slid past dents and scratches that Missy herself had put there. Her, and the Others, they'd fought tooth and nail at first. They were unstoppable. They could not be restrained, and yet this place had done just that. The Others recoiled at the taste of their defeat.

Then the hand wrapped around Missy's. It was warm, soft, and unexpected. The Others quieted. Now it was just her in her mind. She looked into the hard blue eyes of the doctor and she felt that maybe...

"You'll be okay." Dr. Chadwick put on an empty smile.

Missy pulled her hand back. She still had pride, after all. She'd kept that.

"Just like that?" She asked.

"Well... no. There's paperwork and there's, well, we'll call it an 'outstanding issue.'"

Missy raised her eyebrows. She'd been getting better at practicing expressions. She'd never had to do that with other people. Apparently, it was how people functioned, yet it all seemed so imprecise to her.

"When you were..." Dr. Chadwick hesitated.

"Miss Mania." Missy could say it now. The memories of the monster she'd been, the amplifier she wore like a crown, the madness of the Others, she knew they were her. Still, she refused to think about the things she'd done. That was still too much.

"Yes, when you were... *her*, you 'erased' more than just memories. There's still some confusion over what was real and what was fabricated. One of those situations revolves around the subject of who you really are. It seems you've made several false identities."

Missy nodded along. She didn't remember it herself, but as Dr. Chadwick spoke, she felt the memories the Others had. She could feel them share the sights, sounds, and thoughts. They'd turned the mind of a postal worker once and forced the man to make her into someone else, at least on paper. There were other memories like it. Missy knew about them, but they lay beyond her control. They belonged to the Others, not to her.

She wished she had something better than marshmallows to wash the taste away.

"So, according to all official records, you could possibly be one of three people."

Dr. Chadwick pushed her chair back and opened her accordion-like case that she'd set on the table. She pulled out three manilla folders, placed them down, and pushed them over.

Missy set the bag aside and examined the files.

"Marjorie Jalen, Melissa De Mar, and Marie Menoit." The doctor read the names on the labels. "They're all a little different, so it's up to you—"

"Not Marie."

Dr. Chadwick raised her eyebrow.

"Can't take your name." Missy explained. "It's yours."

The doctor remained quiet as Missy read through the other two. They were similar. Both Marjorie and Melissa had been born to rough families. Both had younger sisters. Both had watched their siblings die under tragic circumstances.

Neither of them were true. Missy knew that much. The Other's memories from before were unstable, blurry, often inconsistent, but she knew enough to see that both of these people had been fabricated by the Others. The fact that they said she had a sibling told her that.

Still, whoever she'd been, she didn't want to be her anymore. Whoever had been in control back then had turned her into a monster. She could be better than that. Missy *would* be better.

"Melissa." She pushed the folders back.

"So that's your name?"

"It will be." Missy's eyes met those of the doctor.

Dr. Chadwick nodded and put the files away. "I'll let them know. Once you are, well, 'Melissa', then it shouldn't take too long. There is... one last thing."

Missy grabbed the bag again. Cheap plastic crinkled.

"You'll get your things back." The doctor's voice was low. She was trying to be calming, it never really helped, but she tried. "Everything you came in with: all of it."

Plastic crumpled louder.

The amplifier.

"If you want us to keep it, I can—"

"No." Missy shook her head.

No matter how much she hated it, the psionic amplifier was hers. It would be a reminder of all the things she'd done, like an alcoholic who kept a bottle in his desk to keep himself sober, something that they have such a connection to that even looking at it floods them with all the pain and anguish it caused.

It would be her little talisman of regret.

"I'll take it all."

Dr. Chadwick watched for a long moment. She looked tired. Her face casted with wrinkles and dark, swollen bags below her eyes. Missy knew she had made things hard on everyone, *especially* on the doctor. It was one of the reasons Missy tried so much to be better now. She tried her best to make up for all the things she'd done before.

"Alright." Dr. Chadwick stood up with her case. "That's all I need for now. Congratulations, Missy."

"Uh… Thanks." Missy looked down at the bag in her hands. Her fingers had torn holes into the plastic. The smell of sugar and fruit flavoring surrounded them. "Doctor…"

Dr. Chadwick turned.

"I can still come back, right?" She forced her hands to relax, "When… after I'm out and everything?"

"Of course."

Missy let out a long breath and stood up. "Okay."

She made sure to pick up all the marshmallows that had fallen and pack them away. She stood there, holding the plastic bag, hands strategically positioned over the holes. The air rushed out against her skin as she squeezed. She let her mind stretch out a bit, felt the complicated neural activity of orderlies and patients and janitors and secretaries. She felt all their lists and worries. She let it all mix around within her. All this life in this tiny place… and there was so much more outside.

"It'll be fine." Dr. Chadwick said as she opened the door. "You've come quite far, after all."

Missy nodded. She hoped it was far enough.

\*\*\*

The institute was quieter than most. She'd read that in the minds around her. Most of the people who worked here came as veterans from larger, busier facilities, lured here with promises of better pay and fewer patients.

The only downside was that they had to work in the place that held her: Miss Mania, the psychic supervillain.

The buried fear that those smiling faces had locked down deep inside irritated her. It was like a little kernel of corn stuck between the teeth of their thoughts. Every action they took, every task they planned, it always moved around fear.

They knew she was watching them, that she could peek into their heads like they would look into a glass bottle. All of them suppressed their impulses because of it. Occasionally, they would get an orderly who didn't care about that, or anything else. The kind of person who tortured the patients that couldn't complain about it. There had even been one who had covered up a rape. He didn't see it as wrong so he had no impulse to conceal it.

Missy's tongue still soured when she remembered that particular mind.

He'd fantasized about her. They'd been strange things to experience. Miss Mania would have just destroyed him, taken all the little parts of him that'd turned him into a monster and replaced them with memories of agony and confusion. She would have turned the man into a raving, tortured lunatic.

Missy, however, told Dr. Chadwick.

Then the man was gone.

He'd been escorted out of her range and none of the other staff knew what happened. Missy assumed that he'd been brought before the proper authorities, but it was unnerving how they hadn't let any information filter back, even the guards that took him away knew nothing.

It could have been because it was something that no one cared about. Dr. Chadwick was the only one who knew the whole truth, and she was the one person Missy couldn't read.

The end result of it all was that the institute kept its very small complement of patients, and its very large and nervous staff. Missy was glad for the first, and annoyed by the second. She used to enjoy being feared, but now it was just something she itched to remove.

The other patients were all special cases. Some were powered; some were just placed here because they needed extra care.

One that was a bit of both was Leaning Lena.

Lena had broken her spine the same day she discovered she had the ability to fly. She'd been thirteen, feeling top-of-the-world, flexing her power for the first time. She was spending her birthday speeding through the air, when she misjudged her height and garroted herself on a power line. Her vertebrae shattered upon impact. The only reason she'd survived was because a hole had been ripped in her neck, allowing her to breathe despite the blood and bone that should have choked her to death.

It was a sad life to read. Even when Missy had been under the control of the Others she hadn't messed with Lena. Lena was neither a threat nor entertainment. She was just a middle-aged woman with a crooked body sitting near the window and leaning against the little headrest on her wheelchair.

She was the one person who was never afraid.

Missy plopped down beside her and pulled a strawberry marshmallow from the bag, tore the candy apart, and pushed one half into Lena's mouth. She felt the appreciation through the privacy of her mind.

Lena couldn't speak, or move, or even control her bowels, but she could talk to Missy. Missy could look inside.

*You look like you're in shock.*

"Yeah." Missy said aloud as she rolled the marshmallow half around between her fingers. Lena's mind gathered information and connected it. She may have been an invalid, but her mind worked just fine. Years without distraction had sharpened her observational and analytical skills to the point where they approached the level of a minor superpower.

Missy felt the memories Lena had. She felt them collect details like the fact that Missy had not been taking her medication. She felt the itemized list of things seen, said, and remembered about her. Lena sifted through it all with lightning efficiency.

*Could it be...*

Missy felt the idea solidify. She nodded her head and felt the shock and sorrow strike the former flying girl.

*They're releasing you.* The thought was a statement. Lena didn't doubt herself too often. *I never thought I'd see it. You must have considerably impressed the good doctor.*

"I guess." Missy mumbled as she chewed. "I don't know if I'm... ready."

*The Others?*

Lena was the only one who knew about the Others. Missy never described them in detail to Dr. Chadwick. The doctor was still a walking, talking person, one that Missy couldn't read, after all. There was a limit to how much she would reveal to someone outside her control. Lena, on the other hand, had never been a threat.

The woman had been ready to die for decades. She held no ill will toward anyone. She had no secret plans. She didn't lust after men or plot revenge or fantasize about violence.

Lena just sat and watched the world, trying to understand how it all worked.

Missy had offered to show her what it was like to know everyone's mind, but Lena had declined, saying that it took all the fun out of guessing.

They finished their marshmallows and Lena called for another.

*Where will you go?*

The question rattled through Missy as she supplied them both with more treats. She didn't know. She never thought that far into the future. In fact, once Missy had established herself as the one in control of her body, she'd only ever hoped to be the one that woke up in it each morning. The best future for her had been about the location of her mind, not her body.

Her greatest fear was to wake up one morning and find herself locked away and one of the Others in control. To find that she could only watch while one of them destroyed everything she'd worked to build. The fear of being locked away like Lena, only worse. Lena never had to worry about her body rising up and ripping apart the minds around her, leaving them dead or insane.

"I…" Missy spoke just to pull her thoughts away from her fears. "I don't know."

*Do you have anyone you care about? Anyone you wish to see?*

She didn't. Her family had been some of the first people Miss Mania had 'disposed of.' She held no remorse over that particular act. The Others remembered those minds; they saw the sickness inside all of them. Removing them from the world was the one bit of good they could all claim, even now.

She'd never made a friend before.

Friends were people who bonded over the same likes and activities. There was no one else who liked diving into the minds of others and forcing them into enslavement. Miss Mania had always been alone, from the first day she'd found she could open the little locked boxes behind people's eyes. Missy was even lonelier.

"No, I don't have anyone."

Missy waited while Lena gathered information once more, synthesizing a simulacrum of what it must be like to be psychic, then recoiling from the extrapolated answers.

*Is there a place you'd like to go?*

Missy shook her head.

*Then... What do you want?*

The curiosity and sadness in those words tasted sour to Missy's mental senses. She could feel all the things Lena would miss about her. It was strangely personal to find that anyone cared at all. She was so accustomed to reading fear, that this sorrow, the sorrow that Lena was losing her only friend, hurt even more.

A few seconds later Missy found herself crying. She'd never cried before. One of the Others always took over before it got that far. They screamed at her now. They wanted to rise up, and lash out, to do all the things that would stop the sadness.

She found that she didn't want it to stop. She wanted to sit there. She wanted to cry.

Eventually the Others settled, and Missy fought against her body as her chest convulsed and her eyes blurred. This was all so new to her. These kinds of feelings were usually washed away under anger or pain.

It was worse when Lena cried with her. There was a resonance of sorrow between them. Lena cried because she was losing the only person in the world she could talk to, and Missy cried because no one had ever been sad to see her leave.

It was only after someone noticed them that she made an effort to dry her tears. It was one thing to collapse in front of Lena, it was quite another to unravel like that in front of anyone else.

In that moment, as she wiped the tears from her eyes and straightened her back in a way that Lena could only envy, she knew what she wanted.

"I want to find him." She said it before the thought had even fully formed.

*Find who?*

"The one that caught me." Missy's thoughts jumbled. "The hero.... Psyconic. That was his name. I want... to thank him."

*For not killing you?*

Missy shook her head. That wasn't it at all. She wished she'd died back then. In a lot of ways that would have made it easier. It was harder with all the guilt she'd had to live with, all the lives she had taken or destroyed. She carried debts so black and heavy she worried they would drag her back to madness every time she closed her eyes.

"For stopping me." Missy paused and found the words weren't quite correct. "For stopping *us*."

*Oh… I see.*

Again, Missy watched as Lena's mind collected and organized, restructuring everything she knew about Missy around this new set of data.

She would miss that.

*He may not be happy to see you.*

"I know."

*It's been six years. He'll be quite hard to find.*

Missy nodded.

*Are you thinking of using your powers?*

The words made Missy think about the amplifier. She would get it back. Thirty minutes ago, she had promised herself she would never use it again, then with just a few words Lena had placed a seed of doubt in her mind.

"I don't know." Her hands tightened on the plastic of the marshmallow bag, her fingers pressing into the holes they had made before. "I might."

There was another swirl of emotion and thought inside Lena's mind. Only this time, it was too quick to track, too messy. The information flowed together in a way that was both expedient and disorganized. It was all so fast that Missy couldn't track it. She'd seen this happen before. People could be overwhelmed by their own minds, stripping them of their ability to even track their own thoughts.

She watched in tense fascination, wondering what was going on that prompted such a storm of activity inside her friend's head.

*I hope you find him, Missy.*

The surprise of how earnest the thought was put a few more holes in the plastic bag.

*I really do.*

\*\*\*

# Chapter Two

The next few days rolled by in a fog of anxiety and discomfort.

This was the first time in Missy's life she felt anyone would miss her. She desperately wanted to sit down with Lena and feel through her mind, yet at the same time she couldn't bring herself to do it. Every time she thought about it, she found she couldn't even reach out to try.

She was used to ignorance, fear, worry, hate, revulsion, or even concerned caution.

Lena hadn't felt any of those things, and Missy didn't know how to handle it. She just wasn't equipped with the tools needed to navigate these new waters.

So instead, she avoided her. She knew where Lena was at all times by reading the orderlies and knowing when they moved her. She wouldn't touch Lena's mind. She was afraid of seeing things she couldn't handle, or something worse.

What if Lena hated her now because she had abandoned her? Lena was anything but stupid. On one hand, Missy would feel more comfortable with the hate, but on the other hand it would hurt so much more to read that from her friend. A friend. She'd made a friend. She didn't know how to handle being a friend.

Looming above it all was the prospect of leaving.

Missy had absolutely no idea how to handle that.

All of that wasn't the worst of it. The worst of it all was the fact that ever since the conversation with Lena, the Others had been silent.

The Others were always there. They were like hearing

a crowd in the background of a movie. The constant rumbling and talking filled out a scene, but for Missy they filled out her mind.

Now they were silent.

Missy curled herself into a ball on her bed. The bag of marshmallows was now just a pile of plastic scraps on the floor. Tearing the material apart had helped for a while but now she didn't have it any more. The silence taunted her.

With a grunt, she flopped over, feeling the heat and dampness of the sweat on her back.

She did what she always did when she couldn't live with her own mind.

She reached out.

After a minute of scanning the thoughts around her she found a young man ordering flowers in the break room. He was new here, so Missy hadn't learned everything about him yet. She knew he wasn't a transfer, which was unusual. He was, instead, a gifted student who had heard about the institute and became fascinated with it.

Missy read about herself in the young man's mind, he looked at her so clinically and from such a distance. She couldn't blame him for that. It's not like she had ever talked to him. She never really needed to talk with anyone, not really. She only asked people to do things for her now because Dr. Chadwick had once demonstrated why it was preferred over Missy's more *direct* commands.

Missy rolled over, back into the patch of cold sweat as she remembered that particular day in all-to-vivid detail.

\*\*\*

She'd only been at the institute for a year at that point. The staff was smaller and every single one of them feared her. The orderlies were convicts, the mentally diminished, or both.

She controlled them as she wanted to. She made them dance, or fight, or scream; whatever whims she fancied at the time.

And Dr. Chadwick was the only one who stopped her.

The doctor would storm in, her face a scowl of concentration and fury. She'd push a button and Missy's mind would be filled with electrical chaos. Then the orderlies would restrain her and she'd end up in a chemical fog for some unknown amount of time.

Even that hadn't stopped her. She would wake up, scan minds, get bored and start it all again. She'd take a body and tell it to go find a knife and bring it to her. She'd take a hostage or attempt to remove her restraining collar, and each time Dr. Chadwick was watching.

Each time it was Dr. Chadwick that stopped her.

A year of this had done something to the psychiatrist. Missy could see it now, in hindsight. She'd pushed and pushed and eventually she'd pushed too far.

She'd been sedated after another of her little tantrums where she'd made the entire staff stand on their heads until they passed out.

But when she woke up, she'd found she wasn't in her bed. Instead, her arms and legs were strapped and bound to metal. It smelled of oil and ozone. She'd scanned the entire institute and found not a single mind within her grasp.      For a moment she thought she was alone.

For a moment she thought they had strapped her to a bomb. They were done with her. This was her end.

She lashed out, reaching, stretching, trying to find any mind she could take, any tool she could use.

She found nothing.

Still, she fought. She struggled in mind and body. The Others took turns, switching in and out of her mind. Each of them screaming or shouting obscenities. Each one of them failed to find an escape.

"Are you quite finished?"

The words caused her entire body to convulse. Missy remembered that. She'd thought she was alone. When the words reached her ears she twisted and turned, muscles tightening in her gut.

She'd tried to turn around, to look at the doctor.

"LET. ME. GO." She remembered the rage she'd put into each syllable as she scratched her skin against the metal frame.

Then her body moved, but it wasn't the way it should have. Her legs lifted her and took a step. Missy couldn't speak. The pure shock of finding her body moving against her will paralyzed her.

Yet she kept moving.

She was turned around to face the doctor standing behind a table. There was a remote control in Dr. Chadwick's hands, one of the video-game-type, but bulkier. It had dials and levers and loose wires hanging out of it. The table between them was covered in different objects. Missy hungered for them. There were scissors and a scalpel. There was electrical tape and tools and a large binder that seemed to be full of instructions.

"This is what it feels like, Mania." Dr. Chadwick hadn't gloated about it. She said the words plainly and firmly.

Missy's hand was pulled forward. She fought against it, but her muscles were weak and ineffectual from years of ordering others to do everything for her.

Her hand moved on its own. It reached forward to the table and grabbed the scalpel. Missy shuddered as her own fingers were forced by clamps of metal to grab the surgical knife. She screamed and shook as the knife rose up and grew closer and closer until it was all she could see.

It stopped there.

The scalpel was poised in the just the right spot to cut through and remove her left eye.

Missy knew this because she'd done it to one of the

orderlies two weeks earlier with a kitchen knife. She'd laughed as his mind had crumbled under her assault.

Now it was happening to her. This was revenge.

The scalpel stabbed forward and Missy screamed. She lost control of her bladder. She felt the warmth cover her legs. There was pure, unmitigated terror in that moment. She shrank back but the metal frame kept her from going anywhere. She was trapped, no longer in control. Even the Others abandoned her. They left her alone there, alone with the fear and the pain.

And she was going to die.

Missy didn't know how long she stood there, squeezing her eyes shut and fighting her own body. It was probably only a handful of seconds, but it had felt like years.

Then she'd opened her eyes.

The scalpel had stopped half an inch from cutting. It was so close she couldn't focus on it. Missy's breath was ragged and low. She realized she had pissed herself. She was confronted with the memories of when she had laughed at others who had done the same thing.

"This is what you've done." Dr. Chadwick dropped the words like a weight. "Do you understand now?"

She pushed a button on the remote and the scalpel jumped from being in front of her left eye to her right.

Missy screamed and fought. She threw her body against the bolts and clamps that kept it still. She earned bruises and shots of pain but she found no retreat. She found no control.

Dr. Chadwick had control.

Missy turned her eyes to the doctor, looking at the nasty scar on the side of her head that kept her from being normal, that kept her from being controlled. Missy had never hated that scar as much as she did right then.

"Please…" She found herself saying.

"Did they say please, Mania?"

Missy stopped struggling. They had. So many of them had. She'd heard the panicked wailing of thousands of minds.

In that moment, that spare moment, she realized that she was them. All the things she'd done Dr. Chadwick could do to her.

"No. No, no, no…." Missy heard herself say.

"I think they did." Dr. Chadwick moved a dial and Missy's fingers pressed even harder into the scalpel handle. Her bones ground against each other, almost breaking. "I think they all did."

Missy almost said it again, to beg with 'Please' and 'Mercy.' Once more she realized it would only hurt her position. This was her. She was looking at Dr. Chadwick but she was seeing herself. Only… Miss Mania would have laughed. She'd laughed as the knife cut into the orderly's skull. She'd laughed at his screams.

She'd gone too far. Oh, how she had gone too far. This was the end.

Her muscles relaxed. She'd expected this ever since she was captured, ever since she met the doctor, ever since they found a way to keep her confined. It was finally over. Her long, chaotic existence was at an end.

Missy closed her eyes.

Then the doctor pushed a button and her hand let go. The scalpel clattered away. Missy's eyes snapped back open as she was forced to take a step forward.

Was she being made to walk over the knife? She didn't know. She couldn't move her head to see. She was completely at the doctor's mercy.

Her body leaned over the table, placing palms flat on the surface as her weight shifted onto them. She moved forward against all of her control. She was moved right up to the doctor's face. She was forced to look into those bloodshot, tired eyes, and chapped lips. She was forced to see every twisted bit of flesh in the massive scar that ran above the doctor's ear.

"Is this fun for you?" Dr. Chadwick whispered. "I can't imagine how. It all seems so… cruel."

Missy tried to look away, listening to the panic and fear of the Others as, for the first time, they refused to take over. They'd abandoned her. They left her to deal with this torture. The Others only wanted to be part of the fun, not this.

"Miss Mania, are you ready for this to end?"

She wasn't. She wasn't ready. She didn't want it to end, but she'd known it was coming. It was the only answer, after all.

Then, a needle stabbed her in the neck.

\*\*\*

That was five years ago.

Five years and she could still feel the metal bindings on her skin. They squeezed her now, making it hard to breathe.

Missy sat up and stripped herself of her sweat-soaked top. The cold clung to her shoulders and back as she sat there.

She felt exposed and vulnerable, but even the lightest touch of the cloth on her skin felt like those bindings. It felt too close. It felt like the clothes were controlling her, that they'd stop her from moving, that they'd come to life and move her around.

All the things she'd done.

The scalpel before her eye.

The screams of the orderly as she'd laughed.

It all bled together in her mind. The days after had been the only time she'd ever had where the Others had been silent. She hadn't missed them then, and she didn't miss them now.

It was what would happen when they came back that was making her sweat.

Missy stood in the center of her room, shaking and shivering. Her heart was a peal of thunder in her chest. Her eyes twitched to the corners. She was looking for them: the Others. They would come back. She was sure of it.

She grabbed her head in both hands and opened her mouth to scream.

The doctor might hear.

They might keep her here.

For a moment the possibilities bloomed inside. She was safe here. This was all she'd known for six years. Yes, she could 'relapse.' She could become unstable and they'd be forced to keep her here. She could…. She could just….

She could be like Lena.

The prospect soured. She knew Lena inside and out. She was a woman prepared to die, struggling to find some spark of life after being removed from all that made it worth living. An outside observer of humanity because she had no choice.

Missy could do it.

But then she would never find Psyconic.

She would never tell the hero all the captured thoughts she wanted to say.

Missy forced her arms down. She swallowed the scream and straightened up, sweat burning cold as it trickled down her back.

She opened her door and stepped out into the hall. There were orderlies and others around but she knew where they were, knew where they were going. They were easy to avoid. She cut around and through the corridors and halls, moving out of sight just as a janitor would turn to look in her direction.

After a few minutes of this she was standing in the common room.

Lena was there. Her chair was parked before the largest window in the place. It was dark outside with only a small circle of grass illuminated by some security lamp far above.

Missy stood there, mostly naked, shaking and cold.

She reached out. Her arm shook and her fingers twitched inward and out. She pressed her hand into the short, unkempt hair of her only friend.

She read the mind inside.

*Good evening, Missy.*

She jumped a little as the words hit her.

*I saw you in the reflection on the glass.*

Missy's muscles unknotted, and she let her hand relax on Lena's short-cut hair. It was clean and soft.

*I wasn't sure if I'd see you again.*

"Sorry." Missy found herself saying. "I... I don't know how... how to—"

*I know.*

The swell of emotion and complex matrices of information that Missy read in Lena's mind made her cry once again. Lena had dissected her, cut her behavior and words apart and had, over the past few days, put together a sketch of what she must be feeling.

And gotten it almost exactly right.

She'd only missed the part about what Dr. Chadwick had done to her so long ago.

Yet, all of it was overshadowed by a bigger question in Lena's mind. One which she immediately asked.

*Missy... why in the hell are your tits out?*

So Missy told her.

She stood there, shivering under cold sweat, and gave Lena all the pieces she'd been missing. She talked through the entire night. She spilled everything out to the one person in the world who just might understand.

\*\*\*

# Chapter Three

Missy woke slowly and in stages. Over time, she became aware of the fact that she'd fallen asleep with her head in Lena's lap. This was well proven by the soggy patch of drool that had been deposited in Missy's hair during the night.

And she was still topless.

And they were still in the common room.

She wondered why no one had woken her, or covered her up, or called Dr. Chadwick. Then she remembered who she was to them, she was the monster. You don't wake the sleeping monster, even children know that.

Eleven other people were currently in the common room. Each one was busy pretending they didn't notice the half-naked psychic asleep on the crippled lady's lap.

Missy moved through their minds and in doing so must have somehow betrayed her wakefulness to Lena, for the first thing she read was a message from her friend.

*There's a blanket you're sleeping on. Take it.*

Missy sent her own burst of thankfulness straight into Lena's mind, then chastised herself. She shouldn't do things like that any more.

"Thank you." She whispered as she lifted her head and stole the medical-issue blanket off of Lena's lap. It was small, thin, and itchy... but it was enough.

Missy wrapped herself up, got to her feet and crossed the arena of curiosity with her head held high.

Pride was a funny thing. She spent all night bawling her eyes out like a child, but that was fine because no one had been watching.

This was different.

These were people who would talk about it. They could spread rumors and innuendo and they could ruin any chance she had of leaving. Part of her would be fine with that, but part of her was angry that she'd already put herself through so much over the choice to stay or go.

She'd been contemplating doing something she'd promised Dr. Chadwick she'd never do again when everything changed.

Simon, an orderly with red hair and a long-distance girlfriend that he spoiled, was the first to look at her face. Missy felt him read the red, puffy eyes and her crusty cheeks.

All the thoughts inside of him shifted in an instant.

He wouldn't tell anyone. In fact, he told himself right there, while Missy looked at him, that he was going to ignore her state completely.

He turned away and moved off as if he hadn't seen anything.

Missy stopped in her tracks. She wasn't sure what had just happened. It had been too quick, too complicated, too much tied up with the young man's own memories and feelings.

Then a nurse by the name of Agatha saw her face. The same reaction. A quick reversal, a touch of sadness, then of fierce determination. Agatha wouldn't tell anyone, furthermore, she planned to bring Missy a fresh cup of hot tea once she was settled.

Missy looked at the others around the room and one by one they shared variations of the same reaction. Only one of them was different, a younger girl who did physical rehabilitation. She, instead, made it a point to ask Agatha what she should do.

With that, Missy was left with a mess of unanswered questions.

She was standing there, holding a blanket over her chest, eyes red and swollen from tears, and an entire room of people pretended they didn't see her.

Missy was tempted, just for a moment, to drop the blanket. To really test them and their strange new conviction. She didn't understand it. She wanted to poke it, probe it, pry it open and read the reasoning from their heads.

The Others would have done that, but she wasn't them. So she left.

In fact, she fled back to her room, where she found that her sheets had been laundered and a fresh set of clothes had been put out for her. All of which shouldn't be here. They didn't take the laundry until after breakfast.

Missy wondered if the outside was like this: No schedule, no consistency, people just acting on *impulse* for everything.

Could she handle that just as herself?

She ran a hand over the fresh clothes. She'd been so vulnerable, so embarrassed…. And somehow that had protected her.

None of it made sense.

She dressed slowly, taking her time as she tried to piece it all together. One look at her face had changed them. It had to be the eyes. They saw she'd been crying. They saw she'd been weak. Why did that protect her?

It didn't make sense. Weakness was something to leverage. When it was made known, you latched onto it and used it to push people to do what you wanted. It was what she'd always done, it was what she often saw in other people. So many of them planned and plotted on how to use friends, family, co-workers.

The cold shiver struck her skin and soul as she put the new shirt on.

It was what she'd always done.

Except she'd never done it to Lena or Dr. Chadwick. One because she'd never needed to, the other because it was literally impossible.

Missy dropped down on the fresh sheets and felt her bones and muscles shake as her mind wobbled through the back end of her life. All the Others, they had exploited weakness because it was how they'd been used when they were young. They weren't raised to be people, after all.

Missy wasn't like them anymore.

Missy was the better one.

Dr. Chadwick told her she needed to believe that. While she thought she did, now it was up for question. If she might be mistaken about something so simple for so long then what else was warped because of the Others? Was she closer to them than to actual people?

The Others resurfaced with a roar, screamed a resounding 'Yes' to her question.

Missy whispered a quiet 'No.'

Those people had all ignored her. She wouldn't let that be forgotten. She felt... something. She wasn't sure how to explain it. She felt like she owed something to all of them. She was unsettled by the feeling. What was happening that made people so confusing to her in just the past few days? The world used to make so much sense, and now, now that she was about to leave, now that she felt she was truly making progress...

Now it was all changing around her.

Missy sat on her bed and, for the first time in a long, long time, she sat there alone with her own thoughts.

\*\*\*

The next day Missy woke to find evidence that someone had been in her room.

Sleeping was her only real weakness. When she'd been Miss Mania, she'd taken incredible precautions to protect her body while her mind slept. One time she'd even smuggled herself into a time-locked bank vault just so she could rest without worrying about supers and assassins.

It'd been one of the hardest things to adjust to when she'd first come to the institute. Dr. Chadwick herself had medicated Missy every night to make sure she slept. The fear Missy held that someone would finally end it all while she was deep in the darkness of sleep had been overwhelming.

Yet every morning she woke up. Every night they let her live to rage and scream.

She knew they had access.

She knew they had the keys.

Missy was their prisoner, after all.

Still, it was unsettling this time to know that they had come into her room in the dead of night and been beside her, just inches away while she slept.

All of this should have been secondary to what had been left behind, but for some reason it was the violation of privacy that concerned her more. It was far more concerning than the fact that her Psychic Amplifier was sitting there on the table beside her bed.

She called it hers, but it really wasn't.

The Others shook and offered up the memories of it; memories of Miss Mania prying the fantastic machine off the dying body of a former hero. She couldn't remember his name. He'd been young and brash. He'd thought his mental powers were a match for her. He'd thought the amplifier gave him unstoppable power.

Missy had read the hubris in his mind. She'd learned everything about him in minutes. She hadn't cared about any of it except for the little device he'd found. If the idiot kid hadn't had the amplifier, then she probably would have just avoided him.

The silver circlet he was so proud of was the entire reason Mania forced a dozen strangers to rip him apart.

She shivered at the images the Others showed, the sounds, and the smells. Her hands shook as the feelings were offered up to her. She felt the screaming of those minds as she used them as puppets. She wondered how much she'd hurt them. Did they sleep at night? Did they find some way to deal with the horror of it all?

She curled her hands into fists and squeezed her eyes shut.

That wasn't her. She was just living in the body where it happened.

The Others did that.

She was the power that kept them back, kept it all back.

Missy opened her eyes and forced her hands open. She pushed the terrible hospital blanket off and started her morning routine.

She brushed her teeth in the small sink. She wished she could change clothes, but shower time wasn't until later and she wouldn't get a fresh set until then. Not like yesterday when they'd brought her clothes early. Now they were back on schedule. She crouched on the floor in her sleep-wrinkled clothing instead. She stretched her hands out across the small space between the bed and wall, arched her back and felt her spine pop. She curled her toes against the thin rug and rolled her neck around.

Her muscles ached with relief as she stretched them all one-by-one.

Then she stood. The Others always seemed a touch quieter, her mind always a little sharper, the day a bit brighter after her morning routine.

Only then did she regard the amplifier.

It was a small thing, basically a thin circle casing built from stainless steel with five upstanding prongs. Missy had opened it up once and found the casing protecting some intricate technology that might as well be magic. She never did find out who built it, even the hero who had come after her had been ignorant of the technology's origin.

None of it mattered. What mattered was the fact that it extended the range of her powers almost infinitely. From what she could tell, it multiplied the natural mental ability of the wearer in an exponential fashion. A weak mind might be multiplied to being strong, a strong mind multiplied up to being psychic.

For Missy, though, it made her unstoppable.

She reached out and touched the center of the five prongs. She let her finger press into the casing. She wanted to know that it was real and not some elaborate illusion crafted by the Others.

The cold of the metal told her it was here, the unfolding power in her mind told her it was real.

She was uncertain what to do next.

She needed someone with a different set of skills, someone smarter.

If Missy was to be completely honest with herself, then she had to admit she wasn't well educated. She'd never needed to use her own mind. Tests had always consisted of reading the answers from the minds of other people. Tricks and locks and everything complicated in the world were easily bypassed by finding a brain with the answers.

It had been difficult, at first, for her to realize how ignorant she truly was. Her sessions with Dr. Chadwick had shown her just how much she relied on seeing inside people. Faced with an unreadable, unanswerable problem had been like facing a set of stairs after never using your legs.

The amplifier in her room was a mystery. One she wouldn't act on until she had more information. She scanned the minds of the institute staff and the only thing she'd found was that Dr. Chadwick had come in before sunrise this morning and gone straight to Missy's room.

Missy pulled her hand back from the device and sat down on her bed. She reached out and found Lena's mind. She was sleeping, her brain shut down to the most basic of elements while it repaired and restructured. Missy could feel it all, the subtle lines of neurons firing as they shuffled memories and information back and forth. The sleeping mind worked just as hard as the waking one, just with different tasks to accomplish.

Missy watched it all while she decided what to do next.

The Others would have wrenched Lena out of her sleep immediately. It would be easy. Just pinch a few of the right receptors and the brain comes roaring to life.

Missy wouldn't do that.

Anything the Others urged her to do was usually something she should resist. She had learned this lesson over and over. Lena told her once about having a conscience, a quiet piece of your mind that lets you know what's right. Missy figured she had the opposite of that. She had a dozen voices that screamed at her to do wrong.

So she considered other options. She could still wake Lena, in a quieter, gentler way. She'd push on a few external stimuli until it tripped a wake response. Lena would never even know she'd been adjusted.

Still, the fact that the Others wanted to do nearly the same thing gave her pause. A year ago, she would have done it. Even now, she wasn't exactly sure why she was hesitating except for the strange feeling that it was still somehow wrong.

A year ago Missy would have never considered the third option of just waiting until Lena woke up.

So she sat there, wrestling with her patience and her need to understand why Dr. Chadwick would leave the amplifier in her room. Why now? She'd expected to see it again. She'd expected to get it back as she was processed out of the facility. To put it in her room was unexpected. She didn't like it.

And she couldn't read Dr. Chadwick's mind to find the answers.

It was frustrating. She hated questions without answers. The world was better when all the answers were just there for the taking. Mysteries were terrible things.

Missy didn't want to wait.

She reached for Lena's mind, reached into her sensory processing center, her mental fingers poised over a nexus of bioelectric impulses.

The Others surged with fevered excitement.

She stopped. She could do it. Just a touch and she wouldn't have to wait any longer. Just the gentlest brushing that no one would ever know about.

Except the Others.

Except Missy.

She paused.

She withdrew her attention back to herself. She sat there on the bed, hands curling and uncurling over the white fabric of her pants. She would know. That was the part that was important. She'd never be able to talk to Lena without remembering that she'd messed with her head. Even if it was just a little, even if it was for a good reason, even if no one else knew....

The Others would hunger for more.

Missy laid down and stared at the pitted acoustic tiling above. How was she going to do this? How could she make these kinds of decisions on the outside?

She reached into her own brain and looked at its strange and overly-complicated architecture. Her mind was dozens of times more complex than any others she'd known. Everything was interconnected with an extra array, extra processing, extra everything. It was all twisted and reversed and built around clusters and nodes she didn't understand. Normal minds were no mystery to her but this mind, her own mind, was.

She wished she could put herself to sleep. Or purge the memory of the circlet being here. She didn't know how to do either.

Instead, she rolled over, pressed her forehead against the cold cinderblocks of the wall, and tried to get to sleep the old-fashioned way.

Or at the very least, pretend to.

\*\*\*

# Chapter Four

When Missy felt Lena's mind creep toward wakefulness, she crowded around its edges, becoming the mental equivalent of someone pacing and muttering outside a shop that should have opened ten minutes ago. She fidgeted and bobbed from thought to thought just beyond.

She didn't need to explain why the item was dangerous. Strange as it might seem, Lena knew more about Missy's past than Missy herself. Well, perhaps not more, but certainly more clearly. Missy had only shattered, broken pieces of her life from before. She remembered through the eyes of the Others, and they only showed her what they wanted to show.

Lena, however, had been watching her from the day Missy first stepped foot inside the institute. She had a fully organized description of nearly everything said or done. Missy read it all as it flashed through her friend's complicated thoughts. It seemed cruel of fate that a mind so beautiful was locked away in a broken body, but then again, fate had not been kind to either of them.

*It's a test.* Lena concluded after she was satisfied with her analysis, *Possibly even a trap.*

Missy sat up from the thin hospital mattress and turned to regard the amplifier. She could feel the Others scrambling, shouting at her to take it, give it to them. They knew that with the circlet on her head no one could stop her from leaving. Her skin crawled at the things the Others screamed at her. There was so much they hungered for, so many terrible things.

*Missy?* She felt Lena ask. *Are you still there?*

Yes, yes, she was. The Others weren't in control, *she* was. She sent the thought back, then she got herself out of bed.

She wondered if that's how they'd captured her. Had Psyconic known enough about her powers, about her past, to knock the circlet away? Had he happened upon her while she slept and taken the amplifier? Had he used it himself? Maybe that was it. His name implied he was psychic as well. She wanted these answers from the Others, but they seemed to be similarly ignorant of how they had been captured.

Or at least they pretended to be.

She couldn't trust them. Beside the anomalous Dr. Chadwick, they were the only people that could ever lie to her, and they did so with great abandon, but she could trust Lena. Lena couldn't deceive her, while also being much more intelligent than her. If she thought it was a trap then Missy agreed.

She would leave the amplifier where it was.

It took her several minutes of telling herself this before she got up and realized that it was time for breakfast.

She spent the rest of the morning with her body following her routine while her mind lingered on the power sitting in her room. Dr. Chadwick had to be watching. She wouldn't leave something so dangerous just sitting there without a contingency. What if some other psychic knew about it? What if it hadn't been planned? What if they wanted her to take it and she was failing their test?

The worries gnawed at her as she ate, and then showered, and then gave her quick instructions to the orderlies about how the other patients were feeling today. She made a point of it to mention Lena had been a bit uncomfortable as she slept and needed to be shifted in her chair. Then she explained that Franklin was going to be agitated today because he'd had some disturbing dreams and that Kylie was hiding symptoms of a stomach problem.

Then it was free time.

Missy found Lena and sat with her. They had given her a cushion for her chair and propped her up at a more askew angle than usual. Missy read that Lena was mostly satisfied with the change.

She was never *truly* comfortable, but there were degrees of discomfort. Sometimes you just hoped for a level that might be ignored for a time. Missy understood that. Lena's body was akin to the voices in Missy's head. Both were constantly there, screaming and clawing and wanting something that couldn't be given.

Sometimes, though, sometimes you could forget the screams just for a moment.

"How long do you think they'll leave it there?"

Lena's mind processed the question as Missy watched.

*They may not remove it at all. It is, after all, something of yours. Yes, it was stolen, however, given that you often fabricated false memories of the past, you may be the only one who knows the truth. You may know that the amplifier isn't yours, but it is entirely possible that they are under the firm belief that you built it and own it.*

"Oh." Missy wondered if she had done that. Did anyone else remember the brash hero that had come after her with the amplifier? Did anyone remember his name at all?

*Dr. Chadwick herself said that it would be returned to your possession. This is perhaps their way of observing how you deal with the power that it offers. If you abuse the power here, in this place, Dr. Chadwick can come and remove it. It would not surprise me at all to find out that she is hiding nearby, in case she needs to step in and stop you from becoming a problem.*

Missy's skin crawled along the backs of her forearms. It was distressing to think that there was a person hiding out there, a mind she couldn't see. Fully capable of doing anything to her at any time. She knew this was how other people lived their whole lives, but for her it all felt… unnatural.

"Do you know what I… what I did before when I had the…?"

Lena showed her what she remembered. News reports from hours and hours of sitting in front of a television while she couldn't move nor control any of it. Her distaste for the media and her critical analysis of how they manipulated the facts colored each of those memories.

Yet, they also contained the fear and sorrow of hearing what Miss Mania had done. She left only confusion and death behind her. One day a city street would be a fine place, then they would wake up two days later to find their friends and family butchered and their own hands holding the knives that had cut them apart.

The worst part was that as Lena showed her this, Missy felt the Others remember with her. She saw the hidden bits in flashes. She saw how she wrenched control from a young man and forced him to stab his father to death. The Other who offered the memory did so with excitement and hunger for more.

Missy just leaned forward and tried to keep her breakfast from returning.

*I'm sorry.* Lena's mind called out. *I didn't properly anticipate that—*

"It's fine." Missy lied. No one could read the horrors in her mind but her. That was how it should stay. Lena couldn't lie to her, but she could lie about this. "I need to remember. I need to know why I can't ...can't…"

*Take the amplifier?*

Missy closed her eyes and took a deep breath while she projected her confirmation.

*They shouldn't do this to you.*

"No." Missy shook her head then quickly regretted it. "They should. I deserve much more, so much more."

*You don't.*

For a moment Missy found a picture in Lena's mind, a great desire tied to the image of reaching over and rubbing Missy's back. All of it was superimposed on how a teacher had done the same thing for Lena when she'd been sick as a child. The warmth of the touch was clear in Lena's mind. The calming, stomach-settling effect even more so.

It was strong enough that the memory alone calmed her just a little.

*I watched you.* Lena reminded her as her thoughts quickly cut back to the index of observations from the first year Missy had been admitted. *I noticed you came out in the quiet, in the late times. The Others, as you call them, they were monsters, but then there was you: the one who was quiet. The one that allowed everyone to relax and catch their breath.*

Missy read on to what was unsaid. Lena had dubbed the personality 'The Sad One' in her own thoughts.

*I don't think you were ever the one responsible for those things.*

"I didn't stop them."

*Do you believe you could have? On your own? While they were in control with the amplifier?*

Missy tried to answer this but she couldn't. So much of her life was made up of broken memories scattered about in disconnected and nightmarish pieces. It was possible that Missy didn't even know who she was back then, much less who the Others were or what they were doing.

"I don't know." Missy's voice fell into a whisper. "I can't…. remember."

*Then it's not your fault.* Lena laid the words down with weight behind them. *Yet it has become your responsibility. When you leave here, you know that the world will only see—*

"I know." Missy's voice turned harsh. "I can read it all."

For a moment Lena attempted to imagine what it must be like to read every thought around you. As intelligent as she was, she fell far short of how disturbing reality could truly be. How many people entertained thoughts of murder, fantasized about sex with the people around them, spiraled around horrifying memories that buried them in guilt or desperation. Happy thoughts were so few and far between.

Missy wondered if it was possible to share her experience in some way. She could change memories in other people, could she also give them?

Maybe one day she would try to, but she didn't want to give Lena any taste of what her powers actually felt like.

*Are you really going to go?*

Missy found that she was, despite everything.

"Yes."

*To find Psyconic?*

"Not just that." Missy felt the complicated jumble of emotions inside of her and tried to untangle it. "I want it to make sense. I don't understand who I am, who I really am. I want to know how we became… that."

*Do you know where to start?*

Missy nodded. She knew a place. A place where low level grunts and second-class heroes hung out. Minor villains, neutral parties, the occasional vigilante, they all ended up drinking together, swapping stories, and settling old feuds with the occasional brawl. She'd spent more than a few nights hiding out in the back alleys of bars and basements of long-abandoned buildings. The nearly-empty, half-destroyed section of the city that no one wanted. It was worth nothing to villains and there's nothing worth saving, according to the heroes. It was the place where the forgotten and unseen gathered, swapped laments, and got blind drunk.

"Yeah." She answered. "I'm going to Two Town."

\*\*\*

# Chapter Five

Dr. Chadwick pushed the bag of candy across the table.

It was some sort of peanut butter treat this time. Missy preferred the marshmallows because they were easier to share with Lena. However, she'd never talked about her preference.

"Good morning, Melissa."

Missy jumped. It took her a few moments to realize that Dr. Chadwick was waiting for her to say something back.

"Morning." Missy frowned a little. "Why... Why'd you call me that?"

"It is your name now, remember?"

"Oh." Missy hadn't really thought about the whole thing with her name since last week. Who cared about a name, anyways?

The Others surged and screamed inside of Missy's head. She closed her eyes and fought against the impulse to bring her hands up to her temples. She shoved the voices back, tightening her mental noose on each one of them.

"Melissa."

Missy opened her eyes.

"You aren't wearing the amplifier."

Missy shook her head.

"Can you tell me why?"

It had taken Missy some time to learn when she should lie about things. As a villain, she never had to lie... or tell the truth. In fact, as Miss Mania she never even needed to speak. The cabal within Mania just took what they wanted from other people; they made them speak for her. Like when the Others had taken control of an opera singer for a month. They'd forced the poor man to sing anything they wanted. Who needed to lie when you could just command?

It was one of the many reasons she found conversation uncomfortable.

"I don't need it."

Missy winced as the words left her mouth. It felt weird… because it was both the truth and a lie at the same time. It was true that she didn't need it here. Her powers naturally covered the entire facility. That was enough for her, but not needing it didn't mean that the Others didn't hunger for it with raging want. They needed it more than they needed Missy.

Dr. Chadwick watched her for a minute. Missy shifted her weight in the hard metal of the chair.

She knew that the doctor was thinking about her, judging her, weighing in her mind all of Missy's faults and mistakes, but Missy couldn't read any of it. She didn't know if Dr. Chadwick was about to order someone to cut her throat while she slept, or if the doctor was just wondering if she should bring sandwich cookies next time.

If there was a next time.

Missy straightened up in the chair.

She hadn't really been paying attention to the days. Other people did that so she didn't have to. She might not see Dr. Chadwick again. It was a strange thought. She wasn't sure how it made her feel.

Missy reached out and rummaged through the mind of the woman who ran the front office. She didn't approve of Mrs. Hiln. The old secretary looked down on everyone she met and never admitted to any mistake of her own, all the while saying things like 'Heaven help me!' and 'Lord, give me strength.' However, she was always thinking about what day it was and what was coming up in the next week. She tracked time like it was a venomous snake slithering closer and closer to her.

"You understand you're being released tomorrow."

Missy jumped again. The words came at her without preparation. It made her angry, just a little. Doubly so since the doctor was answering the question she was just trying to answer.

"Yes." Missy remembered to speak after a moment.

"Do you want us to call anyone? Friends, family?"

"Why?"

"So they can pick you up." Dr. Chadwick spoke with the same calm, collected manner she usually did, but Missy thought for a second that she was speaking a bit faster than usual.

Missy took the bag of candy in her hands and began squeezing the air from one side of the bag to the other. "Why would someone do that?"

Dr. Chadwick looked as if she was going to say something. Missy tried her best to anticipate the words. After a moment, the doctor pulled back and made it clear that whatever she had been ready to say was now gone.

Out of Missy's reach.

"I was... terrible to people." Missy stated as she trapped all the air in the bag in one corner. "No one will come to help me unless I force them to."

"Mis—"

"Which I'm not going to do." Missy's hands tightened on the bag, making the corner balloon even bigger. The sounds of stressed plastic surrounded her.

"Then what will you do?"

Missy shook her head. She focused her attention on the candy bag corner. All the pressure in one spot, held there, chained there underneath everything else. The air wasn't useful for the candy. It was just there.

"Where will you go?"

Missy paused before answering, preparing to commit to it when she said the words.

"Two Town."

Dr. Chadwick froze.

Missy had learned over the years that this meant the doctor had encountered something unexpected, and she was making sure she didn't react in a way that could be read by other people. She really didn't need to do that with Missy, though. Missy was a terrible judge of emotions from faces alone.

"Why?" The question finally slipped past the doctor's lips.

Missy wasn't sure if she should say. Would it change anything if she did? If she told them who she wanted to find, would they think she was out for revenge? Would the board and all the people who decide her fate in rooms far away believe her when she said that she just wanted to thank the person. That one person who finally got her to a place where she could become something other than a terrible collection of enraged personalities.

"There's someone I want to see." Missy let the trapped air escape back into the rest of the bag, "I want to see how they are."

Dr. Chadwick leaned back in her chair and rubbed the side of her head. Her fingers ran back and forth over the long scars there.

"Are you ready for this?" Her voice was tired and low, it showed more than it usually did. The hand she was rubbing her scar with seemed to shake.

"I don't know." Missy answered honestly. "But... I want to be."

Dr. Chadwick let out a long, heavy sigh, then stood up. "Then that'll have to do."

\*\*\*

Missy never had to guess where people were. She did have to learn what obstructions were between her and the minds she read. Mapping things out was one thing she actually did well. Learning the institute hadn't been hard. She'd even scoped out the places she wasn't allowed to go. People only moved through certain patterns; the places they went showed her where each door was. Of course, she could read all of that from their minds, but it took time and effort to piece together the strange bundles of sensory information that people really used to navigate. There was a dishwasher volunteer whose eyesight was so bad that he found his way entirely by smell, and other people weren't much better in that regard.

All of this allowed Missy to know how to find the person she wanted to see. Lena was once again at the window. It was raining outside. It was strange that you couldn't hear the rain anywhere else in the building but there. Its chaotic rhythm was only heard because of the glass it crashed into.

Missy sat down beside Lena and began the process of opening the candy bag and unwrapping one of the pieces. She spent her focus on that for as long as she could. She hadn't had a lot of simplicity in her life, so she tried to embrace the small things. Small things like opening containers, or even leaning on the dishwasher's mind as he stood back there, lost in a world of smell and hearing and touch as he performed the same action over and over again. His mind was so free to wander.

Still, Missy couldn't be too jealous. Lena lived in the far end of that measure. A world that only lived inside of her head. All Lena had were the memories of her youth before the accident. There were so many regrets, so many wishes for things she had missed the chance to do; boys she should have kissed, food she should have tried, things she should have told her family.

Now it was all locked away.

To everyone but Missy.

The candy finally released from its shell, and she broke it up even further before feeding it to her friend.

"It's tomorrow."

*I know.*

"I...I'm not ready." Missy knew she would get in trouble if anyone heard those words. If there were listening devices or hidden cameras or some sort of omniscient superhero keeping tabs on things...

At the moment, though, Missy didn't give a shit. She wanted to tell Lena.

Lena's mind did what it always did. It pulled the information in and connected it to a network of everything else she had ever learned about Missy. Things changed, values moved, positions warped, and the entire web of information that Lena thought of as Missy changed its shape.

*Will you ever be?*

Missy shook her head.

*Then perhaps this isn't the place to really learn how to be a normal you.*

Missy unshelled her own piece of candy as she thought about this.

*Tell me about Two Town.*

Missy grinned in spite of herself. It was one of the few memories she had that didn't horrify her. They weren't wild, violent, terrible things. This was because when Miss Mania had been in Two Town... Missy had actually been there.

"It's a hidden corner of the city." She began. "In the old part that used to be slums. There's this bowling alley there, the kind with the neon sign from the sixties. At night it's all pink and blue and has this hum...."

Missy paused as she tried to explain it.

"...the kind that prickles the skin when you walk by. There's a bar across the street, but it's also a diner. It's full of freaks. All the tier-two powers go there. All the harmless and weird ones. It always smells strange, sometimes sickening, but never the same. The food smells like food, but there are powers that leave slime trails and emit gasses and turn wood into onions..."

Missy ran out of steam for her words and ate the candy while she gathered enough for more. She'd never needed to talk much. Missy thought once more about putting her memories into Lena's mind, to make Lena feel everything that she did, to make her understand why the place meant so much.

She wouldn't, though. Two Town was for Missy. Giving those things to Lena wouldn't be right for either of them.

*You loved it there.*

"No." Missy shook her head. "Mania didn't love anything. She was never herself for long enough to. Two Town just felt... safe. It was a place to get lost. They never noticed me...her....*us*. When they did, we'd just wipe the memory away."

Lena processed all of this for a minute.

*Sounds like Mania was very lonely.*

Missy winced. Lena had a way of surprising her even when she could read her thoughts. It was like they came too fast to anticipate. Lena would cut away all the distractions and find something interesting to pounce on.

She would've made an incredible lawyer.

"It was. It's like... being everybody kind of makes you into nobody."

Both of them were quiet for a time, listening to the rain and the crinkling of candy wrappers.

*Do you think he'll be there?*

"Psyconic?"

*Yes.*

"I don't know." Missy shook her head, "But everything comes through Two Town. I... I think there will be someone who knows. Then I'll read them and... That's..."

Missy stopped for a moment and stared down at her hands.

"That's not wrong, is it?"

Lena gave her the mental equivalent of a shrug.

*Wrong for you is a tough line to mark.*

Missy didn't laugh exactly, but she huffed in a way that could have been one. She ate another piece of candy and thought about it. Would the Others think it wrong to just read what she needed from the minds around her?

No. They wouldn't even consider it.

It was probably a bad thing to do, right?

Yet... no one was ever hurt when she read them. It's only after she...

The Others surged forward with offerings of the things she had done. Memories soaked in blood and pleading and the widening eyes of horror.

The candy Missy had been poised to eat was no longer appealing. She fed it to Lena.

"He should have killed me."

Lena's mind jumped with confusion.

"When he caught me." Missy explained. "I'm not... worth this. The cops should have killed me... but they didn't. They sent me here. They spent all this time and money and..."

Missy felt the last words in her head so much that she couldn't say them. All the people she'd killed. All the lives she'd ruined. The survivors hurt even more, the people she left with horrible nightmares. The people who would look at her and see nothing but a monster.

That used to fill her with power.

Now it overwhelmed her in a different way.

*You want to know why.*

Missy nodded and closed the bag in her lap.

*Knowing may not change anything.*

Missy nodded again. She read the memories that came with Lena's words. Lena learning how she'd been paralyzed never really helped much. It was just a thing to know. It changed nothing about her situation or her life.

"I know." Missy whispered. "He may hate me... but I

want to find him. I want to know… I want…"

The rest of it was too jumbled up inside of her. Missy wasn't sure what she was after. Maybe all she really wanted was to know where she came from, where her personality fit in the chaos that was Miss Mania.

*I hope you find it.*

Somehow, the earnestness in the thought helped. Missy held the feeling close, pressing her mind into it. She didn't deserve Lena.

"I'm going to miss you." Missy's voice was just barely a whisper.

Lena's heart mirrored her own.

\*\*\*

# Chapter Six

Missy sat on the cold metal bench while the rain poured down around her. It was especially loud against the scratched and faded plastic above.

She'd expected more.

Even though she hadn't known what her last day would be like, she hadn't expected it to be so long, awkward, and boring. Lena had already said all she wanted to say, and Missy had as well. The strange part was that Dr. Chadwick hadn't said anything to her. In fact, Missy had only seen her once, and she'd been standing all the way down the hall with a strange new expression on her face.

Maybe Missy wasn't the only one who was bad at goodbyes.

It all felt disappointing. After all those weeks of tension and fear, most of her last day had been taken up by paperwork.

There was one thing that had been interesting. Missy had only noticed it today, as she was struggling with some form in a stack of so many others like it. One of those was designed so that each question you filled out had a paragraph behind it that said something like: 'If you answered yes to questions 4, 7, and 11 in this section then you must also fill out section C through H of part 14.'

The whole thing was like the worst choose-your-own adventure story ever created. One that made you do all the work of writing it.

It was twice as annoying because Missy loved those books. Not because she read them herself, but because one of the Others had given her a memory once. It was a memory from when she was very young, sitting in a classroom and reading twenty small minds while they all read through the same book... but with *different* results!

Young whoever-she'd-been-at-the-time was entranced. She wanted to find out who would get to the real end, the end where no one died or got shipwrecked or something. So she'd sat there with her book closed before her, hopping from brain to brain as all the children around her read and chose and tried to find a way out of the paper labyrinth.

Then the teacher smacked her desk with a ruler and screamed at her for not reading.

After that, the memory was a lot more like the other memories that the raging personalities gave her, full of power and madness and an anger that only grew stronger as time moved on.

Missy shivered in the cold and hugged the backpack in her lap a little closer.

No, the thing she'd noticed was the people at the institute didn't think of her as Miss Mania, not anymore. While the receptionist helped her with the forms, Missy read the young woman's mind to try and understand what she was missing.

The young woman called her Missy.

Ideas of people in a person's brain are different from the ideas of people in a book or a file. A name isn't just a name, it's a face, a collection of details, snapshots of their favorite clothes, how they laugh, how wrinkled they are around the eyes, how fat they are.

In the mind, a name is more like a police witness file. It's a random assortment of details all smushed together into a ball of information that most people absorb quickly and efficiently.

It's a bit more difficult when you're reading it off of them, though. You have to take the time to pick apart the memory wad. Missy had never really noticed when they had changed how they thought of her. She'd never been so bored or so curious as to examine the name-wads.

The forms were *really* boring, though.

So Missy had picked at it while the receptionist found and fixed little mistakes. She thought of Missy as a small, awkward girl. Girl, not woman. That bit had stung a little. There were fragments of thoughts, like how she sat with Lena all the time, bits about how she gave her briefings, a lot about her facial and verbal tics.

Yet the fact that she shared a body with those that orchestrated the death of thousands was buried so far beneath... that it was almost never thought about.

Missy marveled at that. It was like they wanted to forget who she was. She was certain that Dr. Chadwick remembered, and those that gave her orders were probably not of the new opinion. The rest of the world would look at her and see a monster.

Except for a handful here, in this place.

Missy turned and looked at her reflection in the scratched-up plastic siding of the bus stop. Pale, so very pale. Her eyes were open and scared, hair messy and flat from walking through the rain. She didn't remember what she looked like as Miss Mania, but it probably wasn't this. Maybe they wouldn't notice her.

Missy hugged the backpack again and set her chin on it. All her things were in there. The suit was in there, and the amplifier. There was also some money, some probably-expired tampons, a disconnected cell phone, and two sets of civilian clothes.

There'd also been a pair of shoes, but Missy had put those on. They were comfortable... and probably expensive. She replaced the empty spot in the backpack with the half-eaten bag of candy from yesterday.

Reaching out, she found not even a single mind around her. The institute had turned out to be quite a ways out in the wooded foothills of the mountains. She'd had to walk to the bus stop in the rain for an hour. She didn't mind. It'd been six years since she'd felt rain on her skin. The cold and trembling and the smell of it all...

...it felt new.

Yet now she was soaked, and her body kept shaking and the nice shoes were covered in mud and not a soul was around. Not a single mind to read, to distract her from her own mangled thoughts. The Others were nervous about it. People's minds were power. Without them...

Missy shivered again and looked out into the rain.

She had more than enough money to get to Two Town. She just had to take this bus to the terminal then book another bus back to the city. That couldn't have changed much in six years. Some things seem to stay the same no matter how much time passed. Taxis were always disgusting, bus lines were always slow and full of crazies, restrooms in fast food places always had that smell of not being washed enough.

Missy's mind prickled as she sensed someone come into range, then it was several someones. The bus was coming. The driver was in his forties, tired, bored, and expecting to pass this stop without a pause. He hardly ever saw anyone out here. It was just a place between two other stops.

Missy made sure to stand up and push her backpack out so its bright purple color would catch his eye in the rain. She was also prepared to nudge him if he still didn't notice.

That wasn't a bad thing, was it?

She wished she could ask Lena, but Lena was out of range.

She *could* use the amplifier... but there was a great amount of fear about that, fear that it would be too much to handle after all this time. If she lost herself again then the Others might take over. Missy didn't want to take the chance. The memories the Others shared to torture her were enough. She didn't want to sit in the back of her own mind while they made her nightmares come to life. Again.

She distracted herself by reading the other minds on the bus. Mostly tired folks on the way to visit family. There was one young man who was suffering from some mental affliction or drug use. He was hard to read, his thoughts crashing and skipping all over from one thing to another. He'd recently gotten some money, but he was afraid of something, like there was a person in the dark who talked to him. His mind moved so fast between these things that Missy couldn't find the real problem in all the mess.

She moved something in his head and made him fall into a restful sleep.

It might have been wrong, but the bus driver would wake him up when they got to the city... probably. Plus, it felt like he hadn't slept in days.

The bus came into sight, and Missy felt the mild surprise of the driver as he saw the backpack and the mousy little woman holding it. He performed the complicated action of slowing the bus to a stop in the pouring rain on a road covered in mud and potholes.

Then Missy climbed aboard, paid the driver, and sat down in a seat near the front.

She put her head on the backpack and decided she wanted to sleep as well.

So she did.

***

# Chapter Seven

Two Town was not what she remembered.

Missy stood on the sidewalk, staring at the spiderwebs of cracks and missing pieces of aged cement that lay scattered around her. The Two Town in her memory never had a cracked sidewalk. There'd been a minor heroine called Caulky who fixed them all. She'd made it a point of pride to keep every wall, street, and sidewalk smooth and clean.

Now it looked as if a wrecking ball had rolled through the main street and taken everyone with it.

At least the rain had stopped.

Missy looked up and watched the mottled gray of the clouds above her. The smell of rain still hung heavy in the air. It smelled like wet dust. Missy breathed slowly, deeply. She closed her eyes. It had been so long since she'd smelled anything but air conditioning.

The bowling alley was still here.

Missy knew it. That was the one place that couldn't die. Its unlit neon silently proclaimed that 'Rawlin's Bowling!' was the place to be. It'd been one of the twin hearts of Two Town. The bowling alley was the place to drink during the day, and Meribelle's was the place to drink at night.

Which was why it was such a shock to find the doors were locked.

She tried to open them several times, fists tight and shaking the handles like they were two, cold metal necks. She heard things rattle on the other side, yet the doors did not give. Missy turned to run across the street. She hadn't run in years. Her body complained with every step.

The Others woke inside and found the smell of her panic enticing.

Missy found the exposed skeleton of the canopy that once hung over the entrance to the late-night diner. It used to be pink, not a regular pink, but rather a red that had faded in the sun for twenty years until it was pink. Now it wasn't even there.

She grabbed the doors in both hands and she pulled.

Chains rattled.

The word *'Closed'* on the sign within mocked her.

This was all she'd had.

This was all she'd wanted.

What could have happened in six years? What took this place from what she remembered… to this?

There used to be food trucks. Always food trucks! Missy remembered that they clogged the street. There were always drunks, and young girls with fake IDs, and the sleazy guys who chased them.

There were Type-Two's: those with powers too weird, specific, or disfiguring for people to want them. The kind of people who could turn your nose a different color, or had hair that tasted like spaghetti, or always knew where to find a pencil.

Missy had been hoping for them.

They were the ones she thought might understand.

Two Town took everyone the world hated and made them all friends…

…and now it was gone.

Missy wandered down the street to a brick stone apartment building. Mr. Fixit used to live there. He'd had a severe social phobia, but he could fix any machine, with or without the parts needed to do so. Everyone would leave their stuff at his door and then come back the next morning and it would be sitting outside in perfect working order.

There was a time when a random thief had stolen everything from the 'fixed pile.' Missy had never seen Two

Town like that. The whole place had organized, hunted him down, and beaten the snot out of him. They'd taken all of the guy's money and put it on Mr. Fixit's doorstep. You could do almost anything in Two Town, you just didn't fuck with the residents.

Missy made it a point to see if he was still there. She could tell, after all, a mind was a mind was a mind. She reached out toward the building and found nothing. Not a soul.

The Others surged inside her. She battled them back, turning her frustration into rage to fuel her fight. The Others staggered away into the dark parts of her mind.

She pushed her senses out, looking for any mind in the area. Was anyone here at all?

Then she touched one. On the far end of her range.

She made straight for it.

The mind was sad, angry, and exhausted. Missy felt her own emotions echoed in it. It was a man. A man who'd been strong. He'd been a hero, but also something less noble before that. The closer she got to him, the more she could read.

He was running a shop now. A place he hated as much as he loved. He wanted to keep everything inside of it while also wanting to see it gone. He was so full of contradictions that Missy almost missed it when she read his name.

Electric Swing!

Missy's step faltered. She remembered him. He'd been a former mob thug who later became one of the informal 'bouncers' of Two Town. When trouble hit, Swing hit back. Of course, no one called him that around here. To everyone in Two Town he was just known as Plugger.

With the ability to power up any device he held in his hands, he rambled about the neighborhood. His trademark had been a metal baseball bat that electrified when he held it. He loved to carry around walkmans and small televisions. He never replaced a battery in his life.

Missy smiled at the memories she had of him, yet the

joy was dulled by what she read of him now. As she closed the gap she saw more and more.

She came around the corner and saw the shop at the same moment that she read what it was selling.

It was full of superhero memorabilia. She could see through the window all the items that were iconic to the people who used to live here: Iron Beak's crow-like mask, Tiny Teke's bag of steel marbles, even the hand-written sign that used to hang on Mr. Fixit's door detailing his services.

Missy stopped reading Plugger's mind and focused on just getting there. She had to see it with her own eyes. All those things: personal, private things that belonged to all the people of Two Town. Why?

She pushed on the door expecting it to open and found it was also locked. She paused and banged her fist on the glass. It rattled the whole door with each hit.

She was angry. The realization hit her mid-strike. She was angry about this! Those things were all a part of what had made this place and here, here it was being auctioned off!

Then Plugger came into view behind the glass door.

He looked terrible. Missy remembered him as tall and strong, muscles always defined in tight shirts, and he always wore a smile on his face. The man who carefully moved around the shelves toward the door had the same body, but the soul had gone out of him. His back was hunched, his face unshaven. The shirt was baggy. The smile was gone from his eyes.

He opened the door without looking at her. Missy read it from his mind. He didn't even want to know who she was. She was just some crazed collector here to buy something.

Missy stepped inside.

Then stopped as her eyes took it all in.

Her hands went to cover her mouth. It was all here! Everyone she'd thought of as being immortal and untouchable was being sold off.

"What happened?" Missy hadn't realized the words

had left her head until she heard them.

"What?"

Plugger turned and looked at her face. Missy felt the reaction.

"Get out!" Plugger roared.

He rushed her, forcing her to back up or be run down. He raised his hand like he was about to strike her with a weapon, but the hand was empty. It grasped at nothing but air. Missy's back ran into the glass of the door. She read his mind with furious intent.

He remembered.

*He remembered!*

Missy's legs failed as she saw from his perspective the things she'd done. The way she had toyed with people. She'd done things to this place, plagued it for weeks. She hadn't been in her worst form, she'd left most of them alive, but the scars from what she'd done had dug deep.

Plugger was focused on one memory in particular. One where Tiny Teke, under Miss Mania control, fired her steel marbles at his head. Teke's beautiful face was so empty as she did it. Her dark hair was pulled back in a perfect ponytail, her tan skin so smooth, her black eyes wide but unseeing. She wasn't there, Miss Mania was.

Plugger had loved Teke. Missy read it in the memory. He'd never told her, but he had. Yet now his nightmares always carried her face.

"Get OUT!"

"Please!" Missy pressed a hand to the side of her head as the Others whispered what they wanted her to do. They didn't like the shouting. They didn't like the threats. They wanted out. They would make it safe. They would make it all *better*.

"Now!"

Missy couldn't take any more. She turned around and pulled the door open just enough for her to leave. She stumbled a few feet out onto the cracked and weathered concrete. Her head was full of all the things she'd been: all those times Miss Mania had played with people, all the lives she destroyed, all the secrets she stole.

Missy stopped her headlong stumble and sat down. Her pants instantly soaked through from the puddle she landed in. She barely noticed. Everything important was happening inside her. She couldn't stop feeling what Plugger had felt as he watched his friends do terrible things to each other.

For some reason she hadn't taken him over. Some great, wonderful joke by one of the Others, perhaps. Missy didn't know.

She just knew that all of it hurt.

And she had nowhere else to go.

\*\*\*

# Chapter Eight

"What's this?"

Missy's head shot up from where it had been cradled in a nest of her arms and knees. She'd found an overhang to sit under while she tried to sort everything out. It used to be the front stoop of the kabob shop. There used to be a smell here, a wonderful smell.

She must have been so lost in thought she didn't notice that someone had walked up to her. Missy reached out to find the mind as she raised her head.

And was confronted with an impossibility.

Her eyes widened as she looked at it. It looked like it was a man, his stature was obscured by a strangely formal suit of black and gray. He also wore a mask, one of those gas masks like you would see in old movies. It had something woven into it, some sort of circuits or lines with other bits that glowed.

He was a total freak.

And Missy couldn't read him.

He was like Dr. Chadwick. He wasn't there... but he was.

The Others screamed at this. Missy, in her panic, forgot to fight them. They took her hands and made them open the backpack and reach for the amplifier. The amplifier would give them the power to see into his mind. It had to!

Then she remembered. She remembered what the Others were. She remembered that the gas-masked man hadn't done anything but ask a question.

She remembered that anything the Others wanted to do was something she probably shouldn't do.

She forced her hand to stop, pausing it in the act of digging through her clothes to find her crown of power. She pulled her shattered self back together.

He'd leaned down for a closer look. Missy couldn't see anything behind the dark glass lenses over his eyes.

"You're Miss Mania."

Missy's muscles would have tensed if they weren't already rigid with fear.

"Who." Missy tried to ask three questions at once, but it all became jumbled in her head while she tried to fight the screaming panic of the Others.

"Apologies." The masked man straightened up. His voice had an odd quality to it, airy and formal, with a whispering rhythm to his words. "I have failed to introduce myself, haven't I? My name is Mr. Keeps. Are you attempting to destroy my mind?"

Missy found she was shaking her head before she'd fully processed the question. She didn't want to do that to anyone, not anymore.

"Oh, I am relieved to hear that." Mr. Keeps' shoulders changed position. "Might I ask what you're doing here? I can't see this area having much value to one such as yourself."

Missy frowned as she watched him. He knew who she was and yet he just stood there, asking her questions. It was like he had no concerns about her at all. She couldn't read him, so perhaps he didn't. If she couldn't read him... if he was immune... if he didn't have any fear of her...

"Are you Psyconic?" Missy got her feet under her and stood up. "Did you arrest me?"

Mr. Keeps hummed to himself for a moment, "No, but the question interests me. I haven't heard that particular name for quite some time."

"Oh." Missy looked down. "Do... do you know what happened here?"

"Here?" He looked up and around. "Oh. You've been

away, haven't you? Well…"

Mr. Keeps hummed once again. It was a pleasant sound, pitching up and down like something a person would sing to themselves while they cleaned their house.

"Please!" Missy said. She couldn't remember the last time she'd had to say it… no, she did. It was when she was in that contraption Dr. Chadwick had strapped her in. That was the last time. She'd said please over and over again.

Mr. Keeps straightened up, "If you wish, you can come with me. I'll tell you what I know, but first I have to make a purchase."

Missy looked from the mask to Plugger's store.

"He won't let me in."

"Hm. Is that so?" Mr. Keeps turned and gestured for her to follow.

Missy followed the strange man. He wasn't very tall, barely an inch or so more than Missy herself. He moved strangely, like his left leg was stiff. He'd swing it out and back in with each step. Yet, he kept a quick pace in spite of it, forcing Missy to rush after him.

He knocked on the shop's glass door with a repetitive tap.

Missy felt Plugger's mind recognize the pattern, mentally grumble and sigh, then begin his trek to open the door. He was still raging in anger and fear at seeing Missy. The magnitude of those feelings made her step back. She pulled herself behind Mr. Keeps for a moment, then remembered he was someone she couldn't read. He could be planning to kill her, to strangle her to death and she wouldn't know. Missy took another step back.

The door opened.

"Creeps." Plugger growled.

"Mr. Swing, I believe you have something of interest up for sale? Shall we negotiate?" Mr. Keeps seemed to ignore every part of Plugger's mood.

"Fine."

Plugger turned around, leaving the door to fall shut behind him. A gloved and besuited hand shot forward and caught it before it could close. Missy read from Plugger's mind that this was the standard routine.

"I've brought a new friend with me." Mr. Keeps announced after he was already inside the doorway, holding it open.

Plugger knew.

Missy saw it in his mind. He knew exactly what the words meant. He turned around with the full power of his rage and anger and everything else. He looked past the masked man toward Missy. She cringed at everything she felt. Her face reacted against her will.

Then she felt it all melt away.

She looked up and saw and read nothing but tiredness in the old bouncer. He looked at her and she looked at him and something changed. The anger came back after a second, but it was muted, like a shadow of what it had been. Missy didn't understand what had happened, but she was grateful for it.

Then she realized her hands had grabbed onto the strange suit Mr. Keeps wore. She'd done an excellent job of wrinkling his left sleeve.

"Sorry." Missy let go and stepped back.

Mr. Keeps glanced back at her. "Hm?"

"Sorry."

This was too strange. She pressed a hand to the side of her head as the Others demanded to be let free. This Mr. Keeps was an unknown. The Others hated the unknown. They wanted to have full control over everything around them. Half of them were screaming at her to kill him, the other half begging her to run.

The worst part is that they were right. She couldn't read him, so he *was* a threat. He was protected from her power.

So was Dr. Chadwick.

But she knew Dr. Chadwick… sort of. She didn't know this one. She couldn't see his face.

Yet she'd just cowered behind him like a little girl.

Missy pressed her hands against her head even harder as she tried to sort it all out, all while Mr. Keeps moved further into the store, leaving her behind.

"I've heard you found something new." He was saying.

Plugger only grunted, but Missy read the information in his mind. He'd found a hairbrush in an online auction. He'd snagged it knowing that Mr. Keeps would pay for it. It supposedly straightened anything tangled that it was rubbed against.

Missy heard it hit the counter and Mr. Keeps hum with delight.

"You know what it is?" Plugger asked.

"I do." Mr. Keeps' voice was definite. "This is Debutant's Brush. Quite the find. Did you know it works on internal organs as well? Rub it on a man's stomach and, well…"

"It's five thousand."

"No, it is not."

Missy read that Plugger needed at least sixteen hundred for it in order to pay his bills. He wanted more, but he would take that. She wondered if she should tell Mr. Keeps. The masked man seemed to be aware of the game and was playing it well as they haggled back and forth over the price.

Which left Missy to explore the shop. There was so much here it was nearly overwhelming. Mesmerizmo's crimson top hat sat on a shelf next to Whipcord's high heels. Momentary's stopwatch hung from the ceiling on its chain, right in front of—

Missy gasped.

"You can't sell that!"

Once again the words had left her mouth without her meaning them to.

The men stopped their haggling to look at her. They followed her gaze, and Missy felt Plugger's reaction so much that it made her flinch.

Hanging from the ceiling was his trademark electric baseball bat. A yellow tag dangled from the handle, stating its price.

"My dad always told me to sell anything I haven't used for five years." Plugger said. "It's been six."

"But..." Missy couldn't look away. What had happened here? Plugger... he'd never... The one she remembered...

Except those weren't her memories. They were the memories of the Others. The broken pieces of them. Or were they hers? Missy grabbed her head again and pulled her fingers through her hair. She scraped her fingernails along her scalp as she tried to untangle her mind. Nails dug into old scabs and scars, guiding her along the way they'd been before.

It was nothing like she remembered. She'd just wanted... she'd wanted *one* thing.

The Others surged and she faltered.

Then Mr. Keeps put a hand on her shoulder.

The Others stopped. Everything stopped.

"Are you alright?"

"No!" Missy screamed. "No, It's all wrong! Where are they? Why is..."

"Why do you even care?"

Missy looked up and over at Plugger. He stood back behind a shelf, only his head and shoulders visible. His face was tired, his mind full of muted anger.

"I..." Missy struggled to find a way to say it.

If Lena was here, she would ask her. Lena would know. She'd have the right words to say, the kind that would make him understand that all she wanted was... all she wanted was...

"I just want to find someone who would understand what it's like." She found herself saying. "What it's like... when you're trying to be better."

A memory flickered through Plugger's mind. Missy felt it. It was something he kept guarded, something important.

She took herself out of his mind. Some things were private. She'd been learning that. That memory seemed like it was probably one of those things.

"You won't find it here." He said after a long moment had passed, "Two Town's gone."

"But why…" Missy lifted her hand to point at all the things around her.

Her finger stopped at something pinned against the wall. It took up a huge space, centered and adorned like one would do for the flag of their beloved home country. She felt her breath catch inside of her.

"Is that…?"

To everyone who didn't know, it looked like a pair of XXL purple sweatpants. They were stained and scuffed and there were bits of thread that had come loose near the knees and cuffs.

Everyone in Two Town knew those pants.

"Yeah." Plugger moved around the shelf and walked up beside Mr. Keeps.

"Baller would never have given them up!"

"Baller's dead."

Those two words answered all of Missy's questions.

Ball Return, known to everyone in Two Town as 'Baller', had been a tier-two hero. He owned *Rawlin's Lanes*. He was the heart and soul of Two Town. It wasn't a great heart, it'd been smokey, dark, and smelling vaguely of vomit, but that was the blood of the place. Two Town was a place where the muck settled.

Baller had hung out with losers and drunks. He'd always been overweight and foul-mouthed, often needed a shower, and only wore the cheapest clothes found in dollar stores.

And he took care of Two Town.

"Heart attack." Plugger went on, "Yelling at some kids for scuffing up the lanes."

"Oh..."

Plugger only grunted in response.

"Do they still...?" Missy asked.

"Yeah." Plugger nodded, "I tried 'em on once. Just to see. I pulled two eight-pounders from it, the kind for kids. It felt... Well, it was like the dang thing didn't want to do it anymore."

Missy remembered Baller back when she'd been incognito among the crowds. He'd been massive, and the pants were always on him: bright and recognizable. Everyone knew he could reach down into that elastic waistline and pull out a bowling ball. Dumbest power ever, but it was his, and he made it his own.

"Pay him two thousand." Missy said to the silence. "For the brush."

"Hmmm." Mr. Keeps hummed into the silence. "That is acceptable."

"Fine." Plugger agreed.

"And take your bat back."

Missy knew she was pushing things. She knew she wasn't welcome there. She knew she brought nothing but painful memories and fear. Still, she couldn't let Plugger sell himself in this place. As much as all the other pieces of the past hurt, that one hurt more than just her. She could feel it. She knew. He'd been waiting for someone, anyone to tell him that.

She could do that much for him.

Plugger didn't say anything about it. She didn't expect him to. He moved to the counter and he finished selling the brush to the masked Mr. Keeps. All the while, Missy stood where she'd been, looking at every stain and every torn thread in the extra-large pants pinned to the wall.

"How much?"

"For what?"

"For the pants." Missy didn't look away from them, forcing her to talk louder.

She still had money in her pack. It was supposed to be for food and lodgings and all the other things she'd need over the next few days, but...

Some things just seemed more important.

\*\*\*

# Chapter Nine

"May I ask a question?"

Missy paused in her struggle of stuffing the sweatpants into her already-full backpack. There was no way she'd be able to do it without removing something else, but the fight was taking her mind off the fact that she only had a few dollars left and night was coming. Mr. Keeps had earned himself a few questions by now. She didn't know who he was, or what he was doing here, but a single question couldn't hurt, could it?

"Yeah." Missy mumbled as she tried folding the sweatpants up in a new way.

"Did you spend all of your money on that?"

Missy paused once more, letting the pant legs unfold and flop down until they dragged along the damp concrete.

"Yeah."

"May I ask why?"

"Because they don't belong there." Missy told him. "Can I ask you something?"

"Of course."

"Why do you want the brush?"

Mr. Keeps looked down at the bright pink brush he held in his gloved hand.

"That answer requires a rather, hm, complicated explanation."

"If I'm being honest, so does mine." Missy grunted as she tried to shove the pants into her bag one more time. "Hey, um, I think I'm supposed to say thank you for—"

"Are you hungry?"

Her first thought was that it was extremely rude of him

to interrupt, her second was that yes, she was actually starving, but the recent stress had made her forget.

Her third thought was realizing she didn't have the money to pay for anything.

"Yeah, but I can't—"

"I'll pay, given the circumstances." He pointed toward the purple sweatpants with a gloved hand. "It may give us the chance to explain ourselves."

Missy immediately formed a response to refuse. She was already in the debt of so many people, she wasn't sure she should establish the pattern even further.

"You're quite the curious individual." Mr. Keeps' mask made a heavier breathing sound for a second, almost as if he was laughing inside of it, "It is not every day one meets a supervillain, especially one who spends all she has on... that."

Missy looked down at the sweatpants and then back up at Mr. Keeps.

Both Plugger and Mr. Keeps had known who she was from the very start. If this was how it was going to be wherever she went, then what kind of place was going to give her food and shelter? With everything else going on, she almost forgot who she was to this world.

"Oh." Missy grabbed a handful of the purple fabric and pulled it up off the ground. "Okay."

"Do you have a car?"

Missy shook her head.

"Then we can take mine."

Missy hesitated. It was common sense not to get into a car with a strange, masked figure with a creepy voice. Lena would have probably thrown a fit if she knew that Missy was even considering the idea.

For most people, this was correct.

Missy wasn't most people.

As long as there was a mind somewhere around her, Missy was never really in danger. She always had tools to use.

Still... here, in this place. There was no one but Plugger and Mr. Keeps.

Missy dug around in Plugger's mind for a moment. She was hoping to find out more about the masked man. The only things she found was that he came in every time Plugger found an item or artifact that could be dangerous. He paid for the items with prepaid credit cards and then he left. He never took off his masks or gloves. He was always polite.

He drove a noiseless van.

That last little tidbit was interesting. She wanted to pull out more information about it, but Plugger's mind knew nothing else.

"That seems like a bad idea." Missy said after her mental exploration.

"Understandable." Mr. Keeps nodded along as he led the way around the corner and out onto what had once been the main drive of Two Town.

There was a van parked a few feet away. It wasn't windowless or rusted. It was, however, an ugly tan color and both of its back tires were flat.

"Tell me," Mr. Keeps slowed and turned to look at her. "Has a bad idea ever stopped you before?"

Missy looked over at him. He was tilting his head at her, his gas mask making his expression unreadable. Yet, for all of the things telling her she shouldn't go anywhere near him, there were a handful of things telling her she could.

"It has." Missy could hear the screaming of the Others inside her head. "It's been stopping me for many years now."

"Ah." Mr. Keeps straightened up, "Then I believe I understand. Well, if this is our goodbye, then I must say it was fascinating meeting you. You are not what I expected."

"Uh… thanks?"

Mr. Keeps nodded once, his head dipping a bit sideways with the motion, then he moved past Missy with his strange little walk and unlocked his van. Missy stood there, watching his actions as he climbed inside.

More than anything in the world, she wished she could read his mind. Why couldn't she? It was both puzzling and frustrating. She wanted to know what he knew about Psyconic. He'd known the name when she'd asked about it. She wanted to know about the brush and why his van had flat tires and didn't make noise.

She wanted to know a lot of things.

Even more, she didn't want to be left alone in this abandoned place with a bitter and angry shop owner as the only mind nearby.

"Wait!"

Mr. Keeps stuck his head out of the open window of the van.

"I'll come, but... don't fuck with me."

Missy tried to sound like the Others. She tried to channel the smallest piece of their sadism and hatred, just enough to inspire a bit of warning fear.

"Fair enough." Mr. Keeps called back.

The door on the other side of the van opened, and Missy hustled to get inside. It was a bit of a trick to drag the dangling leg of the sweatpants in after her, but eventually she managed to get everything into the vehicle and close the door.

Inside it was both clean and messy. The front cab was kept immaculate. The old plastic dashboard was faded, but clean. No dust or pop stains or any of the other bits that Missy remembered being standard for people's cars.

Behind the front seats, however, was a different story. It was filled with an assortment of strange and mysterious objects all tied to the walls or floor. In the middle of it all was an empty space and something that looked like a disco-ball-tiled surfboard set in a metal frame, bolted to the floor of the van.

"What's that?"

"Sky Raider's hoverboard." Mr. Keeps answered as he

pressed a few buttons on his steering wheel.

The hoverboard lit up, shining golden light through the van. Missy felt herself being lifted up, but there was no roar of the engine, no other indication that any kind of machine had turned on.

"My van has undergone some 'personal' upgrades." Mr. Keeps explained as they swept forward down the road without any sound of tires crunching over asphalt. "It saves on expenses."

"Oh." That was all Missy had to say.

For the next few minutes Missy worried. She worried about where she was, how far up the van could go if needed, she worried about the other items in the van with her. She was really worried about why she couldn't read the mind of the man driving and what he was hiding under that mask.

Then she felt the people.

There were so many of them!

They touched her mind and thoughts and emotions flooded into her. First it was a dozen, then two, soon it was hundreds. Missy held her head in her hands again as she tried to control it. The most minds she'd faced in the institute and on the bus ride here had been about fifty. This was so much more.

"Do you like Mexican food?"

Missy didn't recognize that the question had come from outside her head until a few seconds had passed. She was significantly late in answering.

"What? Yeah, sure."

"Very good."

The van turned without a sound and Missy was thankful for it. Any more noise and she would have begun to panic. There was so much, far too much!

It started coming back to her. How the Others... or maybe even herself as well, had filtered it all out. She recreated the strainers for thoughts, blocking out the mundane but letting the highlights drift through. The crowd became more like static. It took effort to maintain it all, but not nearly as much as trying to keep her thoughts straight when the world was shouting at her.

It was only after she got it all organized that she realized she didn't really know if she liked Mexican food.

She hadn't had it for years.

***

# Chapter Ten

The restaurant turned out to be a small room wedged in between a discount tire store and a nail salon. The smell of stale tortilla chips was pervasive.

Missy was getting better at filtering out the mass of minds around her. She barely felt most of the people here. Only one person leapt out as interesting. He was smiling and talking to the waitress, working very hard to maintain the illusion of happiness.

Inside, he was seething with rage because his wife hadn't ordered his drink for him while he'd been out having a smoke. That wasn't the real reason for his anger, but it was the current excuse for it. In his head he was imagining in great detail how he was going to 'teach her a lesson.'

Missy twitched at the images. They riled the Others up. They felt the rage and they wanted to be part of it. They wanted to see it now, instead of behind closed doors like the man wanted. If they'd been in control, they'd have pushed him, made him scream and rant and break his wife's arm right here.

She reached inside the man's head and did something else instead. Rooting out the cause would take too long, but she could pinch a few things, twist a few others…

She heard the grunt of pain because she was listening for it.

Now every time the wife-beater got angry he would receive a paralyzing migraine.

It didn't fix the problem, but perhaps it would give him the motivation to fix it himself.

Missy looked up to find that she'd sat down and had a

menu in front of her. The bizarre Mr. Keeps sat across from her, gloved hands folded over his own menu.

"Are you going to keep your mask on?" Missy wondered aloud.

"For the moment." Mr. Keeps answered. "I'm not particularly hungry. I was more concerned about you."

"Oh."

Missy turned to the menu since she didn't have any idea how to respond to what he'd said. She'd been hoping to see his face, or at least read something about him from the people in the restaurant. However, the people here recognized him but ignored him. They'd seen him before. He'd become 'normal.'

She didn't have any content on him at all.

"Why did Plugger call you 'Creeps'?" Missy asked as soon as the memory popped into her head.

"I'm afraid I have many derogatory nicknames."

"Why?"

"Well…" Mr. Keeps unfolded his gloved hands and looked down at them. The dark plastic of the mask gave nothing else away. "I can answer both that and your previous question through an explanation of my past. Tell me something, how young were you when you realized you were powered?"

"Six." Missy blinked when she realized that she knew that about herself, when so much of that time was locked away in the memories of the Others.

"Ultimate appeared when I was just about that age. Are you old enough to remember him? The first hero, the 'herald of the powered age,' the 'hero of the world.'"

Mr. Keeps paused and seemed to be lost in some distant memory.

"When other heroes appeared, I realized there was a chance that I could be one of them. That superpowers might be something that could be achieved. There were those who found their powers in machines and chemistry… I believed I could be like them."

Mr. Keeps looked down at the menu, "But I wasn't the type to make those kinds of discoveries. It turned out that I was particularly untalented."

"But your van—"

"Is not really my work." Mr. Keeps shrugged, "Also, it jumps ahead in the story."

"Sorry."

"For years I tried to be a hero, but by the time I was… seventeen, I think. Was it? Yes, seventeen. By that time, I had realized that I was just a mere human, and destined for merely human things."

"But—"

"Yes, my mask, my clothes, well…" Mr. Keeps looked down at his hands, "Next question: Do you remember the names Zenithette and Ninefire?"

Missy shook her head. To be perfectly honest, the Others had never really noticed anyone unless they could be made to amuse them in some capacity. The fractured remains of Missy's memories were a bit different, but they were all too incomplete to make any sense of.

"I was a big fan of Zenithette." Mr. Keeps hummed again to himself. "She had this suit with- Well, I was a young man, and she had a certain appeal to that kind of youth. Regardless, she was forced into battle against the villain Ninefire. Unfortunately, their battle took place where I happened to live."

Mr. Keeps stopped speaking for a long moment. Missy blinked as she realized she'd stopped paying attention to the other minds around her. She'd been so focused on the story she'd been ignoring everything. She'd even been ignoring the man with the Missy-induced migraine muttering to himself at the next table.

"Hi folks!"

Missy jumped as the uniformed intruder swung toward

them. On instinct, Missy read her mind. The waitress was thinking about her tired feet, worrying about the blisters on them. She was scanning the table, analyzing if they were going to tip well and what level of friendly charm she should push her voice up to.

"Can I get you anything to drink?"

"Water, please." Mr. Keeps' voice was a bit lower than usual, losing its light and airy tones.

"Uh, lemonade?" Missy asked in panic. She liked lemonade, she thought. She had a memory of it, at least.

"Regular or pink?"

"Uh… pink?"

"Alrighty, are you ready to order or do you need a few minutes?"

Missy blinked as she read in the waitress' mind that she knew the answer. She'd already pegged Mr. Keeps as being ready and Missy as not, yet she was still asking. The strangeness of it kept Missy from answering for a moment.

"Uh… no, not yet."

"Well, I'll be right back with your drinks, take your time!"

The waitress scuttled off, mentally cursing her sore feet and slow patrons.

Missy shook her head. There were so many things people lied about, the strangest, smallest things. They even lied in their questions.

"What happened?" Missy turned her attention back to Mr. Keeps.

"Ninefire killed my family."

It took several seconds for Missy to understand everything in what he was saying. It hit her in waves, the way he'd stopped speaking the same way, the way he'd talked about heroes, the way he folded his hands over the closed menu.

"I'm—" She started to say.

"I woke up in my room, but the rest of the apartment

was gone. It'd been... melted away." Mr. Keeps tightened his fingers together. "I believe they died quickly. Yet, in that moment, at that time, it didn't matter to me at all. I always saw those fights, those great clashes of power against power... I saw them as something glorious and amazing and..."

The waitress zoomed by and sat their glasses on the table. Mr. Keeps took a moment to unstrap part of his mask, moving it aside to reveal a clean-shaven face with twisting, shining patches of pale scar tissue covering his cheek and chin. He lifted the glass and took a long, slow drink.

Missy did the same, finding that her mouth was suddenly dry.

"I was one of the first to leave the wreckage of the building." Mr. Keeps lifted his head. his scarred chin shining under the fluorescent lights. "I couldn't feel my wounds, you see. They had burned too deep, or perhaps I was in shock, or perhaps I've just blocked out the memory. I do remember that the sky was nothing but smoke, the ground was covered in pieces of building, glass, concrete..."

Missy had read these kinds of horrors before, from other people at other times. She'd even caused some of them, her and the Others. She knew them all so well, knew how they stained a person, yet hearing it this way and being unable to see it all inside of his head. It was different.

She felt... powerless.

"I found their bodies, the supers I mean." Mr. Keeps continued. "Zenithette had so many burns on her that I only knew who she was by her shoes. Ninefire was still burning, but his neck had been broken. His suit's flamethrowers were still launching blue fire into the air."

"What... what did you...?"

"I stole the suit." Mr. Keeps looked up. "And I took her shoes. I took them both. I found a suitcase and used it to carry the things I couldn't wear myself. I'm not sure how to explain it, but there, in all of that, I *hated* that someone like

Ninefire had those powers. That someone who'd destroyed my life could build something so amazing when I could not! He didn't deserve it."

"And the shoes?"

"I took them to keep them safe." Mr. Keeps said. "The whole world was burning around them, and around me. If I hadn't taken them, there would be nothing left of her. She deserved something to be saved. She deserves to be remembered."

"I…" Missy realized she had no idea what to say. She'd never felt like this for another person. She wished she could read him so she could reach inside and wipe those memories away.

"It was then that I realized something." Mr. Keeps went on. "I realized that all those fights, all those battles… They leave behind so much destruction… and loss. I couldn't stop that, of course. Yet as I walked past firetrucks and military convoys with my stolen suit and suitcase, I realized that by keeping powerful items like these away from men like Ninefire… that perhaps could stop something else from happening."

"Oh."

"So I let them declare me dead. They never found my body and there was so much that had been turned to ash it wasn't an unreasonable conclusion that I had burned away to nothing. Ninefire's suit kept me alive, and eventually healed me in a way I still don't understand. I found a shady man and sold him the shoes for enough money to buy a new name. Zenithette memorabilia was going at a premium since her death, and the shoes still had her ashes smeared on the soles, so…"

Missy almost asked how people could spend money on something so terrible, then she remembered that she knew more than anyone how terrible a human mind could be.

"Now I gather all those little dangerous things left behind." Mr. Keeps paused to take the brush out of his pocket and lift it up. "I scavenge the battlefields, buy from shops like those of Mr. Swing's. I purchase from the internet and any other source I can find. I collect what is hazardous, and resell what is not. I don't know how much I've done, but I have to believe that for every flamethrower suit and EMP cannon I keep hidden away that there are disasters I have prevented from ever taking place."

"That's…" Missy once more found conversation difficult.

It was all so much easier when she could just read people and never talk to them.

"So that is why I bought the brush, and why some people find me… distasteful." Mr. Keeps' mouth tried to smile but the scars twisted it.

"You're… like a super-janitor!" Missy finally found something to say.

His laugh was so loud that it made Missy jump. She disliked things that surprised her. She had to fight the Others down as the laughter faded.

"That is… Well, that is a fair way of putting it."

"I like janitors." Missy told him, "At the institute where… where I was. They were always looking for problems and fixing them. They always had a plan. Everything they ran into was something they knew how to clean or fix."

"You spent a lot of time with them?"

Missy opened her mouth to say yes, then realized that she'd never spoken to any of them. She'd just sat in her room and read their minds, riding along on their thoughts without them ever knowing she was there.

"No, I guess I didn't."

Mr. Keeps tilted his head but said nothing.

Missy turned her attention to her menu. All the pictures and words were overwhelming to someone who hadn't chosen her own meals in years. She finally decided to go with the largest picture on the middle part of the menu: the burrito special.

A special sounded right.

The waitress swung by a moment later and took their orders, giving Missy a moment to process everything that she'd just heard.

He could be lying.

She didn't know if anything he'd said was the truth.

Yet the scars on his face seemed real enough.

Still, without being able to read his mind, she had no idea if he was Mr. Keeps or if he was the Ninefire villain he talked about.

She wished Lena was here. She would be able to look at him, weigh him with her clever mind and point out all the little things that told her so much about everything.

But she wasn't.

Missy looked down at her own hands, curling them inward and out for a second. She looked inside and asked herself how she felt.

"And you?"

"Hm?" Missy looked up.

"Why did you purchase Ball Return's pants?"

"Oh." Missy's mind skipped to a different track. "He's... he was important."

"Why?"

"Because..." Missy bent her head back and looked at the colorful paper mâché decorations that hung from the ceiling. "Because he was more than he was."

She knew she wasn't using the right words and once again wished for Lena.

"I don't know how to say it, but people... they lie."

Mr. Keeps gave his scar-twisted smile once again.

"They lie to make themselves more than they are, but Baller didn't. He lied to make himself less. He lied to make himself someone everybody could talk to. He was..."

Missy grabbed her head as the noise of other minds grinded against her nerves. There were so many people!

"I'm sorry, this place makes it hard for me to think."

"Hm?" Mr. Keeps looked around, then straightened up a bit, "Oh, I see."

"Can we...?"

"We can order the food to go, then return to a place that is, perhaps...somewhat quieter?"

Missy nodded as she felt the Others writhe under the noise in her head.

Dr. Chadwick had told her she was ready, but the noise of it all...

Missy wasn't so sure.

\*\*\*

# Chapter Eleven

Two Town was an empty calm.

Missy stood with her hands on the top of a concrete barrier. Mr. Keeps had driven them out to an abandoned parking structure. It seemed to be as far away from people as you could get in the city.

Still, she stood there, her hands pressing into the gritty concrete, her mind focused on just breathing in and out. She tried to ignore the echoes and screams within. The Others were tearing at her, wanting her to go back, wanting the noise.

Missy wished they would all just shut up.

"Talk to me." Her voice was low and raw.

"Talk to you?"

"I need the distraction... please."

Mr. Keeps had kept his distance until now. He'd stayed by the van while she'd wandered around the abandoned rooftop, pacing over the faded yellow lines and trying not to think about what had happened here. Now, he moved toward her, his mask still loosened and the takeaway boxes from the restaurant held in both hands.

"You said that Ball Return lied to make himself less." Mr. Keeps stopped a few feet behind Missy, "What did you mean?"

Missy shook her head and tried to focus. The memories from that time were blurry, scattered. Trying to remember what she'd meant was like hunting jello with a tire iron. She'd find it, then it would just wiggle away.

"He..." Missy squeezed her eyes shut. "He saved a girl."

"Oh?"

"During the day he just drank and sat around… and people hated him." Missy opened her eyes as the memories came easier. They weren't her memories. They were Baller's. She'd stolen them. She should have felt guilty, but instead she felt like a part of the man still lived in her. He was gone. All those things she read from him were also gone… except in her mind.

"But at night…" She struggled to find the words. "At night he watched out for people. He'd take these walks, up and down the back alleys of Two Town. He…. didn't sleep well. Never had. So he walked, and he called rides for drunks, and gave directions. He would just walk around and… and there was a girl."

"Who was she?"

"I don't know." Missy shook her head. "Baller didn't know, so I don't. She was just a girl. She'd been roofied. Baller could spot a drunk at a dozen paces, but she wasn't just drunk. He knew it. He also didn't like the man with her. He was grabbing her, dragging her toward his car. Baller only had seconds to understand what was happening… but it took him no time at all to decide what to do."

Missy paused and let go of the concrete, standing up straighter. She looked out over the city and the sky over it. It was nearing sundown. The gray clouds were glowing with streaks of orange and red.

"Most people dither." Missy's lips curled over the word. "They try to weigh everything. They worry about being wrong, they worry about getting hurt, they worry about someone coming after them if they do something. They just stand there while bad things happen."

"And Ball Return did not?"

"He reached into his pants… these pants." Missy pulled the purple cloth up out of her backpack. "He pulled out a bowling ball and charged the guy. Hit the jerk right in the back before he knew what was coming. No one expects people to act that fast. The girl was so drugged she didn't even scream. She just stood there, wobbling back and forth. Baller hit the guy a few more times, then took the girl to *Meribelle's*. Big Bitty was there. He took care of her."

"And he lied about this?"

"Yeah." Missy nodded. "Told Bitty to lie for him too. He didn't want anyone to know. I've seen...no, I've read people…"

"You read the past in other people's memories."

"Yeah. They lie… they lie like this because they feel guilty about hurting people. Baller didn't feel guilt. He didn't feel pride either… not for hurting someone. He just felt… he felt nice. He'd helped the girl. That's all he wanted. Yet he lied about it. The girl didn't remember a thing and the wannabe rapist had his back turned during the attack. The bowling ball disappeared into the same place it came from… no evidence, no story. It was only known to him and Bitty."

Missy took a deep breath. The Others were quieter now. The world was quieter now. All she could hear were the distant thoughts of Plugger, a few other minds, and the wind.

"Fascinating." Mr. Keeps crossed the last few steps between them, coming to stand beside her. The smell of food came with him. "As someone who also prefers to work without recognition, I respect him for what he did. Although, to be completely honest, I hide out of fear. It's a reasonable fear, I believe, but fear nonetheless."

Missy used to laugh at the fear inside of people. She'd thought it was a weakness. No, not her… or did she? Was it her or the Others? She looked down as Mr. Keeps offered her the box of Mexican food. She took it in both hands, it was still warm and the corner was leaking.

She'd always been afraid. Even back when she'd been Mania, she'd been terrified of being caught while asleep. She'd undergo elaborate measures to protect her dormant body from attack. She knew she was hunted… but she was invincible any time she was awake.

Now it was almost backwards. Being awake was the risky part.

She sat down on the cold concrete and opened the box. The promised burrito was inside, along with a set of plastic utensils.

Mr. Keeps spent a moment levering himself down to the ground across from her. His leg seemed to give him trouble. Even as he sat down, he didn't cross his legs like Missy. Instead, he kept one leg forward and to the side. Once he was settled, he opened his own box and began to eat.

"Fear isn't bad." Missy said to the silence.

"No, it is not."

Missy let out a long, slow breath, then she turned to her own food, finding that she was hungrier than she'd been in a long, long time.

\*\*\*

# Chapter Twelve

Missy was scraping the last bits of refried beans off Styrofoam when Mr. Keep's hand appeared in front of her. It was holding a crumpled wad of cash.

"What's this?" She asked.

"Two thousand was a bit less than I expected to pay for that brush." Mr. Keeps' voice sounded different with his mask loose. It was clearer, stronger. "And I know you need it."

Missy licked the beans off of the fork, then put the utensil down. She took the money. There was something like five hundred dollars in the wad.

She just sat there holding it. There was a ritual that went with taking money. She'd noticed it in passing, but not enough to remember all of it. She desperately tried to piece it all together, struggling in silence until Mr. Keeps leaned over and whispered to her.

"Most people would say 'Oh no, you don't need to do that' or just 'Thank you.'"

"Oh." Missy looked at him. The mask was dangling away from his chin, showing more of his scars and stubble. "Which should I do?"

"Personally, I'd go with: 'Thank You'."

"Thank you."

"You're welcome."

"Why are you being nice to me?"

"Because I don't think many people will."

Missy opened her mouth, then realized she had nothing to say. Talking was more work than she'd expected it to be. Instead, she stared down at the empty container in front of her and wished it contained just a bit more.

They sat in silence for a while with their own thoughts. Missy began worrying about the money he'd given her and tried to understand if that made her owe him something. She'd never had to care about such things before. Dealing with an unreadable person was even stranger when they weren't a doctor in control of your life.

The wind picked up around them.

Missy had to tighten her grip on the box and napkins and plastic utensils. Somehow, the wind made it even lonelier here. The silence in her head was relaxing, but the old nervousness was setting in. In the distance she could feel Plugger's mind grumbling away at everything that had happened.

He was taking the bat down from the ceiling.

Missy felt something. It was like the first two pieces of a huge puzzle had been put together. It was a small thing, but it felt like it was a beginning. One thing set right amidst the brokenness around it.

Something like a wind chime began to sing behind her. It was a pleasant sound.

"That's… not good."

Missy looked over at Mr. Keeps. He was busy trying to lift himself off of the ground, but his one leg was making it difficult.

"What is it?"

Mr. Keeps didn't answer. He had gotten up and was staring at the van. He shoved his meal trash into a pocket with the ugly sound of Styrofoam rubbing against itself. Then he began searching his other pockets.

"What's going on?" Missy got to her feet.

"SAD!" He shouted back.

Then he found what he was looking for: a box of earplugs. He opened it and emptied the box into his gloved hand. Only two came out. He looked down at them, then up at

Missy, before closing his fist.

Missy frowned and tilted her head. "I'm...sorry you're sad?"

"No, not that sad, S.A.D. Sonic Assault Drones. PMC tech, banned for domestic use. That doesn't stop them, of course. They still show up here and there when the right people are paid to cover it up. Hmm. Hmm." He said this in a rush while he put the earplugs in. "We should get back in the van."

"Uh..." Missy froze. This could be the trap she'd expected. She'd get in the van and then he'd hurt her. He'd steal her away. He'd keep her and...

The Others surged forward and offered her memories they'd taken. All the terrible things that can happen to a woman under such conditions. Her head filled with screams and pleading and the echoed anguish from thousands of foreign memories.

Mr. Keeps, however, remained unfazed.

He'd already moved to the van and was climbing into the driver's seat. He stopped right before closing the door, leaning his gas-masked head out to yell at her.

"Quickly, please!"

Missy took the plastic knife from the box. She held it hidden, pressing it flat against her wrist. Then she followed. She opened the door and was considering all the possible dangers when something happened.

Missy could feel another mind.

It was very close to her.

No, not close. It was right where she was.

Her head began to ache and her ears began to ring, but that was secondary compared to the strangeness of feeling a mind that wasn't there. She touched it and found it was her mind... again...

Then there was a third copy, then a fourth. She'd never before been able to read her own mind before yet now there seemed to be copies popping up all around her. She moved in to touch one, wondering what she would find. *What would she find- What would she find- What would she find- What would she find- What would she find- What would she find- What would she find- What would she find- What would she find—*

Missy gasped when the cycle broke.

She was no longer on the outside of the van, she was inside. She was lying down.

She sat up, but too quickly so she banged her head on the low roof. A yelp escaped her lips as she grabbed her head.

Her hands looked wrong.

They were gray. In fact, everything was gray. There was also music. A saxophone and piano were warring far away in the distance. She looked down to find that she was laying on the shiny surfboard in the back of the van. It still glimmered, but now it was dulled and blurry.

She turned around to look toward the driver's seat. Mr. Keeps was there, staring up and out of the front window.

"What—"

Mr. Keeps spun around to face her. Missy felt the Others surge, offering her fears and worries about everything that might have happened while she was trapped in whatever that was. It made her body itch to think about the fact that she'd been moved, and she didn't remember any of it. She'd been through that at the institute and the memories she had of those times made her skin crawl even more.

"Oh, good." Mr. Keeps dropped his head an inch, as if his neck had been kept stiff until now. "It worked. I was worried that—"

"What happened?" Missy found she wanted to scream, but she didn't have the energy to. "Why's everything gray?"

"Well," He glanced out the windshield for a second before turning back. "I don't know what happened to you, so I cannot assist you there. What I know is that you froze in place. You weren't doing anything but standing there, stiff as a board. I had to move the van around and load you into the back before the drone spotted you."

Missy remembered the echoing feeling of reading her own thoughts. She'd been trapped by it somehow. How was that even possible? She searched again with her mind and found none of the other copies of herself.

"As for the new color scheme…" Mr. Keeps pointed to a small coin that was floating in the air next to him. Missy hadn't noticed it before. "This is Phil Noir's lucky coin. It changes reality to fit his old-movie-inspired preconceptions."

"So we're… in a dream of his?"

"In a way, yes."

"So we're safe?"

"No."

Missy grabbed the sore spot on her forehead and glared at him.

"To the outside world we look the same, this just changes how we perceive it. The important part was hearing, though."

Another piece clicked together in Missy's head.

"The saxophone?" She listened to it for a moment, wailing and tooting in an ungainly rhythm. "It's doing something?"

"Exactly." Mr. Keeps turned back around in the seat and grabbed the wheel. "I wasn't sure, but I thought it might block the sound waves, stopping them from causing further injury, especially given your condition."

Missy ran her hands over her body, searching for anything that might indicate that Mr. Keeps could have done something to her. Her skin crawled and her mouth soured at all the things the Others insinuated inside.

"You touched me." Missy whispered as the saxophone trilled in the distance.

"Pardon?"

Missy shook her head. She tried to shake the Others away. They always clouded her thoughts. Whatever they wanted her to think had to be wrong. It had to be. She should know this by now.

Then she caught the edge of something.

Her whole body stilled as she focused on it. One of the Others had a memory: their memory. It was the memory of Mr. Keeps loading her onto the shiny surfboard. Missy grabbed it with such ferocity that the Other personality gave it up before realizing what was happening.

Missy watched. The Others had been able to see through her eyes while she was locked in the loop. They'd tried to take over, of course, but the sound affected those that got too close to the surface. This one had lurked below, watching as Mr. Keeps had driven the van around so she was near the back of it. She kept note of the way he hesitated as he pushed her over and pulled her body up onto the surfboard.

Then he'd rummaged around the back of the van, ignoring her body as he pulled strange items from boxes and cans until he found the coin. He stared at it for a moment, then climbed back into the driver's seat.

He removed one of his gloves.

Missy watched in estranged fascination. This was a memory that was hers and also not hers. She watched from the corner of her eye as the glove was removed to show skin striped with thin scars. His nails were too long. They needed to be trimmed. He held the coin in his hand and flipped it.

It hit the ceiling, bounced away, then stuck in midair. The world went monochrome in an instant.

Then the memory ended.

She blinked and realized that Mr. Keeps had been saying something.

"What?" Missy's voice cracked, so she cleared her throat. "Sorry. The sounds…"

"I can see the drone." He repeated. "It's up there."

Missy climbed forward to look. She noticed that his gloves were back on his hands now. That meant there was still some part of what happened that she didn't know about, but she had the one piece. Part of her wanted to find the hiding Other and learn more from it. What else had it seen? What else had it watched from the back of her mind?

But there were more important matters at the moment.

Missy squeezed between the seats, her fears put to rest enough that she would be able to sit beside the strange, unreadable man without having her skin crawl and stomach heave.

He'd done nothing. She knew that now.

Yet there was a shiver deep inside. Even the concept of that fear gripped her. She found her hands shook so much she pressed them into her thighs as she settled into the passenger seat.

Then she looked out to follow his pointing finger. She saw the drone out there, painted in the same grainy monochrome as the world around them, yet stark black against a sky of gray. Just a mere speck in the distance.

"How'd you know it was coming?" Missy asked as she pieced together everything in her head. "You yelled about it before it…"

"My lovely junk collection." Mr. Keeps answered, "The crystals of…something, can't quite remember at the moment. They sing with certain sound waves. I've kept them in the van ever since my first encounter with a S.A.D."

"Oh."

Missy turned to look back at the piles of small boxes and strange items behind her. There had to be at least a hundred different objects there. She couldn't see crystals in any of them.

"Not there," Mr. Keeps reached over and opened the glove box, displaying a small pile of miscellaneous items, including three blue crystals on a chain. "Here."

The chain was tangled. Missy fought the urge to pull it out and untangle it.

"What are we going to do?" She closed the glove box

with care, so as not to disturb the pile. "How long does the coin last?"

"To answer both questions: I don't know."

Missy looked up at the drone.

"Do you have a ray gun?"

"No."

"Or some other type of gun?"

"I do not." Mr. Keeps sounded annoyed at his own answer.

"There has to be something here that you can use, right?" Missy looked around at everything behind her. "You have the crystals and the coin and—"

"Most of it is sadly ordinary." Mr. Keeps sighed and shook his head. "I use it as camouflage. Look."

He dug down into a pile behind him and pulled out a jar with some coins in it. They were of all shapes and sizes.

"This is where I keep Noir's coin." He explained. "None of these here have any powers, but his coin does. I wanted to make sure that if anyone ever stole the van, and knew what they were stealing, that there would be another problem for them to solve. So, unless they know exactly what they're after…"

"Oh." Missy looked at the pile of junk with new eyes.

"I have a few special things, mostly harmless, usually items that can be used to alert or protect. I don't keep anything powerful in the van, with the exception of the surfboard. That was a practical choice." Mr. Keeps let out a second long sigh. "I'm afraid that nothing else is going to help us with the drone."

"The board?" Missy pointed. "It was made to fly, right? How?"

He didn't answer at first. He turned to look at it.

"I… can't fly it that high." His shoulders hunched a bit. "Even if I did, we don't know what else the drone might be capable of, or who its target is."

"It's me." Missy said this without any doubt. She

wasn't the greatest thinker, but she had some experience with people trying to kill her. "No mind for me to take over, a weapon that keeps itself at a distance... it's after me."

"Oh."

"Sorry." Missy reached into her pocket and felt the wad of cash that he'd given her. Her hand tightened on the bills. "You can go. I'll—"

"If only we could lure it down." He interrupted, maybe he hadn't heard her at all.

Missy blinked. She knew everything about Two Town. It was where she hid. It was where she'd felt safe back when most of her was a monster.

"I know a place that might help." She spoke a little louder this time. "Do you know where Mr. Fixit used to live?"

Mr. Keeps nodded.

"Take me there."

"The coin won't move." He pointed at the silver disc hanging in midair between them. "I'd have to stop it to—"

"It's okay." Missy straightened up in her seat. "I'll tell you where to go."

***

# Chapter Thirteen

The underground garage was darker than she remembered. No power meant no lights, turning the once-bright haven into a dark cavern of pillars and shadows. Abandoned, rusted wrecks littered the area. None of them had wheels or engines. They'd been stripped bare.

Missy had been astounded by this when she'd woken up. She'd tried not to read her own mind this time, but the more she resisted the more painful the sound had gotten. It became too much and Missy submitted to the loop. She only fell out again when the floating van cruised deeper into the underground levels of the garage.

"The noise stopped." Missy reported.

"What?" Mr. Keeps' voice was louder than normal. He looked over at her, then removed enough of his mask to pull out an ear plug.

"I said the noise stopped."

"Excellent." He put his hand back on the steering wheel, earplug still gripped between his fingers. "How'd you know the gate would be unlocked?"

"Fixit left the lock broken, he… wanted visitors."

"I see."

Mr. Keeps parked the car in the far corner of the garage behind the shell of an old pickup truck. He turned the hoverboard off and climbed into the back to begin the process of unbolting it from the frame of the vehicle.

Missy had nothing to do, so she focused on how she felt.

The drone had to come after her. If she was out of sight

for too long then they might think she'd escaped. If they were watching... if it wasn't some automated machine...

There were a lot of 'ifs' in the plan.

She should just go underground instead. She remembered how and where. The drone was after her, if she left it would probably leave Mr. Keeps alone.

Which also left Missy alone.

She turned to watch the gas-masked man as he stumbled around the surfboard and released it from the steel clamps that kept it in place. His mask was still half-open, but she couldn't see his scars in the darkness. He was only a shadow with two glassy, reflective lenses.

He could be her enemy.

He could still be planning to kill her, or worse. He'd talked to her, helped her, given her money... all the things a man could do to lure a woman into their trap.

Missy's skin crawled once more.

What should she do?

She was about to open the door to tell him that she'd leave. She'd deal with the drone somehow. There were too many people hurt by her actions already. She didn't need anyone else added to the list. Two Town was full of bolt holes and hidden exits, it wouldn't take her long to find a way out.

Then she felt the mental echo of her own mind again. The little crystals inside the glove compartment began to chime quietly.

"It's coming."

"Oh, goody." Mr. Keeps grunted as the last clamp came off the surfboard.

The entire van fell a few inches. It hit hard on flat tires and sent both of them into the air for a second.

Missy panicked during the moment of freefall, her hands grabbing onto the door and dashboard in an effort to convince herself that she wasn't going to fall out of the van. Her hair fell over her eyes in a tangle after the jolt. She stared at the mess of black obscuring her vision.

"Use the brush!" Missy shouted.

"What?"

"The brush... thing. It straightens tangles, right?"

"Yes...But I doubt the drone—"

"Have you ever seen anything wired without tangles somewhere?" Missy grinned in spite of herself. This was some Lena-level brilliance she was dishing out.

Mr. Keeps was silent for a minute, then pulled the surfboard off of its mount with a screech of metal against metal.

"That's... not a bad idea, but I'd have to get close to—."

"Leave that to me."

Missy popped open the glove compartment and the door, grabbed the tangle of chiming crystals, then jumped out.

Her feet hit the cracked concrete and she ran. She ducked around the bare metal frame of an old sedan and moved along the back wall of the garage. The crystals in her hand rattled louder, their once-delicate chiming turning into chaotic clanging. Missy's head shivered with disorder. The echoes of her own mind spread out in a cloud around her. She tried not to touch them, but her brain was built to seek out minds and interact with them. It was second nature to her to tap into every new mind she noticed.

Every time she even brushed one of the copies another would spawn. The headache came soon after. Then she heard it coming. She heard the whir of the motors as the drone grew closer and closer. It grew louder and the pain inside of her grew with it.

She shuffled out into the open. She couldn't run any longer. The world seemed to tilt from left to right, her feet not falling where they should. Everything felt wrong. It felt like she was in the middle of a crowd of herself. The crystals clenched in her fist screamed with her. They sounded like a truck full of metal piping dumping everything it carried onto the highway at full speed.

Then she saw it.

It was larger than she'd expected. It had to be a good six-feet across. Four black propellers spun in a noisy blur as it drifted along. It moved slowly through the darkness, a large camera lens shining like the bulbous eye of a deep-sea predator.

Then it turned and saw her.

Missy let her legs collapse. The world was wrong. Everything turned and twisted to the right. She dropped the crystals and tried to hold on to the ground as it slid away. The crowd of herself began to scream with the same pain she was experiencing. All the anguish wasn't just inside her head, it was all around her. She had no place to run, no place to hide.

The drone maneuvered closer, making Missy bare her teeth and curl up into a ball.

It was too much. It was all too much.

She stared up from the ground at the dark monster as it crept closer and closer, its singular eye locked onto her. There was no mind to read, no face to look at. Someone had built the perfect psychic hunter and it had come to kill.

Missy had a hard time breathing. Her muscles were too tight. She glared at the thing, wondering how long until it killed her. She felt the food inside surge back up from her stomach, but it couldn't make it past her clenched throat.

Mr. Keeps arrived.

He was lying flat on his stomach on the glittery surfboard, one arm gripping him in place while the other was thrust forward with the brush like it was a knight's lance. He moved terribly: in short, jerky turns and bursts. He lurched over above the drone, reached down with the brush and swiped it along the top of the machine.

Missy gasped as the sound stopped. Her mirrored minds vanished. The pain and discomfort stayed, but enough of it was released that she found herself taking one giant breath in relief.

Her muscles had been locked so hard that she hadn't been breathing. She gulped for precious oxygen while trying not to vomit.

At the same time the drone lost three of its four engines. The one remaining made the entire machine flip over, away from Mr. Keeps. It hit the top of another abandoned car, its remaining propeller hitting something and throwing out a splash of sparks and sound. It skittered in circles, falling from the top of the car onto the concrete before finally dying.

Then all was quiet.

Missy focused on breathing and not throwing up. She could do that. She'd just eaten that food and she was not going to waste it.

"I hope... this is the last time I have to do that." Mr. Keeps' voice echoed from somewhere else in the garage. His voice reflected the same manic fear inside Missy. It sounded so childlike, so raw.

Missy laughed, then immediately threw up.

\*\*\*

# Chapter Fourteen

Mr. Keeps drove the van in silence while Missy curled up in the passenger seat. Her arms and legs kept shaking, her eyes hurt, and her throat burned with the taste of acid and refried beans.

New minds were popping up around her as they drove. It was dark out, so many of them were tired. They were thinking of sleep, of going home to family, of sitting down and relaxing. Missy picked one of them at random and tapped into their thoughts. It was a young guard for an empty lot. He was about to hand his shift over to the next guy. He was looking forward to cooking a nice steak and watching soccer. His feet were sore and his back hurt, but he was at peace with the world around him.

Missy wanted that.

She wanted a world that wouldn't try and kill her.

"I should go back."

"Hm?" Mr. Keeps hummed at her. "To Two Town?"

"No, to... the institute." Missy tightened her arms around her legs, "It's safe there."

Mr. Keeps said nothing, so Missy drifted out to other minds. Men and women all going about their days. Most of them were busy working or driving. This was obviously an area of town that was not residential.

"Are you sure?"

Missy pulled her thoughts back and considered the question. She missed Lena. That was first and foremost. She could talk to her. Lena always had answers. Dr. Chadwick was there as well, but Missy realized that she didn't respect the doctor as much as she feared her. There was a difference now that she'd met another person she couldn't read. There were also familiar minds back there, all the people who had lied to protect her just the other day. She still wasn't sure why they'd done that, but she felt safe around them because of it.

Yet to go back would mean admitting defeat.

It would be turning her life into Lena's. Missy knew Lena's regrets more than anyone else. If she went back, Lena would scream at her for giving away her one chance to be out in the world.

"No." It was possibly a lie, but Missy knew it had to be her answer.

They lapsed into silence once again. Missy gazed out of the van's window at the passing buildings. They all looked to be abandoned. They had dirt-encrusted windows and every metal part of them had been stripped of paint and infected by oxidation. The van turned down a small alleyway between two of the more dilapidated structures. There wasn't a touch of life in either of them.

They coasted over a road that would have shaken both of them to death had they been riding on tires. It was torn up from years of harsh winters and no repairs. Missy unwrapped her hands from her legs and looked forward. They were heading toward a bridge piece between the two older structures. It was newer, cleaner, and it had one of the metal doors that rolled up for heavy trucks.

Mr. Keeps pulled the sun visor down and pushed the button on a garage door opener.

Missy watched in fascination as the metal door slid sideways into the wall, instead of rolling up.

"Where are we?"

"This is my place." Mr. Keeps answered as they pulled into the garage. It was small and bare of furnishings. "I like to think of it as the Keep Keep."

Missy snorted, then winced at the way it made her

throat feel. "That's terrible."

"Perhaps that's why I enjoy it so much." Mr. Keeps flipped a switch that shut off the hoverboard, letting the van fall onto its flat tires with a thump.

Missy unwrapped herself and pushed on the door to open it. Her legs were still weak and unsteady, so she hesitated a moment before sliding off the seat onto the hard floor of the garage.

"This place, I built it to protect things that could be 'misused.'" Mr. Keeps said as he walked around the van. "I don't have many niceties, but it's a safe place."

Missy watched as he opened the door the rest of the way and held it for her. Once again, she felt the fear. Every show, every book, every unending terror she'd read from the minds of other women told her this was a bad idea. He was going to hurt her, attack her, do something to her in her sleep.

All the same things Miss Mania used to do.

Missy clenched her teeth together as the Others made her remember all the awfulness she'd been a part of. She'd destroyed people. She'd destroyed Plugger. She didn't even remember doing so, but he remembered.

She tried to shut the Others out as they rallied against her. She closed her eyes and took a long breath. She sensed the other minds in the distant factories and lots. Some were strong, some had guns. They were things she could use.

Then Missy heard the door shut. She opened her eyes to find that Mr. Keeps had stopped holding the door open and gone inside. He'd left her in the garage with his van and everything in it.

And somehow that made her feel better.

***

# Chapter Fifteen

Ten minutes later Missy let herself inside.

She'd gone outside first. The garage door opener had been left in the van, so it was easy enough to arrange an escape. She'd stood there in the cool wind of the night, her throat burning and sour, the Others screaming at her to leave.

She'd met two people today. One of them had hated her, the other had put himself at risk for her. What would it be like if she left? What kind of hate would she face? How many would see her face and know her?

The hardest thing to consider was this: how would she react?

When Plugger first realized who she was, she'd panicked. She'd read his anger and grief and she'd fled. She didn't want to lose control. She didn't want to use her powers, capture his mind, and force him to go away. That was Miss Mania, not her.

Yet that begged the question of what *should* she do?

That was the real problem.

She still wanted to find Psyconic, but without Two Town, she didn't know where to start. Visiting a library would put her in contact with people. Was she able to handle that? She didn't know.

So Missy turned around.

She hit the button to put the door down, and went inside.

Dealing with Mr. Keeps was like how normal people lived, wasn't it? She reached her hand into her pocket and felt the wad of money he'd given her earlier. He'd been nothing but kind to her. Still, not knowing every part of his mind made her skin itch and shiver.

Then again, the whole world made her feel like that.

Once more, she wished she could talk to Lena.

Missy found the inside of the warehouse to be similar to the back of the van. There were rows of shelves packed with crates and labeled with sticky notes. Here and there, objects that were too large or too strange were awkwardly positioned between or around the other boxes. There was an oversized tuba sitting up on the third shelf to her right and a large aquarium painted black sitting next to it.

She moved down the rows slowly, reading labels and examining some of the stranger objects. A large glass bubble was floating alone on a lower shelf, slowly tapping against the sheet metal around it. There was another shelf that seemed to be covered in a pink moss that showed signs of being trimmed back with shears.

When the shelves ended, she found herself looking at a small office and some other area behind it. There were several little rooms that seemed to exist out by themselves in that area. She wanted to investigate, but for now she focused on Mr. Keeps.

He was inside the office. Missy could hear the little sing-song humming he did. She moved closer and pushed the door open. He was placing a blanket and pillow on an old, orange couch in the corner near a refrigerator. There was a small kitchen area next to it, the kind with a sink and overhead cabinets and a small, collapsible table. On the other side of the room, near where Missy was watching from, there was a desk, computer, printer, and a fax machine. All the things a person would need to live and work in the same place.

Missy watched him. He hummed to himself as he set the pillow down and shook open the blanket. Then he turned and moved past the refrigerator to the small kitchen. He got a plastic cup from the cabinet overhead and filled it with water from the sink. He set the glass on the table. There was only one chair for it.

Missy moved inside and shut the door loud enough that he'd notice.

"Ah." He turned around and nodded toward her. "I don't have much, but I hope it does well for the night."

"Thanks." Missy said it too quietly.

She cleared her throat and winced at the taste before trying again.

"Thank you." She said.

Mr. Keeps just nodded then shuffled off to another door.

"There's a bathroom here." He opened it to prove his point. "And I have a small bedroom over there."

He pointed at another door a few feet away.

"If you need anything, just knock."

"Phone." Missy found herself saying.

"Hm?"

"The, uh…." Missy tried to remember what the paperwork had said. She'd almost forgotten it amidst everything else. In the long, drawn-out process of her discharge from the institute they had mentioned something about calling in.

Missy moved over to the table and began to unpack her bag. The sweatpants and psychic amplifier came first. Then came her clothes and her toiletries. Lastly, she pulled out the crumpled up sheets of her discharge papers. She flattened them out as best she could and tried to find the section.

"Daily check-ins." She announced as she found it. "I need to call them."

"I see." Mr. Keeps looked upward for a moment, like he was staring through the ceiling to the darkness outside. "There's a phone on the desk."

Missy turned to search for it. It'd been hidden behind the monitor when she'd first looked around. She grabbed her paper and shuffled over, then lifted the phone and stared at it.

She'd never used one before.

Phones were for talking to people. Missy never needed to talk.

She stared at it for a long moment before she put it down and pushed the numbers on it in the order she read on the paper. She picked it back up and listened.

A voice came on the line but it didn't sound right.

Missy listened and frowned as the person told her to press more buttons for different things. Was she an inpatient? Outpatient? Appointment?

She stood there in mounting confusion until she heard something about check-ins, but she missed the number it told her to hit, forcing her to wait until the whole thing looped around a second time.

By the time she hit the right number she was scowling at the crumpled paper and its instructions.

"Check-In Office, how may I help you?" A young man's voice said through the phone. He sounded real, not like the other voice.

"My name is Missy."

"Full name, please?"

Missy paused. Her name. The name she'd had to choose. She tried to remember it. It had to be on the paper, right? She looked down at the crumpled mess and tried to find a mention of her.

"Are you still there?"

"Yes!" Missy hissed at him.

There! She found it.

"Melissa De Mar."

"One moment, please."

Suddenly there was music: really terrible and loud music. Missy held the phone away from her ear and glared at it. She began to understand why people hated making calls.

"Alright, Ms. De Mar. You are confirmed for check in.

May I ask if you have found a permanent residence yet?"

Missy glanced at the couch in the far corner.

"No."

"Is this number where you can be reached until you find a residence?"

"Uh…Yes?"

"Excellent. This has been recorded in your file. Thank you for checking in and we will talk to you tomorrow, Ms. De Mar."

Missy nodded then pressed the red button on the phone.

She turned to find Mr. Keeps watching her with his head tilted slightly to the left.

"What?"

"Nothing." He shook his head. "You just don't strike me as a 'Melissa.'"

"I'm not."

"Is that so?"

Missy moved over to the table and took a drink before she answered. Washing the taste of acid from her mouth.

"I don't know my name." She put the glass down slowly. "One of the Others does."

"Others?"

Missy paused. She'd forgotten that he didn't know.

"They… they're the other people in my head." She tried to explain. "The ones who had control back when I was…"

"When you were Miss Mania?"

She nodded.

"How many are there?" Mr. Keeps sat down in the kitchen chair and gestured toward the couch.

She moved over and sat down. The blanket and couch were both soft. She needed soft.

"I don't know." She shook her head as she looked inside and tried to measure it. "Maybe ten?"

The Others grew agitated at her probing so she pulled back.

Mr. Keeps placed his hands on the table and looked down. "And now you have control?"

She nodded.

"Completely?"

Missy hesitated before shaking her head. It was never a complete thing.

"I have to keep fighting them." She answered. "If I let go…"

"I see... Is there something I can do?"

"Don't make me scared." Missy wrung her hands together. "Or angry."

"Those things agitate these 'Others'?"

Missy nodded.

"I will keep this in mind." He stood up straight once more. "With that, I am going to retire. If you are hungry or thirsty, you may use the kitchen. The light switch is over near the wall by the bathroom. Have a good night, Miss De—."

"Missy."

"Have a good night, Missy."

And with that, he left.

She wondered if he slept in the gas mask and suit.

Something about the thought made her smile.

Missy considered turning the lights off, but after everything she'd been through today, a little light sounded better to her. There'd been too much darkness, too much that was unknown. She pulled the blanket up and flopped down onto the couch.

Closing her eyes, she reached out to the other minds around her. Tired, working minds. She watched them toil and daydream and grumble as she drifted off to sleep.

\*\*\*

# Chapter Sixteen

For six years Missy had woken up in the same bed at the same time every single day. She'd had the same pillow, and the floor was exactly the same temperature each morning. She knew where everything around her was, even in perfect darkness.

Tonight, she woke up to all of it being wrong.

She threw the covers off and tried to roll over, only to find the back of the couch was in her way. Rolling the other direction, she found the floor was too close. Her feet hit hard against the thin carpet and concrete.

It took her several seconds to remember everything. The Others were fully riled by the time she did. It took her much longer to quiet them.

Then she did what most people who wake up in the middle of the night need to do.

If there were any vestiges of sleepiness or confusion left inside her mind, the coldness of the toilet seat burned them all away.

When Missy left the bathroom, she knew she wouldn't fall back asleep. The air here was cold; cold enough that she took the blanket off the couch and wrapped it around her shoulders. Her fingers and face tingled with the chill.

She left the office and wandered into the warehouse. It was dark, yet there were a few points of strange light upon the shelves. One of them was the large, crystalline bubble she'd seen earlier. It glowed with a shy, yet scintillating rainbow of colors.

Missy watched it as she reached out to touch the minds

outside. There were only a few, mostly men. Night shift people with night shift problems. Arguments with wives and husbands over how they never saw each other, missing their kids, not sleeping well even at the best of times.

It was all so... mundane.

She'd gotten used to the minds in the institute. There were minds so broken and twisted that they couldn't handle the world around them, and there were minds of the people trying to keep the broken ones safe. There'd been a man named Stephen who lived in the room three doors down from Missy. The room had to be retrofitted to have only nails holding things together. Stephen hated screws. He would tear his hands up trying to take out every screw he could see.

Missy had spent a lot of time reading his mind. She'd found that everything wrong with him was because of a single night in his childhood. His schizophrenic father had barged into his room, placed his hand on the wall, then used an electric drill to force a screw through his flesh and into the wallboard.

Stephen broke that night. He didn't understand why his father would do that. It scared him, tortured him. Every night the memory was there in his head, begging for an answer.

Missy didn't know the answer either. Perhaps if she'd met Stephen's father, she would have been able to provide it, but that had never happened. Yet the way that Stephen's entire personality warped around that one memory, that single unanswerable question... It was both fascinating and terrifying.

Pulling the blanket closer, Missy turned away from the bubble to look back at the office.

Mr. Keeps was also fascinating. She couldn't read him. She shouldn't be able to trust him. Yet she was standing here in his home, nearly defenseless.

Missy would have doubted her own sanity if she wasn't fully aware of how ridiculous that would sound to the other voices in her head. The institute may have released her, but Missy wasn't cured. She merely kept things under control.

There was a difference.

Maybe that was why she was here.

She'd grown... accustomed to madness.

This place had its own madness. Missy looked back at the shelves and her eyes caught on a small doll. There was a light that flickered over it, like a projector with a bad bulb. It would light up the doll's face for a moment, then it would flicker black, then come back on. There was no source for the light, and every time the light came back the face showed a different emotion.

Missy watched as it flickered from happy, then to angry, then remorse, then back to happy.

It was an object of madness. A dozen faces in one place. She felt a kinship with it. She walked closer, watching as the faces flickered faster and faster.

Then it went dark a bit longer.

When the light came back it was red. The eyes of the doll were now black. Its teeth were sharp. It screamed at her.

The Others screamed with it.

Missy all but ran back to the office and shut the door. She stood there shivering, not because of what she saw in the doll, but because she was worse than it. She was like the doll, only all the faces were evil ones. She was the only one who wasn't.

But was she?

Missy stood there in the darkness, her hands holding the door shut. Her mind rattled with the image of the doll's face. A single question could destroy an entire mind. Stephen's past had shown her that. She also knew the questions inside her had the potential to destroy so much more than herself.

She had to believe that she wasn't the face with the teeth.

Lena had thought of her as 'The Sad One.'

Remembering that helped Missy relax. She was okay with that. She'd be the sad face in place of all the monsters.

Missy moved back to the couch. She decided to forget about the doll. It wasn't important. Tomorrow was important.

She laid back down and tried to think about what she wanted to do.

***

When Mr. Keeps left his room that morning, he found that his printer had been pilfered for paper. He also found a note, a crumpled wad of money that he recognized as being his own, and half a bag of peanut butter candy.

He sat down at the table and read the note. It was very short and written in a childish, unsteady hand.

*Thank you. You were kind to me.*

He set the paper down, leaned back, then hummed a little tune.

***

# Chapter Seventeen

Missy sat in the cab of the pickup truck. She had her knees up and her arms around her backpack.

She'd used her power, used it to convince a dockworker to pick her up. He'd been on his way home from working the night shift. He had a wife and two kids and cared about them so much it bordered on obsessiveness. She'd been watching his thoughts as he saw her on the side of the road. He'd worried about her, wondered if she was okay.

It was nice.

Missy hugged the backpack tighter, sifting through the warmth in the man's heart. He was an only child. His parents died when he was young. He'd been lonely for a long time, and full of grief. His wife meant everything to him. His kids meant even more.

It hadn't taken much to convince him to stop. She wanted to go to the city and he was heading that direction. Her last visit had been too much, too fast, but now she knew what to expect.

She opened her pack and looked at the psionic amplifier. It sat on top of Baller's sweatpants. This time she would be ready. She had something she wanted to do. Having a plan, even a stupid, petty plan helped. If she could focus on something that meant it was harder for the Others to take advantage.

She had something to do, and all she required from the nice dock worker was to stop and let her out on his way home.

It wasn't really abusing her powers. Not really.

***

The library intimidated her.

It wasn't built to be intimidating. It was only two stories tall in a part of the city where the buildings regularly reached ten times that. It wasn't white and marbled or adorned with pillars, instead it was brick and mortar with big windows that had been plastered with letters and art from little kids.

Yet something about it disturbed Missy.

She kept staring at the drawings on colored construction paper. The stick figures and scribbled trees and cars. There was one with an airplane her eyes kept turning to. It was pulling at some scrap of a memory down among the Others. It was agitating not to know, not to understand.

What made it worse was how quiet the Others were. She fought them, but instead of surging with anger or hate, or any of their other wants, it was like they'd formed a wall to lock her out of her own memory.

"Why?" Missy whispered as she stared at the plane with its large, looping wings made out of blue crayon.

The wall cracked. She pushed against the crack as the Others screamed to life inside of her. She looked inside, and for a moment, just a tiny moment, she felt a scrap of something.

She saw herself being dragged away by someone bigger and stronger than her. She was resisting it, digging her heels into concrete. She didn't want to look at the person, so she looked at the drawings in the window instead. She remembered staring as hard as she could at an airplane. The plane itself wasn't important, but as long as she was looking at it then she wasn't thinking about—

Missy snapped back to the present. She was standing there on the street, crushing her backpack against her chest and staring at the library.

The Others were back to normal, shifting and screaming

and thundering against her control.

She blinked a few times, squeezing sudden tears out of the way. That little scrap of memory was hers now. The strangeness of it frightened her. She thought of the doll in the warehouse. She thought about the face that flashed from one thing to another, flicker and flicker and flicker. She felt that.

Missy turned and walked away from the library.

She didn't need to go inside, not really. There were people inside already. Some of those were bored, listless, merely spending time instead of using it. Missy picked at those minds, pushing them to wonder about a hero they might have heard of once, one named Psyconic.

One by one, the bored minds were turned to get on the computers and search up the old hero. They idly browsed through the mess, and Missy watched them from her head as she paced the sidewalk outside.

There was a park nearby. Missy could see swing sets and a rusted, paint-chipped climbing area, the older kind that looked like a dome made out of triangles. There were park benches as well, their bleached wood stained with decades of bird droppings.

Missy found herself there before she knew it. There were only two other people in the park, the weather being too ugly and cold for most to enjoy. It was a father and his young daughter. He was sitting on the other bench, watching his daughter hang upside-down by her knees from the top of the dome.

Missy watched through his eyes for a moment, then turned her attention back to the minds inside the library. They'd found nothing new or interesting. Psyconic had disappeared six years ago. He'd never had a heavy presence in the news, but there were traces of everyone on the internet. There was always a fan site or news post or something.

Yet, for Psyconic... it had all ended six years ago. Why?

Missy opened her backpack and looked down at the ratty sweatpants inside. They had a stain on them that was about the size of a quarter. It turned the dark material a lighter, almost lavender color.

What happened to him? Had she hurt him? Had she killed him in whatever encounter had ended her life as a supervillain?

She dug her hands into the fabric and squeezed her fingers, pressing her thumb into the ancient stain. It was all wrong, the world had changed. There was nothing concrete to hold on to. Even this place, worn down by time, and scraped free of paint and lacquer, overlaid with years of bird shit... it still felt like change. It felt like a place that was going to be taken away and rebuilt with cheap plastic and foam instead of steel and grass.

One of the listless found a book about Psyconic and a few other heroes of the time. Missy locked onto the thought and explored the mind that carried it. They weren't a regular at the library, so Missy hopped around until she found one of the bored minds that came here each week. She tapped into her mind and gave it a little push.

A high school girl named Angela found herself really wanting to check out the book then go to the park nearby and read it.

Missy turned her attention away and looked down at her hands. It would be some time before Angela would make her way here. She had competing objectives, such as texting her friends and looking up info about some band they all liked. Missy had distracted her from this, but now she could let her return to it.

She pushed her hands deep into the soft, warm material of the sweatpants, feeling the outline of the amplifier beneath.

In her loneliness, in that moment of wondering where she belonged, where she wanted to be, she wondered if the sweatpants felt the same way. Ball Return's pants had always been more than pants, but she'd never felt like they had a mind, not really. They were more like a force of nature, but here, as she crushed the soft material in her hands, she felt something old; old and strange and lonely.

Missy pulled the pants out and piled them up against her chest as she stared at the spiked circlet that sat underneath them. There was a calling there as well. The temptation, the want, the need for it pulled at both her and the Others.

Missy wondered if she was strong enough.

It seemed like the world was nothing but unanswered questions since she'd left the institute. What had happened to Psyconic? How had Two Town unraveled so quickly? Why couldn't she read Mr. Keeps? Were these bowling ball-summoning pants a sentient thing or not? Why was she so afraid of a kid's drawing? Could she handle the amplifier?

What was wrong with her?

It stung as it spun around her, like stepping on a hive of ground bees and feeling their swarming bites. It thudded in her ears: question, after question, after question…

Missy stabbed a hand down into the bag and wrapped it around the warm metal of the amplifier.

The world opened.

Her back went rigid as thousands of minds became hundreds of thousands. A great clamor of emotion and thought surrounded her, washing back and forth like the surface of a stormy lake. Spikes of anger, fear, hate, shallows of peace, satisfaction, contentment. It all changed, shifted, washed back and forth, swirling low in some places, and soaring high in others.

She also felt the force within the sweatpants. There was something there, but not something natural, it was something created by time and the energy of minds. It was the vestige, a remnant of someone that had existed years ago. It was a spiritual echo, one that weakened unless it was placed with someone who echoed back.

As Missy held both objects, she felt the amplifier tune

itself, not just to her, but also to the nascent mind of the object she held. The mental ocean around her shifted, changing in color, becoming dark with a few bright stars among it; one of them shining brighter than the others.

Missy sought the light. She found a mind like a dusty beer bottle, gritty, cloudy with grumblings of a rough childhood and a job he had loved but hated because of those who bossed him around. It was someone who was at his best in the smoke and stench of a bar, who remembered bowling with his father. He fantasized about going back to bad pizza, nacho cheese, and soda in pitchers with those little slivers of ice that got stuck between your teeth.

Missy knew everything about him. It folded into her like taste on the tongue. The pants sang to the song of his mind. She knew where he lived, what he feared, how his arm hurt from a sprain, how much he loved his neighbor's cranky old dog George. She felt it all.

Then she let go.

Her fingers spasmed as she plied them away from the amplifier one by one.

It wasn't the most important answer to everything spinning around inside her head, but it was one that meant something to her.

She knew what to do. She couldn't find peace for herself, not yet, but she could find peace for a pair of semi-sentient sweatpants.

Now she just needed to wait for Angela to bring her the book, then she would visit the post office.

\*\*\*

Finding a box had been easy. Getting a ride: also easy. She just had to ask someone who was already going there and push a little, and Missy had kept enough of Mr. Keep's money to pay for the stamps and stuff.

It wasn't a bad thing.

Not really.

No, the hard part was writing the note to put in the box. What would she say? How could she possibly explain how she'd decided to give a powered artifact to a seemingly random person?

So she stood there in the post office, at one of those stand-up desk things with the pens on chains and the stacks of envelopes and advertisements for stamps. She stood there with a tiny scrap of paper, and she tried to find the words.

The world moved around her. It was amazing how everyone ignored her, even as she stood there for longer than anyone else. The line flowed through but Missy stayed put. The only person who noticed was one of the postal workers behind the counter. She was an older lady and she was starting to get suspicious.

So Missy wrote some of the same things she had told Mr. Keeps. She wrote about Baller and Two Town and what made the pants important. She ran out of space on the first small square and ended up using two more. Her hand hurt after a time. Writing was hard to do when it had been decades since she'd last tried to. She couldn't even remember being taught to write, but she could do it, if terribly.

When she finished the note, it was a mess of crooked lines and letters. Yet she held it in front of her with pride. She'd written a note, a long one. She'd never done that before.

On impulse she grabbed another scrap of paper from the glass slot and an envelope to go with it. She wrote a letter to Lena. She told her that she missed her and other things that sounded stupid as soon as they were put on paper, but Missy was riding high on the achievement of what she was about to do. She let the words stand.

She would use the address on the paperwork in her bag. She would tell them they had to read it to Lena.

When it was all done, when the sweatpants and their

note were crammed into the box and the box sealed up, she got in line with all the other people. No one recognized her. No one even looked at her. The whole thing filled her with the shining touch of hope.

Yet in the back of her mind, she thought about the doll and its flickering faces. How long until it flickered to black?

***

# Chapter Eighteen

It was only after the package was safely mailed that Missy took the time to read the book. There was a bench in the post office. It was hard, but it was warmer than outside and it only took a light touch to smooth away objections in the minds of the people around her.

The book was part of a series. Its cover loudly proclaimed this with the title: 'Unsolved Mysteries of the Super Powered, Volume 6!' Missy started with the index and found that one of the ten stories focused on the aftermath of the fight between Zenithette and Ninefire, she might have to read that one too.

She turned to the third chapter, the one that dealt with the vanishing of Psyconic.

Missy wasn't a quick reader. She'd always depended on other people to read for her, so doing it herself took time and a surprising amount of focus. The upside was that she processed every single word on the page.

Psyconic had only been an active hero for a few years before he disappeared. The book didn't have a clear description of how his power worked, but it seemed he was able to psychically damage his opponents, never enough to kill them, but usually enough to put them at a disadvantage. Descriptions painted him as athletic but probably not that young. He'd worn a purple mask with four silver studs across his forehead, and a matching suit of purple and silver.

By all accounts he'd been more focused on rescues than any other kind of hero work. There were no stories of his fights with big villains, just ones about him saving people who'd gotten in over their head. One story talked about how there'd been a massive brawl after a car full of drunks ran over a gang member's motorcycle. Both sides had quickly devolved to throwing punches and damaging property. Psyconic had apparently walked through the melee, leaving a wake of dazed and confused people behind him. He'd grabbed the hands of a young mother and her child who'd become trapped in the madness, and escorted them out.

The more Missy read, the more she felt like this wasn't the kind of hero you normally heard about. Every page read like he was some god who decided to do a few nice things each day. He had no great enemy or prey. There were no epic fights atop skyscrapers, or stealing a bomb away from a crowd just before it detonated. There was just a man who saw a person afraid and in trouble and decided to pull them out and get them to safety.

Then the book moved on to a story without a happy ending. Missy shook as she read that he had disappeared in Two Town. She read the description of the area and she knew it. It was down past Mr. Fixit's building, off a side street where there had been a gay bar and secondhand clothing store. She remembered the area. There'd been an abandoned courtyard nearby where she'd sometimes sleep at night.

Psyconic had been seen by two witnesses in the area; they were the last to see him alive. They'd noted him walking by in full costume. They said he wasn't worried or scared, but he'd seemed focused, perhaps a bit grim.

Missy paid attention to every word, crawling through the text at the pace of a snail.

He'd been following her.

She was sure of it. The way the witnesses talked about how he'd been focused, seemingly following something that wasn't there. Miss Mania excelled at wiping the memories of witnesses but Psyconic... he might have been immune. They'd seen him, but they hadn't seen who he was following.

Missy half-wished she could remember, but her memories were dangerous things so she didn't wish too hard.

She turned the page and found it disappointingly short.

Psyconic had never been heard from again.

Missy looked at the date: March 7th. According to her paperwork, Missy had been arrested on March 9th. Two days later.

What had happened in those two days?

She closed the book and let it sit on her lap. Psyconic had been following her, a ghost among many, he'd been watching her. He liked to save people, not to fight people. He'd known what he wanted to do.

He'd saved her.

Missy put the book beside her on the bench and pulled her legs up so she could wrap her arms around them and squeeze. She'd always wondered if he'd just been in the right place at the right time, or if he'd meant to be there, and now she knew. She didn't know if this made her feel better or worse.

She had a few more pieces now, like how he looked. The book contained a nice black and white photo of him in costume. He'd looked so serious.

Missy let her chin rest between her knees as she watched the people move around in the post office lobby. Dozens of minds with little tasks to finish, gifts to send, stamps to purchase, people to complain to.

She needed more.

Something had happened, but why had it taken two days for her to be caught by the police? What had happened in the time between?

Missy tried to think like Lena. Lena would want more information. The book wasn't enough. She would need to find out where Missy was brought. There had to be a record, right? There might even be video.

Missy let her knees go and her feet slapped back down

on the floor.

Post offices were very useful places. They could do a great deal more than just mail a package for you, they could also give you a new name, and a new identity, a new self.

Maybe they could give her one that had access to police records.

Missy opened up her mind and began to search.

***

# Chapter Nineteen

Missy hated the police.

Not for the reason that most supervillains did. Cops weren't good or bad, not all of them. She hated them because they were both. As she stood out in the cold, her hands stuck deep into the pockets of her jeans, she read the plethora of minds inside the police station.

There were two officers inside who'd shot unarmed men in the back. One of them was the chief. There were several that were drug addicts that fed their habits through 'confiscation.' There were some that took bribes, some that kicked suspects when they were down, some that encouraged suicides, and plenty who were racist.

Yet that wasn't all of them.

There were the others, the ones who gave their cell numbers out to anyone they thought needed help and then became paranoid about keeping their phone charged, just in case someone might call. They were the kind of people with hearts too big for the world. There were the ones who pulled the others back, who stopped the bad ones from hurting people more than they could.

Then there was the mess in the middle. The ones who could be both, depending on circumstance. There was so much emotion in a place like this, so much rage, shame, fear, and sorrow.

Missy didn't want to go inside.

Which was why she forced herself to do it anyway.

She stepped through the doors and felt the eyes on her. This station was an older one, which meant it was too small for all of the things it had to do. The waiting area was tiny, lined with uncomfortable benches and uncomfortable people who had come down to bail out their drunken relatives. It was a place that smelled of beer and piss and sweat. Missy looked around and waited for the inevitable to come.

It was a bit of a surprise when most of the people just ignored her, but two didn't. Two people inside took one look at her face and reached for their guns. Missy stopped them, of course, holding them back as they fought her in panic and fear. They'd seen her before, watched her when she was the murderer, the manipulator, and the ruiner of lives.

Missy took a deep breath, then wiped their memories of those things. It might be a bad thing to do, she wasn't sure. Yes, she was doing it selfishly to make her life easier, but it would also help them. The things she'd done in the past had been like nightmares inside their heads, things they'd lived through and wanted to believe they hadn't.

She moved it all away from them. Now they didn't know a thing about her. They were never there. Missy shuffled off to the side of the room as she worked on them. Dr. Chadwick would tell her it was wrong. She wasn't sure why, but she was sure she would have.

Missy let go. One of them stood for a second, wondering why her gun was in her hand, but then she put it back and wandered off. The other one was more suspicious, he scanned the room, trying to piece together why he didn't remember pulling his weapon and why his heart was beating so fast.

His name was Brenden Carsi. He was a beat officer, and one of the many middle-of-the road types in terms of morality. This was just a job to him, but he tried to do it well. Part of that was dealing with superpowers. He knew a lot about supers.

So he kept his weapon out, scanning the crowd of people in the waiting area. He knew something was wrong.

Missy frowned at him. Even though he didn't remember, he was still aware that he'd been manipulated in some way.

People like that were too clever for their own good.

She should keep a close eye on him.

Missy crossed the room, dodging an elderly woman who was cursing out her irresponsible grandson in her mind, even while she was attempting to appear calm and collected on the outside. The fantasies she entertained about what she would do with her kitchen knife and her grandson's ear were elaborate.

Yet that wasn't Missy's problem at the moment. She moved to Officer Carsi and looked up into his face. He was a good six inches taller than her. He was also a few years older, a lot heavier, and he had a neck full of loose skin that was less than attractive from Missy's lower point of view.

"Can you help me?" She asked.

His mental confusion and suspicion focused on her and then were pushed aside to make room for this new problem.

"Talk to the desk sergeant. He's right over—"

"I need to know something."

Carsi looked at her, his suspicion jumping into high gear. There was an intricate dance of 'Suppose this' and 'Perhaps that' going on inside of him, with the prevailing theme being that he couldn't be sure, but he thought there was something not-quite-right about Missy.

The man had good instincts. Missy could respect that.

"He's busy." Missy pointed over her shoulder with her thumb.

Of course the desk sergeant was busy. He was currently dealing with the friendly-looking grandmother with the scary knife fantasies. Officer Carsi glanced over and read the scene almost as well as Missy did.

Then there was another moment of change. Carsi seemed to deflate, relax, pull everything out of himself and throw it away like a losing lottery ticket. Missy felt a complex motivation for this, too tangled and knotted to be unraveled in the short time it shot through his conscious thought. The end result was that he shook his head, cursed a few times in the privacy of his thoughts, then waved her toward a desk in the back.

Missy blinked. She wasn't often surprised by other people, but this one had done just that. She followed him to the desk. The nameplate read 'Det. Gilroy' but Carsi sat down in the seat anyways.

"What is it you want?"

Missy hesitated. This wasn't going like she expected it to.

"Well? Are you—"

"Psyconic." She blurted. She snapped her mouth shut, took a deep breath, then finished the thought. "He was a superhero, six years ago."

She watched Officer Carsi's mind as he typed out the name into some sort of records database. He found the info, scanned it for anything sensitive, then turned to look at her.

There was nothing in the file that helped her. Missy frowned as she read the information straight from Carsi's mind. They had almost nothing on him. He'd been a hero, he'd assisted in talking a few people down from tense situations, but there was nothing there about why he'd been tailing her or why he'd disappeared. In fact, the file didn't even say anything about him vanishing. There had to be something. He was the one they told her about. He'd been the one to— Oh.

"Sorry, I want to know about Miss Mania." She found herself saying before she thought the words through, "About when she was arrested."

Carsi reluctantly obliged, typing the name in, but this time he took his time to read the report that followed. For one, it was a class A threat report, which meant it had no less than six pages of warnings about Miss Mania and how dangerous she was. Carsi raised his eyebrows as he read, scrolling through page after page until he got to the bottom.

When he read that section, Missy's eyes bulged.

She'd turned herself in.

She couldn't believe it. She was reading it straight out of Carsi's mind… but she couldn't believe it. On March 9th, six years ago she'd walked into this very police station with a note in her hand and turned herself in. She'd been using her powers, because there were reports that several officers had tried to shoot her on sight but couldn't make themselves pull the trigger.

She'd walked by all of them without saying a word. She went up to the desk and handed them the note, a note that was apparently redacted from the report.

"I want to see the note." Missy told him.

"Look, miss, I can't...I can't…" Carsi looked at her face, then looked at the photo in the file.

Once again, Missy wiped away the last few minutes of memory, then made him close the record. She got up and started looking for the evidence locker where the note was stored.

This was a bad thing to do. She knew it, but what was one more on the mountain of what she'd already done?

She moved through the room like a ghost, smoothing over any objection that was rising with just a touch of her power. A light distraction, a misdirection, a sudden impulse to look away as she walked through a door that should have been secured.

It only took her ten minutes to find it.

She stood there, in a place that should have been restricted to senior evidence officials, looking at a box. She opened it, shifted through the paperwork until she found a photocopy of the note. It was simple, and terribly disturbing.

*My Name is Miss Mania. Please take me to Dr. Marie Chadwick.*

Missy's fingers trembled.

She'd always assumed Dr. Chadwick had been chosen to deal with her because she was the only one who Missy couldn't control. Yet this… this was telling her that it was Mania who chose! Thoughts reeled and collided inside of her as she read the note again and again.

It wasn't her handwriting.

Missy's handwriting was terrible, blocky, childish. The note was written in small, smooth letters. She hadn't written this. Someone had written it for her.

It had to have been Psyconic.

Somewhere in those two days he had defeated her, pacified her, and sent her here to turn herself in. Had the Others known about Dr. Chadwick and never showed her the memories? Had Psyconic known her?

What was the connection? Why her?

Missy closed the box and wandered back out of the station in a daze, barely even stopping to confuse the minds of the people around her.

By the time she stepped out of the front doors, Missy knew where she had to go next. Part of it made her happy, because it meant she'd get to see Lena again.

Missy had to go back to the institute.

She needed answers that only Dr. Chadwick could give her.

\*\*\*

# Chapter Twenty

It had only been a day since she'd gotten off that first bus, now she was sitting on another one as it drove out of the city toward the distant, forested hills.

This bus rattled and jostled its passengers. The cloth covers on the seats were worn and stained. It smelled a bit like old, wet socks, creating a low-grade irritation among the other passengers. That, in turn, irritated Missy.

Her thoughts were annoying enough without the constant itch of other people's. The words in the note bothered her. She wanted to believe they were wrong, that maybe it was all some terrible mistake where the wrong piece of evidence was put in the wrong box.

But it was just her mind trying to escape reality.

The truth was: She was afraid that Dr. Chadwick would lie, or worse, refuse to answer her questions. She was one of only a handful of people in the world who could do that to Missy. How did you find the truth from a mind that can't be read?

How did they do it?

Missy looked around at the other people on the bus. They were all tired, bored, irritated. There were mothers on their way to see their sons, and men on their way to second jobs, others were traveling to purchase something that could only be bought somewhere far outside the city.

How did they just trust that someone was telling the truth? Especially when there were so many instances of that trust being wrong? One of the men on the bus had been married four times. Each time he'd trusted his wife implicitly and each time he'd been wrong to do so. Why? Why continue?

Missy twisted herself in her seat, pulling her legs up and rolling to one side so she was facing the window. The latch on the window was broken. One of the screws that held it in place had snapped in half.

What had happened in the two days between?

How had Psyconic been invisible to her?

Why the note?

Why Dr. Chadwick?

What happened six years ago?

She'd left the institute on a quest to see a man and thank him, now it was more than that. Something strange had happened that day.

In an effort to distract herself, she opened her backpack and pulled the library book back out. She turned to the chapter about Ninefire and Zenithette.

Ninefire's power was turning pain into fire. He used it to enhance flamethrowers and other fire-making machines. Zenithette could dance on the wind. There were pictures of her in the book, showing a young girl posed like a ballerina in the air, right leg back, left leg straight down with her toes curled.

She'd only been nineteen years old.

Missy remembered what Mr. Keeps had said about her body. It was a horrible thing…

…but Mania had done worse.

She kept reading. Slowly, carefully, she pulled the words from the page and made sense of them. Ninefire had been on a quest for revenge. He'd wanted to kill the people who'd put him in an abusive foster home when he was younger. One of those had lived in the apartments that burned down. Zenithette tried her best to stop him, but she was young, new, and inexperienced. Even so, she'd been the only one there.

She'd given her life and still failed.

Missy turned the page to find this thought illustrated by a full-page picture of the building in flames. Giant holes had been gouged out of the side of the structure, each of them belching fire out into the cold colors of black and white.

The story went on. It talked about how no remains had been found of either of them. Both were presumed dead, but there just wasn't enough to survive the fire to be sure. It ended with an interview with Zenithette's mother. Missy couldn't finish reading it.

She closed the book and put it away. Stretching out her mind, she looked through the broken window, reaching for something other than the hard questions that echoed within.

No minds but those on the bus. They were far outside the city now, traveling through a shell of a town. Hundreds of buildings were slowly being reclaimed by the hills, trees and weeds and the creeping red vines of poison ivy taking the concrete and glass and making it their own. She'd heard that all of this land used to have people on it, but the early days of superpowers had killed too many. These were ruins; places ruined by a lack of people, but to Missy they felt quiet and calm.

The bus driver's mind flickered with recognition. They were nearing the stop in the middle of nowhere with the gate.

Missy's stop.

She readied herself to pull the little string above the window.

She tried not to think about the image of the fire in the book.

A place where a hero died, alone and full of pain. Would she find the same kind of answer for Psyconic?

She hoped not.

She still wanted to tell him.

She had to.

***

Missy stood before the gates.

She hadn't noticed a lot of things here on her way out. The fence around the property was larger and more intimidating, with barbed wire and decals that announced it was electrified. There was also a sign right by the gate. It proclaimed in large, bold letters that the institute contained a host of dangerous individuals and that no entry was permitted without authorization.

Missy wondered if they planned to take the sign down now that she wasn't living there anymore.

She shelved the thought, then stepped up to the side of the gate and pushed the speaker buzzer. There was a moment of delay before a voice crackled through.

"Laywater Institute. Please state your name and appointment time."

Missy paused for a second, then leaned in and pressed the button again.

"Miss.. Melissa De Mar." She hesitated. Her chosen name still sounded wrong as she said it. "I want to see Dr. Chadwick."

This time the silence was much longer. When the voice returned it wasn't just some girl, it was the strict tones of Mrs. Hiln. Even her voice sounded holier-than-thou.

"The Doctor is not here at the moment. You need to make an appointment for these things, Missy." Mrs. Hiln's voice cut through the static by sheer force of volume.

Missy paused. She hadn't anticipated this. Dr. Chadwick had always been there, but only because Missy was. She was her counter, the one kink in her armor. If Missy left then, of course, Dr. Chadwick could also leave.

She shifted her thoughts, then buzzed back, "I came to visit Lena too."

Missy sat in the cooling wind, shuffling from one foot to the other as she waited for some kind of response.

Then the gate clicked and rolled open to the sound of grinding motors. Missy didn't waste her chance; she slipped inside and began the long walk down the gravel road.

Whoever built this place had done it near-perfectly. She'd only walked a few dozen feet inside when she started to sense the minds in the distance. The first was Stephen's. His mind was always painted by that memory of his father with the electric screwdriver. Missy rummaged around in his memories as she walked. Nothing had changed for him in his view. The food had been the same, the world had been just as terrifying, his nightmares remained consistent.

There were more as she got closer. Orderlies and other patients. Missy grabbed as much information from them as she could.

Dr. Chadwick had taken some vacation time the day after Missy had been discharged. There were rumors that this was a surprise to everyone as she hadn't given any notice. Still, most of the people understood why. Six years dealing with Miss Mania had been enough.

Missy winced at some of the things she read, the sympathies each mind had for all the horrors she'd inflicted on the staff and doctor.

Then Lena's mind was there and Missy jumped toward it. Lena was in her room. She hadn't been sleeping well lately and had taken to dozing in the common area. Someone had moved her to her bed. She'd woken up a short while later and had just been lying there in thought.

Missy tried to be gentle as she made her presence known.

After all the things she read from the other minds, it was wonderful to feel the joy and relief from Lena.

Missy spent some time just sharing all that had happened, showing Lena memory after memory of Two Town, Plugger's shop, meeting Mr. Keeps, the doll in the warehouse, the book, and on and on.

By the time she'd finished, she found herself at the front doors of the building. She asked Lena to wait a moment while she moved inside.

Mrs. Hiln was there, her head full of Jesus and presumptuousness. She looked at Missy over her thin-rim glasses and demanded that she get a guest badge and be fingerprinted.

Missy obliged, almost wordlessly. She moved through the motions of a security check, knowing full well that all this security had been to protect people from her. It all seemed rather silly.

She did tweak Mrs. Hiln's memories of the fingerprinting. Missy didn't like getting ink on her fingers, so she just made Mrs. Hiln think she'd already done it and passed the unused cards back to her. It made Missy a little bit happier to see the woman hold the cards so proudly, not even checking to see if they were used because Mrs. Hiln knew they had been.

Then Missy was inside once again.

The only difference was the guest badge pinned to her shirt and the strange feeling that she didn't belong here as much as she thought she did.

She made her way straight to Lena. The door opened and Missy saw her friend lying there, her spine so crooked and her limbs terribly atrophied. Not for the first time, Missy wished she could do something to help.

"I'm here."

*You've been through a lot the last few days.* Lena said in her own mind. *But why are you here?*

Missy sat down on a part of the small bed and told her.

She watched as Lena's mind shivered in shock as she explained the note and what it meant.

*Mentioned by name!* Lena practically yelled the thought.

Then Lena did what Lena did best. Her mind pulled every piece of information apart, categorized it, connected it, pushed and pulled and tried different theories. Missy watched in fascination as thoughts and information moved too fast for her to track.

Then it all settled, but Lena was still as full of questions as Missy.

*You came here to talk to Dr. Chadwick.* Lena said. *But she's not here.*

"Yeah."

*You should break into her office.*

Missy's eyes bulged. Lena was never the one to suggest any break in the order of things, yet here in those words burned a fire of curiosity that stripped everything else away.

"I can't do that! They'll—"

*Dr. Chadwick isn't here, Missy.* Lena's mind pushed the idea. *You can do* anything *and they won't know.*

Missy paused.

Lena was right, of course. Dr. Chadwick was the only thing that really stopped Missy. There were cameras and off-site controls, but it had always been Dr. Chadwick who'd been able to respond immediately to anything she did. She was the one person that Missy couldn't deal with.

"Okay." She nodded and stood up. "I'll keep you in my head, alright?"

Lena gave the equivalent of a mental nod.

Then Missy left, and as far as anyone else in the facility knew, she vanished. She moved around the cameras, knowing exactly where to step thanks to the security officer in the basement. She moved past people as they turned away, pushed minds with distractions so she could slip past, and finally made a janitor unlock Dr. Chadwick's office so he could double check that her garbage can had been emptied.

Then Missy was there. She stood in the dark with the door closed behind her. She found the light switch and turned it on, then looked around the room.

She'd only ever seen this office in the memories of others. They never paid attention to the details. It was a stark place. There were filing cabinets and bookshelves but no flowers or pictures on the wall. There were no diplomas or awards. All was bare.

Missy moved to the desk and found it similar. There was a computer and a place for pens and paper.

There was a single photograph in an old, blackened frame.

Missy picked it up to find a picture of Dr. Chadwick with a man. He shared some of her features, especially around the eyes. He must have been a brother or cousin or something. He was too close in age to be a parent. Dr. Chadwick had the scar in the picture, even though it looked like it had been taken quite a while ago.

There was something strange about the picture. Something that made her skin crawl and things itch in the dark places of her mind. More secrets from the doctor. More things she hadn't known.

Missy put it down and opened the desk.

There was nothing interesting inside, just office supplies.

The computer would be a problem. Missy didn't know the password. That had been kept strictly inside Dr. Chadwick's head for obvious reasons.

Which left the filing cabinets.

Missy rifled through them all, finding her case file with ease. She was astounded by its size. Missy had an entire drawer to herself. There were notes, tests, studies, defensive measures and plans. The paperwork went on and on.

The older stuff was near the back. She found the entry forms, the report on the note. No other fingerprints had been found on it, only Missy's. That wasn't terribly unusual. Superheroes wore gloves and masks for the same reason criminals did: so they couldn't be found.

The next reports were more interesting. She fed what she could to Lena, who took it in and processed.

There was an addendum on a report claiming that

Missy's DNA had been found in Two Town. There'd been some of her blood in an alley. However, no victim or perpetrator had been found. The report was filed the day after Psyconic disappeared, but before Missy had turned herself in with the note.

*That's important.* Lena pushed the thought forward. *You were there.*

"I went to a lot of places." Missy mumbled as she moved to the next file. "I just normally wiped away the minds that found the evidence."

Lena considered this as Missy slowly read through the next page.

No one else had been able to track her movements, and it seemed that whoever wrote the file had been completely ignorant of Psyconic's hand in it. Missy frowned. She knew it was Psyconic who'd stopped her. She knew it, but the report never mentioned his name or even the possibility that a hero had been involved in any of it.

How had she known?

*Very curious.* Lena mused on the fact as well. *Perhaps it was redacted?*

"Maybe."

*Yet it doesn't read like that, does it?*

Missy trusted Lena on this. She didn't know herself, not really, but it was odd that there were no black marker spots like the other redacted report she'd read in the police station.

*Either this is an extremely thorough coverup, or you learned about him in some other way. You said the Others can keep memories from you?*

Missy nodded. That was true. Most of her former life was captured in the minds that raged beneath. Some of the Others would love to share the memories, but Missy was afraid of them. Their thoughts were always full of hate and desire. She didn't want to be infected. She didn't want to be like them.

There were good reasons to keep them where they were:

in the dark, pushed away.

*Do you think you killed him?*

Missy froze as the words hit her. She could have. The Others had been in control. Missy didn't remember much about that time. She remembered bits of the police station, the jail, the long nights shivering in chains, but what happened before was blank and empty.

"I might have." Missy admitted.

*Can you ask the Others?*

Missy's burst of feelings about that traveled over the link with Lena.

*Alright.* Lena paused for a moment. *Maybe you can go to the spot where the blood was found? Maybe you'll remember something.*

Missy nodded and closed the drawer. It wasn't much, but it was something.

As the drawer clicked shut, she heard the crinkle of paper. She was still feeding Lena everything she could, so it was Lena who noticed and told her to stop.

*Pull the drawer out and reach your arm back there. It sounds like something caught in the track.*

Missy followed the instructions. It was fortunate that her arms were thin since the gap between the drawer and the top of the cabinet wasn't very wide. She flailed her hand around for a moment before she caught the edge of a paper.

She listened as Lena described how to slowly pull the piece, keeping a little bit of tension and wiggling it back and forth to clear it from the track. When it finally came loose, Missy found herself with a crumpled and torn page out of some kind of classified report.

It was not a psychological report. In fact, it was something that turned her cold from the scalp down.

It was a piece of a military schematic. In the top left corner of the page, it had information in bold, stating that it was page nineteen of forty-eight for 'Project Loud Dream.'

This page seemed to be specifically examining a broadcast system that might work against individuals with 'M-type' mental powers. There were several proposed uses for the system.

The top suggestion was that it be installed in unmanned combat drones.

*Missy, this means that—*

"Dr. Chadwick tried to kill me."

\*\*\*

# Chapter Twenty-One

Missy left the institute as quickly as she could. If Dr. Chadwick found her here, if she suspected that Missy had been snooping then, well, she didn't know what she'd do.

It was hard to say goodbye for a second time. Missy wanted to take Lena with her, but Lena quickly listed all the reasons that made it impractical. She laid it out with the same elegance she always did. Someone like her was too much for Missy to take care of, and too easy to track. Missy could disappear without a trace, but Lena wouldn't be able to.

Plus, it's not like anyone could interrogate or torture someone who was already locked inside their own body.

So, Missy turned in her badge and shuffled back down the long road to the gate. For a moment she thought that the gate wouldn't open, that she'd be trapped inside once more. However, her fears were unfounded. The gate buzzed and rattled and Missy took the long walk back to the shabby bus stop.

She didn't feel like she'd exhaled at all until she fell down into the threadbare cushion near the back of the next bus and felt the minds around her. None of them even noticed her, but she noticed all of them. She had her mental fingers on each brain, ready to seize them if she needed to.

She knew it was wrong.

She knew this kind of behavior was what made the Others into monsters…

…But Missy couldn't stop being herself.

Dr. Chadwick had always been on the verge of being

a nightmare to her. She was something Missy couldn't control. She was something Missy had fought against and lost. Every night when she closed her eyes, she thought of that machine. She thought of the knife poised before her eyes, so close she couldn't focus on it.

Missy bent over as she realized she was breathing too fast. She squeezed her eyes shut and tried to stop the panic, but it filled her like an ocean being poured into a bucket. There was too much of it. The Others surged. They'd been waiting, watching, sitting in the dark corners of her mind for a moment just like this.

Missy resisted for a time.

But only for a time.

She felt herself pushed back. Part of her was relieved. The panic was no longer there. She was in the darkness of the back-mind now. There was no emotion, not really. There was an echo of it, but it was the kind that didn't really touch you, it slid off of the surface like water on glass.

She watched as the Others charged and flickered into the conscious spot. They bit and screamed and tore at each other like a pack of hyenas. Missy watched as her own face flickered between emotions as the Others wrestled to control her. She watched as they grabbed at the minds of the passengers, then released them as another face fought to take hold.

All while Missy drifted in the dark.

She was never meant to be one of those. She could see that now. She wasn't a strong mind. Like Lena had said, she was the 'sad one.' She watched from afar, but soon realized she wasn't alone.

There were other minds here with her. One was fuzzy, indistinct, and small. She tried to reach out for it but it moved further away. The other was even more different.

It sat beside her. She tried to peer inside of it, but this was a mind in her brain. It had all the powers she did. It deflected everything. There was a feeling in it, a feeling of power. No, not power… of certainty. It was like it knew what it wanted to do, even while every other part of Missy seemed to be held in chaos.

She moved closer. She was curious. Maybe this one should take control. Maybe this one was strong enough to—

It grabbed her.

Mental lines of power wrapped around her and she felt the echoes of the panic. It was moving her, pushing her upward. The Others turned to fight her as part of the fray, but the mind kept pushing, pushing, pushing!

Missy gasped as the emotions flooded back. She blinked and wavered as the Others screamed inside of her. They clawed and bit and tore at her with mental fingernails, but now that Missy was aware of it, she could see the other mind holding them back.

Then it all calmed down.

She was filled with even more questions than before, but somehow just knowing that she wasn't alone in the darkness, that it wasn't just her fighting, somehow that helped.

Missy made an account of the people around her. Some were confused, others had headaches, and the driver had thankfully been left alone. No one was bleeding or screaming, so Missy felt that this was a small mercy for her momentary lapse.

She couldn't let that happen again.

If even one person had died…

Missy shook her head. Everything was confused. The sound of blood still thundered in her ears. She needed to calm down. She needed to go somewhere she felt safe.

No. She needed to see that alley in Two Town. She had to look at it herself. Then she had to track down Dr. Chadwick and 'Project Loud Dream.' This was her list, her priorities.

Dr. Chadwick might not be the enemy. She could be just a part of something that ended up using Missy. There was too much she didn't know, too much that the good doctor had tried to hide from her. Before Missy fled the institute, Lena had theorized that the project was probably based off of the tests they had performed there. They used research from Dr. Chadwick to design a countermeasure to psychic abilities.

Missy wondered if they knew how effective it was. Yes, Mr. Keeps had stopped the one drone, but that had been in spite of Missy's weakness. If he hadn't been there, then Missy could have died, or worse.

Still, she had leads to follow. A project name was enough. She just needed the right mind with the right clearance, and she'd unravel everything.

Missy thought about the amplifier in her backpack. She could use it now, find what she needed…

The taste of the Others still lingered in the confused minds of the people around her. She couldn't use the amplifier, not now. If the Others took control while she was using it then she might not get a second chance.

No. She would do this without it.

It was too much power, too strong to use while her emotions still kept her heart racing. She needed calm and focus to handle it. She had neither right now.

Once more she wished it wasn't her. She wished it was someone else in this head, fighting these demons and problems. Lena could have done it better. That mystery mind in the dark of her back-brain could have done it better. Missy wasn't the right one. She wasn't strong enough.

But it had pushed her up instead.

She didn't know what it meant. She wanted to feel safe. She wanted a place to call home, and the only place she thought might accept her was abandoned and condemned.

As the bus rumbled back to the city, a few people heard the quiet sounds of her crying in the back. They did their best to ignore her and let her have her space, but Missy never had space. She always knew. She always felt it all.

***

# Chapter Twenty-Two

Two Town was different at night.

It hadn't been easy to get to. Missy had tried to do the same things she'd done before, but after losing to the Others and the strangeness of all that followed, she felt like she should avoid using her powers too much.

In the end, she found a Chinese place that promised to deliver anywhere. She was still hungry, so with the little bit of the money she had left from Mr. Keeps and a bit of persuasion she convinced them to deliver her along with the food.

So now she was standing on the street in front of Plugger's shop with two bags full of General Tsao's chicken, Kung Pao beef, and crab puffs.

She could feel Plugger's mind. He was much the same as he was two days ago. His thoughts seemed to spark and fizzle with anger, anger born from being abandoned and betrayed by a world he loved. Missy knew he had no reason to open the door to her, but the night had brought true darkness to the old town.

Every building was just a silhouette against the stars. There were no streetlights or neon signs anymore. Missy hardly recognized it like this. It was like a wilderness, but one built of concrete and steel. There were sounds, though, sounds of things that moved in the dark. There were flashes of reflective eyes. It could be just racoons or cats, but it could also be something bigger and hungrier that lurked out in the black.

This used to be a place she'd felt safe in.

She heard the scritching sound of something moving behind her, so she hurried forward toward the light of the shop window. The twenty feet was too short a distance to fully prepare herself.

The memory of her last encounter still stained her mind. The things she'd read from him, the rage that he'd focused on her. It shouldn't mean so much, but it did. Those were things she didn't remember. He'd given her more horrors atop the hundreds she already carried.

Missy wasn't sure she could carry much more.

Pushing the takeout bags in front of her like a shield, she knocked on the dusty glass.

Plugger opened the door and Missy read his mind.

He hated Chinese food. This was abundantly clear by his reaction to the smell of it. This had already gone terribly wrong.

"I, uh…" She tried to think of something to say, anything.

Then his mind shifted.

"Ya know, if you were reading my mind then you'd know I hate that stuff." Plugger said without expression, "Which almost makes me believe you ain't the same."

Things changed too fast inside his head for Missy to track. She didn't know what the right thing to say would be, so she went with the truth.

"I'm trying to be."

"Why're you here?" He asked.

"Had nowhere else to go."

Missy felt the words leave her mouth before she really understood them. It wasn't strictly true, but she'd had nowhere else to go that was so close to where she wanted to be.

Nevertheless, Plugger grunted and stepped aside, leaving Missy enough space to slip through with the takeout bags.

The shop seemed just as different as the town. Maybe it was because the outside was so dark, but inside it seemed brighter and cleaner than before.

The large spot on the wall that had held Ball Return's pants was now the home to a few posters depicting the old place. Missy's eyes lingered on the photographs of the Two Town she'd known before, a place that didn't shine so much as gleam. It was a place that was clean in the afternoon and filthy every morning, a place where smiles and shouts crushed together in a mix of joy and anger.

Two Town was where stories were made.

She turned away from the wall when she realized that Plugger had said something, and she hadn't been listening.

"I'm sorry, what?"

Plugger grunted and moved toward the back of his shop. Missy waddled after, trying her best not to touch anything with the bags of food.

"What did you do with the pants?"

Missy lifted the bags up onto the counter before she answered.

"I found someone they liked."

She hovered over the food. Plugger may not like Chinese food, but she was starving. She'd been so focused on everything else she'd neglected her own stomach. She unpacked the General Tsao first.

"No kidding?"

Missy nodded as she popped the white container open and smelled the spices inside.

Again, there was a massive shift of things inside the old bouncer. Missy felt the edges of it, but she didn't look too closely. As she peeled the paper off of some chopsticks, she realized she was afraid of what else might be there inside his mind.

"Here."

Missy jumped as two plates and a scattering of utensils were dropped onto the counter in front of her.

"Thanks."

Missy chose a fork and plate and began to make use of

them.

"You're really not reading me, are you?" Plugger crossed his arms and leaned back against the wall beside her.

For a moment he looked just as Missy remembered him. The small smile on his lips, the arms bare, and heavy with muscle.

She shook her head to answer his question.

"Why not?"

Missy didn't want to answer, so she stabbed a piece of chicken with her fork and lifted it to eat.

"Stop."

Missy stopped, mouth open.

"I, uh..." Plugger moved forward and opened his hand, "I licked that one before I came out here."

Missy shut her mouth.

He licked it?

She stared down at the fork. It was a bit wet.

The laughter was more of a surprise than any other part of it. Missy found herself nearly collapsing as she giggled and wheezed. Plugger stood by in shock for a moment, but the sounds she made must have been too much, because after a second, he joined in.

When Missy's mind cleared, she looked around and realized the world felt different. That it felt right. *That* had felt like Two Town: gross, stupid, and somehow heartwarming. It was amazing... She'd never really laughed like that before. She'd never had a stupid surprise that was so strong, so unexpected.

"You really aren't like the other one at all." Plugger pulled a pair of stools and cleaner utensils from the back and offered her one.

Missy took them gladly and settled in with the 'clean' fork and began to mix her pile of steaming rice with the glazed meat.

"Um, well. It's more than just me in here." Missy

tapped the side of her head. "There are some who are... you know."

Plugger raised an eyebrow as he poured fried rice onto his plate.

"When they put me in the... the institute." Missy found words a little hard. It was difficult to say things like that to other people. "The doctor scared the Others away, so... I came out."

"But they're still there?"

Missy nodded as she ate. She felt his anxiety as she chewed. Waiting for an answer made the old enforcer tense up.

"They are." She said after swallowing. "But... I've found that there are good ones too."

Missy put her fork down and pressed her palms to the sides of her head. The Others were noisy because she was thinking about them. Yet, she could feel the other two behind the noise. They were like shadows in the distance, caught only when she looked for them.

"It... isn't easy." Missy let her hands drop. "But I think... I think I have help in keeping things together."

"So Mania...."

"Is the bad ones." Missy ate another scoop of food.

Plugger leaned back from his plate of rice and crossed his arms again. He did that when he was thinking. Missy realized this only after watching him with her eyes instead of with her brain. It was amazing that she'd never noticed it before.

"What a fuckin' bastard of a thing."

Missy had a hard time disagreeing.

\*\*\*

Plugger didn't have any real furniture in the back of his shop beyond a ratty military cot and a collapsible table. There was also a fridge, a microwave, and a smallish oven like the kind you'd see in sandwich shops.

She thought she could smell the remnants of burnt toast from it as she tried to make herself comfortable on the shop floor.

The floor wasn't bad. Missy remembered nights sleeping inside bank vaults, abandoned apartments, and even down in the sewers. At least it was dry here, and the burnt toast smell was pleasant-ish.

She pushed the meager clothing around inside her backpack in an effort to make it more pillow-like. Plugger had provided her with a blanket, so she had some insulation from the ground. Still, she shifted and wriggled back and forth.

She'd gotten soft.

Years with a bed and pillow had made this harder. Her body had aged on her while she wasn't paying attention. She felt aches and pains in her feet and back that she swore hadn't been there back in the day.

There was also the fact that in order to make her backpack into a suitable pillow, she'd been forced to remove the sharp, pointy amplifier. It sat on a lower shelf next to the aisle she was sleeping in, between Oxheart's iron bell and a collection of scales that were said to have fallen off of Tributary's back. Both were heroes she remembered from her youth. She had no idea where they were now or why Plugger would be selling parts of them.

Missy shifted and tried to sleep in as many ways her body could contort within the small place between the shelves. It used to be easier. It used to be that she would pass out from exhaustion, and sometimes pain. There was always something that dragged her down to rest.

Here, everything was dragging her up.

There were just so many questions.

Missy didn't enjoy the feeling. She always had answers. She was the one who knew every answer. She knew if Johnny really liked Sally. She knew what the boss wasn't telling his employees. She knew where Allison's husband went every Tuesday when he said he was playing poker with the guys.

This was new to her. All of it.

They wouldn't let her sleep. She wanted to know what Dr. Chadwick had to do with an anti-psychic weapon program and why there was a two day gap between Psyconic's disappearance and Missy turning herself in. She wanted to know why Miss Mania's note wasn't in her handwriting and why it led her straight to Dr. Chadwick.

The worst part was that there might be answers for her.

The amplifier could help her find some of them: right here, right now. She just had to touch it and it would open her mind to so many others. She could find someone who knew, someone with clearance or who happened to be in the right place at the right time to overhear something, to see something.

Missy's hand had already moved toward it, her fingers outstretched, the Others whispering to her about how wonderful it had been when she'd used it before. It'd felt so good to find a home for Baller's old pants.

She almost did it. She almost forgot what it meant when the Others wanted something.

She pulled her hand back and shoved it deep beneath her backpack.

No, it wasn't going to be like that. She glared at the silver circlet. To everyone else it was just another piece of junk in a shop full of it, but to her it was the easy answer. It was the way to get everything she ever wanted.

The problem was that Missy had already had everything. She'd been rich, powerful, subject to no law or restriction. It had turned her into a monster. The amplifier wasn't a crown, it was a shackle. It begged to be used, it made her dependent on it.

She'd lived six years without it.

A night full of questions shouldn't stop her. Even if they were big questions.

Questions as big as the world.

\*\*\*

# Chapter Twenty-Three

Missy woke to the sound of shouting.

She opened her mind to the world and found that there was something terribly wrong. She couldn't focus on anything. Everything seemed foggy and hard to grasp. Still, there was something immediately evident: there were more than two people here now.

She opened her eyes next. She was still in the shop. She was still lying on the floor, but everything was blurry, and her arm hurt like it had been stung. She moved her eyes back and forth, trying to make sense of it.

What was happening? Why couldn't she read them?

"Both down?" It wasn't Plugger's voice. It was someone else. He sounded tense, maybe scared.

"Confirmed." Another new voice. This one was a woman. "Owner's in back. Made it quick."

Missy's heart thundered as she heard the meaning in the words. Still, she felt like she should be more upset. All of this felt like it was happening far away, to someone else. Even the Others inside of her felt sluggish, like they—

No, like *she'd* been drugged.

Missy fought harder to think.

She'd been drugged. That's why her arm hurt. It's why she couldn't focus. She knew this feeling. They used to do this to her for days after she'd had an outburst at the institute. The Others would do something terrible, Dr. Chadwick would stop them, then Missy would come out to deal with the drugs and punishment.

Missy felt herself panic, but it felt as far away as the

rest of her thoughts and emotions. All of her worst fears were coming to life.

A boot stepped through the aisle she was in. It was military, big, the kind with laces all the way up to the calf. It moved toward her as Missy struggled to twitch a finger, to grab a mind, anything.

"She's awake." The woman in combat boots announced.

"Yeah?"

"She shouldn't be awake."

"She's a super." There was the sound of someone spitting on the floor. "This is the kind of shit that happens. Are we dead yet?"

"No."

"Then it's fucking working."

"Should we give her another?" Boots asked.

Missy held her breath. She didn't want another. She didn't want to wake up somewhere else, even more confused. This couldn't happen, not like this. She knew she'd face consequences someday, just like she knew she deserved it. The things Mania had done... that she'd participated in. They deserved to be punished, but not now! She still had questions. She hadn't found him yet. She hadn't told him yet.

"In a minute. Find the secondary, then give her another dose." The man finally responded.

She thought about Plugger. They said they'd taken him out. Had they killed him? Had they just knocked him out? Missy hoped he was just asleep. If they'd killed him just for opening his door to her when he had no reason to...

Now she was angry. Her face didn't show it. In fact, her face was drooling a bit onto the wood floor of the shop. Inside, though, she burned.

The Others burned with her. They liked anger. They liked rage. Even under all the drugs they felt it and wanted to be part of it. They wanted to be part of what would come next.

Missy's hand moved.

"Have you found it?" The man asked.

"Negative." Boots answered, "I checked her bag: twice. It wasn't there."

"Fuck! It's part of the retrieval. We don't leave until we have it."

The amplifier! There were a million reasons why this was even worse than just wanting her. It meant this wasn't revenge, this was about using her for something. No one stole a psychic and a psychic amplifier just for fun.

Missy made sure not to look at the shelf. She knew it was there. If the soldiers here knew what it looked like then they would've noticed it, but they didn't. That meant that they were looking for an unknown shape in the assortment of junk all around them. Just like the stuff in Mr. Keeps' van, it was camouflaged by a thousand other trinkets.

Missy knew. That was her only advantage.

The Others surged together inside of her. They knew what to do. They knew what could let the rage out, what would let them move and touch minds again. They wanted it. They hungered for it.

Missy focused everything she had on turning over. She rocked once, then a second time, then on her third try her body flopped to the side, her arm falling limply into the shelf next to her.

Her hand touched warm metal.

Her mind expanded with potential. Missy fought not to gasp or show any other sign. She moved in her head, instead. She moved to the mind of the woman. Her control was still sluggish, wrong, but now there was a torrent of raw power behind it. The Others were working with her, survival driving them to cooperate. She moved through the woman's thoughts, moving things... changing things... searching for information.

She found the name of the drug they'd given her: Temazepam. It should have knocked her out for eight to ten hours. Luckily, Missy's mind wasn't built on the same architecture as other people's. She was still here, if terribly compromised. The woman was a former military medic. She was a contractor for a private army, working on orders.

There were stimulants in her case as well. Missy didn't know anything about them, but the medic did. There were combinations of chemical compounds floating around in her head, stacked to the side of her thoughts in case she needed them to counter the effects of the sedative.

The woman's name was Patricia.

She was thirty-six. She worked out four hours a day and secretly hated her boyfriend, but kept him around to toy with until she could find someone better. She was a sadist, finding enjoyment in hurting others. This job gave her so much material to fantasize over, so many things she'd done to torture those that couldn't fight back.

The Others loved her. They wanted to read more. Missy pulled their focus back under her control.

She moved through the mind and made a change, made the hands move some bottles and vials around, then wiped the memory away. She could have told the woman to grab her gun, turn around, and shoot the others in her squad. It would have been easy; it would have solved the problem.

Missy didn't want to just solve the problem anymore.

All the time she'd spent with Lena had taught her a few things. One of them being that more information was always worth pursuing. These soldiers didn't know anything about why they'd been sent to kidnap her and steal her stuff. They had orders and a chain of command, but if they brought her back… if they thought she was sedated and no longer a threat.

Then maybe they'd get her close to a brain with some answers.

Missy moved another set of thoughts inside of Patricia.

"Found it!" Patricia yelled as she yanked the amplifier out of Missy's grip with a gloved hand and tossed it to the other soldier.

Missy lost her connection. She felt a bit nervous. This was part of her plan, but losing her power, being unable to focus, unable to touch and control these people, it was a waking nightmare.

"Great." The man walked into the aisle with her, his hand holding the amplifier by a pair of gloved fingers, like it was a toy. "Give her another dose then we'll go."

Patricia nodded. She reached into her case, grabbed a vial, loaded a shot, then shoved it into Missy's arm.

The liquid burned as she pushed the injector. Missy felt the pain, but it was out there far away, somewhere else.

Then the drugs took hold. Her heart pumped faster, the fog grew thinner.

Missy was awake.

Everything in her body felt worse somehow. Her mind raced, thoughts ricocheted off one another. The sound of rushing blood filled her ears. Her hands started to shake. Chemicals fought chemicals within her.

Missy reached out and grabbed Patricia's mind again. She rode with it while keeping her own body limp and silent.

Patricia lifted Missy's body in a fireman's carry. Missy felt it all, but kept it distant. She focused on Patricia instead. She stayed quiet, lurking in the corners while Patricia carried her outside.

Each time there was a doubt or suspicion that Missy's body wasn't quite as limp as it should be, Missy squashed the thought. She kept the medic nice and happy as she moved to a van whose painted panels proclaimed it to belong to carpet cleaners. It was terrible camouflage in a place as dead as Two Town, but they didn't care.

They knew there'd be little resistance. In fact, the intel given to their team suggested that they wouldn't face more than three people.

Why did they think there were three? She made note

of the inconsistency, then kept watching.

There was a gurney in the back. It was kept clean, but Missy read all sorts of memories of it being covered in blood, sweat, and screams. Patricia had done a lot of work in the back of this van, teasing out secrets with carefully crafted pain. Then, even after she'd gotten what she needed, she'd pushed her victims even more. She'd wanted to see them squirm. She did it because there was a need to hurt others, to be in control, but the torture never really made her feel better. It just made the hunger for it deepen.

Missy watched from Patricia's eyes as her body was thrown down on the gurney. She took over for a moment, adjusted her shivering body so she was comfortable, then wiped Patricia's memory of it happening. The other man, Larson was his name, got in the front seat and started the engine. He was a sergeant. Patricia hated him.

That wasn't much of a surprise considering Patricia hated everyone.

They rode in silence, the medic mentally grumbling at her orders not to harm the body. Orders that hadn't existed until Missy had planted them there. The woman fantasized about cutting the flesh between Missy's toes, sticking shards of broken glass within them, then letting her loose somewhere and watching her try to run.

The fantasies moved onward from there, becoming even more depraved. The Others reveled in all of it. They made Missy sick. She wished she could shut it off, look anywhere else, but this is where she had to be right now. Patricia was the one with eyes on her, she had to make sure those eyes only saw what Missy wanted them to see.

The ride was a long one. They left the city, moving out and down along the riverside. Missy read from the driver's mind that this used to be an industrial area before the collapse. Now their mercenary group had taken up residence, turning an old steel mill into a modern-day fortress. There were hidden gun turrets, ambush pods full of soldiers, and sonic weaponry installed all around it.

Missy paid attention to all of this as the driver moved them through checkpoints that looked deserted. The area reminded Missy of where Mr. Keeps lived and worked. There were workers here, just like there'd been back there. These workers were all military, though. All of them were ex-this and retired-that. A great many of them carried the word 'dishonorable' somewhere in their history. The feel of their minds made Missy's skin itch and crawl. She wanted to scratch herself all over.

But she didn't. She stayed where she was, limp and lifeless, trying to fight the terrible things being done to her body. As long as her mind worked then no one would be allowed to notice.

Missy sifted through the minds in the base. There was a commander here. Missy tried to read him but he was too far away, her focus too dulled and twisted. She could only read and control the two in the van. She'd have to get closer to affect anyone else.

She hoped the commander had answers for her. Specifically, she hoped to find out if he knew anything about the assault drone. This base was exactly the kind of place that would keep a thing like that.

The van stopped. Patricia opened the back door and shoved the gurney out onto a landing. The air smelled of metal, rust, and oil. Missy was pushed across the dock to a pair of large doors. She grabbed snippets of information from the minds around her as they moved by.

The drone had been here. A dock hand named Eddie had moved it outside four days ago for flight tests. There'd been a commander there to oversee the process, one named Albright.

Another mind gave her a rumor that they had a new contract, a big, anti-super one. There had been a favor for a favor deal with someone high up in the government. Missy passed another mind, learned that Commander Albright had been pissed about the loss of the drone. There'd been a lot of yelling.

They reached the end of the loading dock and moved into the main section of the base. It was an old steel mill, so it was basically a four-story metal cavern with tracks on the ceiling. Chains and hooks hauling buckets of molten metal used those tracks to move from one station to another. Gigantic, and equally abandoned, furnaces stood at the far end of the place. It still smelled deeply of hot iron and sweat, but overlayed with the scents of gun oil and stale MREs.

The floor had been divided up with prefabricated walls. They were all the same shape and the same shade of gray. Missy read the minds she could, making a map of the place. She found the communications center, barracks, mess area, bathrooms, and gun range. Patricia pushed the gurney through it all, soldiers moving as fast as they could to get out of her way.

Patricia had a reputation, even among them.

Missy found a mind in the medical area. It was that of another medic, one with an unhealthy addiction to opioids. His mind was more unfocused than Missy's with all the drugs in her system, yet one thing stood out as clear: He was very glad that he did not have to deal with this operation.

Missy wasn't being taken to the medical area.

This caused her to panic. She'd expected them to stabilize her and attempt to sedate her even further. It would have been what most medical professionals would have done. Missy hadn't even thought to check Patricia's mind for that information.

She did that now. What she found gave her pause.

The orders were to bring Missy straight to the commander's office, where another individual would take her away. She was never meant to stay; this was just a handoff.

She pulled her focus back and struggled to keep her body still. The drugs were still fighting each other. She'd read the long list of complications from inside Patricia's head. She'd counted on being placed in the medical area, so that she could push the people there to cleanse her system.

Now that wasn't possible. One thing you couldn't push in a military system was a disobedience of orders. Missy had the power to, of course, but the moment she did, it would create a ripple of problems throughout the base. If she'd been in her normal mind and normal body this would've been fine, but she wasn't. Things were difficult enough as it was, like the mental equivalent of running after you'd had the wind knocked out of you.

Missy watched from Patricia's eyes as they passed the medical area. She could still make her stop, make her help, but then Missy could lose her chance. If the alarm went up, there was a good chance that whoever hired them would run. It was the usual response when any group knew she was coming. There was little defense against her when she was awake.

She pulled her focus back even further, keeping only the lightest touch on Patricia to remove suspicion from her mind. Missy focused on trying to calm her own body, her own mind. The Others were agitated under the drugs, alternating between dullness from the sedatives, to raging want from the counteracting cocktail.

The lull of sleep dragged her down. As she pulled back on her power she felt more of the sedative. She wanted to rest, to sleep, to let it all fall away.

Instead, she reached out and grabbed a hold of Patricia's mind, just seconds before drifting off.

Some wakefulness came with it. She was fending off the effects of the drugs by using Patricia's mind. Somehow, she was taking enough alertness away to fight her own incapacity. Missy moved and took the mind of the other soldier in their little convoy. It was difficult to maintain both, but her focus grew with it. The Others raged louder inside of her.

She had no idea why this was working, but it was. She needed to stay in the other minds in order to keep herself awake. Her own body felt awful. Her skin was cold and clammy, her heart was beating too fast, there was a taste of metal on her tongue.

This wasn't good.

They moved toward the old, abandoned furnaces, and Missy felt the mind of Commander Albright.

She leaped for it, trying to focus on it. It was slippery, but she felt pieces of it. The rumors gleaned from earlier were right. This wasn't a contract job. The whole operation had been undertaken to repay a favor. Albright was angry about the loss of the drone, and angrier still that the damned doctor pushed him to eat the loss and keep trying to capture Miss Mania.

Missy paused and tried to dig back in the mind to where it had thought about the doctor. There'd been something there. The closer she got to Commander Albright, the more she could do in his head. It took a few seconds, but then she had it.

And Missy failed to control herself.

Her body gasped. Her eyes opened wide. Her control over Patricia and the other minds shook loose. She felt their confusion in passing, but it didn't matter.

No matter how much sedative was inside of her she wouldn't be able to sleep now. Fear: fear kept her awake. Adrenaline poured through her body as panic mounted higher and higher and higher.

Just down the hallway, standing in the commander's office, was Dr. Marie Chadwick.

\*\*\*

# Chapter Twenty-Four

Missy had mere seconds to react. She made the two soldiers turn the gurney around and tried to push them to leave. This wasn't as easy as smoothing away tiny inconsistencies like making them think she was asleep. It required a stronger, finer control.

Between the drugs and the fear pumping through her heart, her mental grip was imperfect. She'd only made it a few feet when her hold on Patricia's mind slipped.

The medic pulled her gun and shouted. "What the—"

Missy recaptured the mind but it was too late. People noticed, they turned. They knew enough about the operation to be dangerous. They knew the body on the gurney was a super. They didn't know what kind, but the shout and the gun had brought attention.

"Hello, Missy."

Missy swung the bodies of the two guards around. They pulled their weapons and leveled them at Dr. Chadwick. The hands shook, both sets of them, in the same fashion and in the same rhythm. They shook on Missy's thundering heartbeat. She pushed herself to sit up on the gurney. Her body was hot, too hot. She couldn't feel anything but the heat as she moved.

The industrial furnaces loomed behind Dr. Chadwick. Commander Albright stood beside her. Together, they stepped out into the space between the busy military floor and what remained of the foundry's former existence. They stood there on the border of the present and the past, watching her. The commander in his gray merc uniform and the doctor in white.

The base broke into a panic of activity, and Missy did

her best to confuse the issue. Soldiers and workers began yelling at each other. She made the commander tired, pushing him toward sleep with a mental shove. He sat down and collapsed on the floor.

Amidst the chaos, Dr. Chadwick stood there. She wore the same kind of lab coat, the same kind of sensible shoes. She still wore the same glasses, the same cold expression on her face.

She wasn't the same, though.

Her eyes burned, her lip curled.

"Why?" Missy used her own voice as she slipped off of the gurney and tried to stand. "Why…? You let me go."

Dr. Chadwick answered by pulling a gun from her lab coat's pocket and leveling it at Missy's head.

Missy froze and the world froze with her. Dozens of bodies stalling, slowing, stopping as she stared at the weapon.

That could kill her.

"What did you do to him?" The doctor's voice was raw and low.

"What?" Three voices spoke as one.

Missy shuddered as she realized she'd used the mouths of the two soldiers near her as well as her own.

Things were getting confused in her head. She was losing track of who was her and who were other people. She didn't feel right. The Others were scared of the gun. They abandoned her. It wasn't right. None of this was right. She felt her fingers itch to cut something. She felt the urge to run, to hide, to hug her wife close and never let go. No, these weren't her. Those thoughts were from other people. Who was she?

"The night before you left, you said something to another patient."

Missy couldn't stop staring at the gun. She couldn't do anything to stop it. Sure, she could tell the other soldiers to turn, shoot, something, but Dr. Chadwick could still fire. Missy could still die.

Her breathing grew faster, more panicked as she stood beside the gurney, arm gripping the rail, trying to compensate for a body that was full of poisons. She was having trouble judging who she was and who were the people under her control. They were all terrified together; all so similar, yet not the same. Her head swam with contradictions.

"You said 'Psyconic.'" Dr. Chadwick stepped closer, "You said his name. Why?"

Missy tried to step back but stumbled. She grabbed the gurney for support but it started to roll away under her weight. What did the doctor have to do with Psyconic? It didn't make sense. None of this made any sense! She told Patricia to fire her gun, not to kill but just to scare Dr. Chadwick. Patricia's finger squeezed the trigger and the gun let out a soft click.

"No, we didn't give them live weapons." Dr. Chadwick answered Missy's unasked question. "I knew it was possible you'd take them over."

Missy told the other guard to draw his gun and fire. Again, there was nothing but a click. She pushed out a little more, her mind still not working the way it should, her control still thin and erratic. She got another soldier, but found he had no weapon on him.

"Why did you say his name?"

"I…I need to thank… He was..." Missy tried to move back once more, rolling the gurney with her this time. She made the soldiers move in between her and Dr. Chadwick.

The gun stayed on her, though. Every time Missy tried to block it, Dr. Chadwick just moved to compensate. Missy couldn't control her, couldn't stop her. She had no power over the doctor. She was the one who controlled Missy. She had the chair… and the drugs...

"Psyconic." Dr. Chadwick raised her voice. "What did you *do* to him?"

"What?"

"What did you do?" Dr. Chadwick rushed the last few

feet, pushing aside the soldiers while Missy's thoughts screamed and scratched at each other.

The metal of the gun pressed into her head. She stilled as much as she could. Her body shaking, the Others screaming inside. Her tenuous control over the people around her quivered and collapsed.

Missy was alone in her head.

No one else but her.

"What did you do?" Dr. Chadwick's voice was a cracking whisper.

"I don't know!" Missy cried. "I think… I think he saved me."

"How? What happened?" The gun pressed harder into Missy's skin; biting, cutting.

"I don't know."

"TELL ME!"

"I don't know!" Missy felt tears bead in the corner of her eyes as she realized this was how she was going to die. She didn't even understand why. "They won't let me know. The Others keep it from me. I tried… I don't know."

"Then I want to speak to them." Dr. Chadwick's voice was cold, hard.

Missy tried to obey. She tried to reach for them. She had to obey Dr. Chadwick, but the Others didn't want to. There were so many of them. Missy grabbed and lunged at them but they scattered and ran. They were afraid.

"They're scared."

"I don't care!" Dr. Chadwick pushed the gun even harder, forcing Missy's neck to bend. "Tell me!"

Then one of the Others came up.

Then Missy remembered.

She was alone in an alley. It'd been raining. She was in a sweatshirt and jeans. Both were soaked down to the skin. Her arms were wrapped around herself, shivering and clammy. Her mind screaming inside, in pain and confusion. Her feet were bare for some reason. Her toes were black with the muck from the drainage ditch that ran through the center of the alley.

There was a body.

It was that of a young man. He was laying on his back next to the brick wall. He was wearing a mask. It was purple and silver, with points on the side. His eyes were open, but there was nothing behind them. Water ran over his face and he didn't even blink.

Missy's mind screamed as she watched him. It screamed louder and louder. She turned to run away and then she felt something overtake her. Something rose up and wiped her away. The rain and the alley faded to white.

Missy was breathing too fast, the memory hitting too hard. The alley… it had been in Two Town. No cracks anywhere. Caulky always took care of them. The man on the ground was Psyconic. She recognized his suit from the book. What had she done?

"TELL ME!"

"I…." Missy didn't know how to say it. She didn't understand.

Maybe she didn't want to know.

Maybe it was better if she died.

The image of the young man lying there, unmoving, with empty eyes consumed her.

Missy pushed her head into the gun and took a deep breath. Her body still didn't like it. Her mind was still confused and broken. Her heart thundered, her lungs labored… but Missy was fine now.

She should have died six years ago.

Maybe it was better this way.

"I don't know." She said it again, but this time it was with focus. "All I know is that he saved me."

The gun pressed harder into Missy's head, making her stumble back a step and take the gurney with her.

Then there was a sound from far above.

It was a soft, metal chime that reverberated in the large, open room. The world faded, turning black and white around them. A violent saxophone burst forth, competed with a piano to see who could jump from one key to the other in the strangest order.

Dr. Chadwick turned. In that second there was another sound, like a gunshot but corrupted, recorded and played back on a record player. Dr. Chadwick's gun flew from her hand, flipping end over end like it was in some sort of cheesy movie.

Mr. Keeps was here.

Missy didn't know how or why, but she knew that it was him. She let go of the gurney and staggered away while Dr. Chadwick scrambled to get her gun. Missy reached out and controlled Patricia once more. The medic was confused and pissed off, not knowing what was happening. Missy made her think the gun would help. Patricia would be safer if she had the gun. The medic scooped it up, and Missy made her point it at Dr. Chadwick.

She reached out further, moving through minds, moving bits and pieces. She made them tired, she put them to sleep. Then she found a mind that wasn't a soldier. Plugger was here. He was alive!

After the kidnapping she hadn't been sure. It was good to read him again. He was climbing down from a window above, mentally berating himself for joining in on Mr. Keeps' crazy scheme. There was more underneath that, but Missy didn't have time for it.

She moved on, moving from one mind to another. It was slow, but it was the best she could do with the drugs still in her system.

Then everything was quiet. Everyone was asleep except for Missy, Patricia, Dr. Chadwick, and Plugger.

Mr. Keeps had to be here as well but she couldn't read him, of course.

"You... you're a monster." Dr. Chadwick's voice came

out broken and choked.

"I was."

The monochrome dream around them shifted and rippled with their words. Neither of them sounded right, their speech flat and crackling.

"You always will be." Dr. Chadwick glared. "No matter what they say."

"No."

"You know it and I know it." Dr. Chadwick pressed. "You've always known that you're the weak one, Missy. The Others use you. You're there to feel pain so they don't have to."

"No...."

"You're just the punching bag."

"Stop it." Missy put her hand to her head. The Others weren't afraid now. They wanted out. They wanted revenge.

"You're not a real person, Missy." Dr. Chadwick looked at the gun that was pointed at her, then to Patricia who was holding it. "You're a shield, a wall, nothing more."

"Why... why are you...?" Missy's head hurt. The Others clawed at her. They wanted out.

"Because you're the one who t—"

The electrified baseball bat hit Dr. Chadwick in the back of the knees. She went down with a yelp. Then she started convulsing as Plugger kept the tip of the bat touching her after she hit the ground.

A hand took hold of Missy's arm and she winced at the touch, then saw its black-glove and formal jacket sleeve and she knew who it belonged to. Her breathing slowed for the first time in minutes.

"Are you alright?" Mr. Keeps, like all the other voices in the black and white fever dream, sounded scratchy and wrong. It was the same calm, though, in the same professional tone he always used. It was solid, real.

"I'm drugged." Missy told him as he helped her stand up straight. She listed off the items she'd read in Patricia's mind.

"This complicates matters." Mr. Keeps moved around so she could lean on his shoulder. His other hand was carrying a gun, an older one. The kind with the cylinder of six shots in it. Missy didn't know what they were called.

"Would you like to lie down on-"

"No." Missy tried to shake her head. She'd had enough of the beds and gurneys, especially after the memories she'd seen inside Patricia's mind. Instead, she looked around until she spotted the other soldier who'd taken her psychic amplifier.

"He has something of mine. I need it."

Plugger pulled the bat off of Dr. Chadwick and moved to search the sleeping soldier instead.

"Don't touch it." She fought to get the words straight, "Not directly."

Plugger paused, then took the soldier's cap and used it as an improvised glove. He found the circlet and held it up for Missy to see.

"This it?"

Missy nodded.

"Alright."

Mr. Keeps held out a gloved hand. "I can take that, Mr. Swing. Please retrieve the coin in my stead, if you would be so kind."

Plugger handed the circlet over, then used his bat to knock the coin out of the air. The black and white was replaced with color, and jazz was replaced with the sounds of whimpering and snoring.

They stumbled through hallways full of sleeping bodies. Missy wanted to move faster. She didn't want to be here. She'd always been afraid of Dr. Chadwick, but she hadn't thought of her as the enemy in a long time. The look the doctor had in her eyes, the way she said the name 'Psyconic,' there was something there Missy needed to know.

But she couldn't stay here to find out. She needed help.

Her body was still twisting and burning inside.

As if to illustrate her thoughts, she tripped on her own feet. Only Mr. Keeps' grip under her arm kept her from falling over.

He also scared her. She didn't know what he was planning. She didn't know what was true or false about him.

But he was here.

"How did you…?" She started to ask.

"Escape now, explanations later."

Missy nodded. She really wanted the answer, but she was in no shape to push.

Plugger was easier. His mind was open. He was grumbling and panicking and listing all the reasons this had been a terrible idea, including a few that Missy hadn't considered herself. One of them being that they'd now made an enemy out of what looked to be a private military corporation. It had been a job to come after her before, but now he thought he was in way over his head.

Underneath all of that, though, there was something he didn't want to admit to himself. There was a glow of pride in him, colored with the memories of when he'd been at his best. Missy liked that feeling.

They reached a side door to the foundry, and Plugger gave it a shove, holding it open for them.

Missy stopped for a moment, turning to look back. Patricia stood back there. She still had the gun. Missy could order her to aim it at Dr. Chadwick.

She could kill her.

It was possible. It would mean no more trouble.

It also might mean no more answers.

The doctor knew something, more than something. She knew about Psyconic, and for some reason it was important enough for her to do all of this just to ask Missy about it.

There was more to this, there was so much more.

Missy just shook her head and left.

There would be another time and another place for that. One where Missy was whole and in control. She would need it.

They were outside and in Mr. Keeps' van when the gunshots started again. They practically flew down the road and away.

\*\*\*

# Chapter Twenty-Five

Missy dreamed. They were vivid, terrible things. She imagined Mr. Keeps as a giant, his gas mask breathing steam that melted the world around him. She saw Plugger shot to death, bleeding out as soldiers surrounded him, pointing rifles and pulling triggers. Missy tried to reach out and stop them, to control their minds, but she couldn't. Then they would turn and Missy would see the hair and the scars behind the ears and she'd know they were all Dr. Chadwick. She couldn't do anything. She was powerless.

Then it was the alleyway. She was standing there, bare feet black, shivering with cold and shock. Psyconic was lying there in front of her: his eyes wide, his face empty. She'd done that to him. She'd done it.

Then she woke up.

Missy was lying somewhere hard, cold, and wet. She opened her eyes to find herself back on the surfboard in Mr. Keep's van. She had a sheet and a blanket over her, both soaked in sweat. She tossed them off to find her clothes were in the same poor condition. Her heart still felt wrong. It shook and faltered, and she didn't like it. The rhythm of her body was like that messy jazz music from Phil Noir's coin.

"Ehl…" Missy tried to turn over.

"Stay still." Mr. Keep's voice. He was up ahead, driving. "We're almost there."

Missy's mind spun with questions of where they were going and why. She tried to put them into words but once more her mouth just mumbled. She was angry now. She was angry that she couldn't even talk.

What kind of bullshit was this?

She reached out and found that Plugger was still here. He was riding shotgun. He was still worried, but now less for himself and more for her. Missy couldn't talk? Fine, Plugger could help her.

Missy slipped a thought into his head.

"Woah." Plugger said immediately.

"What is it?"

"She, uh… god, that's fuckin' weird!" Plugger leaned over and turned back to look at her. She was breathing hard and staring at him with her dark eyes. Her hair was matted to her head with sweat.

"She, uh, she wants to know where we're going."

"Ah." Mr. Keeps cleared his throat and spoke a bit louder, "We are going to see a friend of mine. She should be able to help you."

Missy dropped another thought into Plugger's head.

"Gah! Will you stop that?"

"What does she want to know, Mr. Swing?"

"What friend?"

"Hm." Mr. Keeps paused as he made a sharp right turn into some sort of tenement parking lot. "That's difficult to explain, and immaterial now as we have arrived."

"Well… good." Plugger was just about to relax when Missy added yet another thought to him. "Fuh... stop that! Now she wants to know what their name is."

Mr. Keeps parked the van and turned around in his seat to look at Missy, his masked face giving nothing away.

"Her name is Madam Lo."

\*\*\*

The first thing Missy noticed about Madam Lo was that she was missing an arm. This was compensated by the other arm, which was twice as large as normal. It was twisted with dark growths of purple and green, and clutched a bright red cane in its grip. The flesh pulsed as Madame Lo moved, slithering over and around itself.

The rest of her was fairly normal. She was of Asian descent. She was short and wide, with large glasses that had to have been bought decades ago. She walked with an odd shuffle. Her long, drab skirt hid her legs, but Missy could read the true depths of her deformity in the woman's mind. The rise of powers among the people came with great gifts, but curses always followed close behind.

Missy had been cursed, she had to admit that. Just as Madam Lo had met her own unfortunate destiny. The woman had only been nine years old when a villain with mutation powers had taken her hostage, seeking to blackmail her father.

Things had not gone according to plan for him.

Missy read all of this as she stumbled to the bed in the middle of Madam Lo's living room. It was one of those you saw chiropractors use, the kind with pieces that were separated and movable, made out of that fake brown leather that felt terrible against your skin. The room itself was small, just part of a normal apartment. It was the place that should have had a couch and television, but instead had the chiropractic bed, a small table with three chairs, a standing lamp with a red, fringed shade, and a large tool chest with drawers labeled with alchemical symbols.

"Lay down." Lo smacked the chiropractic bed with her cane.

The sharp sound made Missy's heart jump. She let go of Plugger's supporting arm and scooted herself onto the bed.

The cane came and poked her, pushed her arms and legs and hips until Missy was positioned exactly where Madam Lo wanted. Missy tried to read the woman, but she wasn't focused enough, so she'd find out what was needed just as the cane jabbed her.

"What's wrong with her?" Madam Lo had a sharp voice, words cut out and dropped without flow.

"She was sedated then given a cocktail of drugs to bring her back out of that sedation."

"Hmmm." Madam Lo leaned over Missy, her massive glasses reflecting nothing but light onto Missy's face. "Where was injection?"

Missy pointed to her neck, then to her arm. Madam Lo bent down over her neck first, pushing Missy's head away with the top of her cane.

"Hmph!" Madam Lo leaned the cane against the chiropractor's bed and grabbed Missy's arm. Her disfigured hand was cold and damp. It felt too large to come from such a small woman. It lifted Missy's arm and Madam Lo leaned down over the injection site.

She took a long, slow breath inward. She was smelling it.

Missy was still having trouble reading the woman. Her brain was as twisted as her body, its architecture expanded, different. There was a second section to how she thought, a section that was alien for Missy.

"Eighty-one dollars." Madam Lo dropped the arm and grabbed her cane again. "Put on table."

Watching from the corner of her eyes, Missy saw Mr. Keeps pull out a hundred-dollar bill, fold it, and place it down. Madam Lo nodded, then shuffled off to her tool chest.

Missy was having trouble with her eyes. She tried to follow things but it was like she was always a little late. She'd move her eyes but she couldn't see for a moment, then things would jump into focus just to blur again. Her chest felt strange, heavy, but her head was light. The shine of red from the lamp made her feel hot, but her body kept shivering.

Missy opened her eyes. Something had happened. She wasn't exactly sure what it was. When had she closed her eyes? Why was her neck burning? She tried to turn her head but found a large, malformed hand grabbing her just as she made the effort. It locked her into place. Missy's breath came faster as her muscles tensed. The hand was clammy, cold, and strong.

"Do not move!" Madam Lo snapped. "Will break needle."

Missy stilled. Now she could feel it, pain in her neck as something pricked her flesh. It was so tiny compared to all of the panic and discomfort in her. Now that she focused on it, it seemed bigger.

Then there was a sharper, more burning pain. Missy's body tensed, but the massive hand holding her head kept her still. Missy felt her fingers claw and curl.

"No move!" Madam Lo's hand tightened on Missy's neck and jaw.

Then even more strangeness came. Missy's tiredness was swept away by energy. Her heart beat even faster in her chest. She started to sweat more profusely. There was another brilliant bloom of pain from her neck, then the hand released her.

Missy gasped and tried to move, but Madam Lo's hand grabbed her arm and lifted it up. Missy looked at the woman. She had a set of three long pins in her mouth. No, not pins, they were needles! Needles without syringes. Madam Lo pulled her lips back and Missy could see that the needles were held tightly between her teeth. One was gold, one looked silver, and the last one was pale and clear. She pulled Missy's arm upward and pushed the golden needle straight into the site of the last injection.

Missy fought to stay still. She didn't dare move with the needle so far into her arm. Her body was full of energy, though. It wanted to run, scream, fight!

The needle turned wet. Missy's eyes widened as she watched it. Madam Lo made a sucking sound and the liquid around the needle flowed up and into her mouth.

Then the golden needle was pulled out. The pain was

startling, but somehow Missy kept herself from flinching. The silver needle came next: another slow push down into the needle mark, another sucking of something from the wound, another sharp pull to remove it.

Missy's heart settled to merely pounding, her arms and legs stopped shaking. Her vision began to clear.

She waited for the next needle, but it didn't come. Instead, Madam Lo stood up and let go. Then the woman lowered her head so her chin tapped her chest. The pale needle glistened, then dripped as Madam Lo spit onto it.

Then she pulled all three needles from her mouth and threw them into a cup on the table. She took the money next, quickly examining it, then pocketing it somewhere in her large skirt.

"She's fine now." Madam Lo glared at Mr. Keeps as she talked. "No food. No water. One hour. Body needs rest too."

"Understood." Mr. Keeps bowed in thanks.

"Tell her she's dumb." Madam Lo went on, "Bad stuff. High-quality, still bad."

Missy thought of saying she could hear her, but there was a lot to be intimidated by in a woman who had just stabbed her with mouth-needles.

"I will relay the message promptly." Mr. Keeps nodded and straightened up.

"Good." Madam Lo picked up her cup of dirty needles and pushed through one of the doors, Missy glimpsed the telltale signs of a small kitchen before the door shut, leaving the three of them alone in the treatment room.

"Well…. That was something." Plugger crossed his arms over his chest. "Where in the hell did you meet her?"

"Hm?" Mr. Keeps had been staring down at Missy. He looked at Plugger then turned his head vaguely upward for a second. "Oh, well… I happen to own her other arm. It's a bit of a collector's item."

# Chapter Twenty-Six

Missy was quiet as they left.

They were going back with Mr. Keeps to his place, or at least Plugger thought they were. Missy had no reason to doubt his thoughts on the matter.

She wanted to lose herself in other minds, but she kept being drawn back to her own. Nothing made sense. Why had Dr. Chadwick been after her? What did she know about Psyconic?

Missy turned over on the magic surfboard, using her arm as a pillow as she stared at the collection of random junk beside her. There was a pile of long, metal sticks. They had a name she couldn't remember. The kind you used to check the oil in a car. One of them had to be special, sitting there amid a bunch of ordinary things.

Missy felt the tears before she even realized she was crying.

She tried to stay silent, but her chest heaved and made her breath louder.

She'd trusted her!

She'd trusted Dr. Chadwick to help her, she'd trusted the one person she hadn't been able to control. Well, she used to be the only person. Now there were two... or was it three if she included Psyconic? No, it didn't matter. Dr. Chadwick had just tried to kill her. Why? Why would it change? What was it about Psyconic that kept tearing Missy's world apart?

She should have left it alone.

With a shaking hand, she tried to wipe the tears from her eyes but it just made things worse. Plugger noticed. He was currently torn between pretending everything was fine and trying to say something to comfort her. The thought alone was very sweet. Missy smiled briefly before everything crashed back down.

She couldn't read Mr. Keeps. He was sitting there, just a few feet away, just like Dr. Chadwick had done for all those years. He was there and he could be lying to her, he could be a monster. Why did he even care?

"Why?" Missy's voice cracked with the word, her throat dry and raw.

Plugger didn't know how to answer. Missy was tempted to dump the question inside of his head again, but she knew he'd had enough of that already. He'd been thinking very kindly toward her, and she didn't want to ruin that.

"Why…. Why did you come… for me?" Missy choked the words out around the sobs.

No more pretending she was fine.

"Hmmm." Mr. Keep's hum had many things in it. Missy couldn't read it, but Plugger could. The former bouncer had extremely sharp senses for things like that. He was like Lena that way.

God, Lena! Missy missed her.

Plugger's mind told her that Mr. Keep's hum was contemplative, reticent. He was in the midst of deciding if he wanted to tell her the truth or craft some sort of lie or evasion. Missy didn't understand how someone could read so much in such a small noise. There was so much she couldn't do, so much of her that was broken.

"I've been studying you for some time now."

The words stopped her tears stopped for a moment. She tried to understand what he meant.

"As I explained before, I take dangerous things and keep them safe." Mr. Keeps continued, his tone deeper than normal. Gone was the mild amusement, the light and airy voice, the chipper humming that filled the gaps between.

Missy knew what he was going to say next. She didn't

even need her power.

"And I'm dangerous." She said it for him.

His silence was her answer. She thought about all her interactions with him.

"Did you follow me?"

"Yes, and also no."

Plugger's mind was very distracting. He was full of strong reactions. Missy pulled her power back so she could focus.

"I waited for you in Two Town." Mr. Keeps' words came slowly, with care. "I've read a lot about you; case files, psychological reports and so forth. Anything that reached the mental health board was copied to me by an acquaintance."

"Fuck!" Plugger breathed. The word took Missy by surprise.

She'd told Dr. Chadwick about Two Town. Dr. Chadwick had seemed surprised. Is that when something changed? He'd read those reports? The reports Missy only recently rifled through. She hadn't read them, though. She wondered what they said about her, but she was far too afraid to ask.

"After we met, and you explained the complicated nature of your mind, I had to abandon my earlier... 'strategy.' So I placed a GPS tracker on your backpack. It's how I found you."

"How long?" Missy pushed herself up off the surfboard. "How long have you been after me?"

This time the silence stretched out for a full minute. Missy found her tears slowing as she waited, anticipating the answer. She didn't know if it would be the truth or a lie... she wouldn't be able to tell... but she needed an answer. She wanted to know.

"Years."

Missy sobbed and fell back on the board. It was too cold, too impersonal. She wanted the institute bed. She wanted clean sheets, the headboard with bars she could wrap fingers around.

She wanted Lena.

Lena was the only one who was safe.

"Why? Why did you let me go?" Missy found the words. "You had me, took me in. You could have locked me away… why?"

"Because that wouldn't work."

The van came to a stop. Plugger leaped out, muttering curses and storming away, leaving them alone with each other.

"If I forced you into a cage, what would have happened?" Mr. Keeps turned from the driver's seat to look at her.

Missy wished she could see his face, even a piece of it like when they'd been eating together. The gas mask was as blank as his mind to her. All she had was words.

"The Others would have come out." Missy answered. She knew the truth. "They would have grabbed minds nearby and had them kill you."

Mr. Keeps nodded.

"You want me to stay by choice." Missy sat up once again. Her arms and legs still shook.

"I want what I've always wanted: to stop a tragedy before it begins."

Missy felt the Others inside of her. They were tired, scared, off balance. They were quiet now, but later… later they would rage.

"I…"

Missy thought about what she was. Dr. Chadwick told her she was just a shield. She was a tool to be used. She was just a personality built to protect the Others from pain.

Was that all?

"I… I'll stay."

A part of her died as she said those words. There had

been that fight, that curiosity. She'd wanted so much to find out what had happened to create her, to turn her from a monster into what she was now.

Yet, it'd brought her nothing but pain and confusion. She'd had enough.

"Are you certain?" Mr. Keeps' voice held so much inside of it, and Missy didn't know what any of it meant.

So she just nodded. She was too tired. Where else could she go? The institute was no longer safe, and her closest friend was trapped there. She had no home, no family. The whole world just remembered her face as that of a mass murderer.

If Two Town hadn't died...

But it had.

"Yeah." Missy forced herself to slide off of the surfboard and stood up. "Where should I go?"

He stared at her for a long and terrible moment.

Then he reached up and unstrapped the clasps from the sides of his mask. He removed it slowly, revealing a face striped with burns. The skin around one eye was collapsed. His hair was gone, burned away. He had no eyebrows and one of his ears was shortened, clipped.

"I am sorry." His voice sounded different without the mask, more solid.

Missy just looked at him. She didn't understand.

"This isn't fair to you." Mr. Keeps said. "But I need to keep—"

"I know." Missy got it. He just wanted to keep them all safe: all the people who'd been like him, all those who didn't know the pain and terror until it crashed down on them from the sky above.

Mr. Keeps replaced his mask in silence, opened his door, and left Missy alone in the van.

The hole in her chest felt endless.

\*\*\*

# Chapter Twenty-Seven

The room was exactly wrong for her.

It was one of those box-looking places she'd seen before in the warehouse. If she'd investigated them that night, what would have happened? Would she have realized what it was for? Who it was meant to contain?

Why did he give her the couch instead? What was really going on inside of his head? Who was he, really?

It was all wrong.

The bed was on the wrong side. Instead of being to the left as she entered, it was on the right. It had no headboard. It was too low to the ground. The small table beside it didn't wobble like the nightstand used to.

It all fit her new world.

Everything was wrong.

For days she barely moved. She would get up to eat and shower and all the necessary things to stay alive, but she didn't live. For the most part, she just sat in bed and lost herself in the minds of the people outside.

She really enjoyed watching Elias Sobzak. His parents were both immigrants. He'd grown up in the city, but knew enough about his past to appreciate everything in his life. He was clever. He was the guy everyone went to when there was an odd problem. He would look at it, ask a dozen questions, circle around it in his mind, gather everything about the situation, and then list all the things he could do to mitigate or avoid the problem.

He was like Lena.

Missy spent hours on end in his mind. She never

touched it, just rode shotgun as he hummed old songs and moved pallets with his forklift, shared his lunch with the other workers, and took life by the moment.

Then he would go home, and Missy would think about using the amplifier to follow him. She stopped each time. Partially because it would require getting out of bed to fetch the thing, partially because of how the Others hungered for it, partially because she hated it for what it was.

Mostly she was afraid of what she would hear if she touched it.

She'd be able to reach so far, maybe even as far as the institute. She might be able to touch the minds there, learn about what Dr. Chadwick was doing. She might learn more about why the doctor hated her so much.

The questions still burned inside, but they remained muted beneath the fear.

So Missy sat in her bed each day, drifting through the lives of others.

Then spent each night in silence and dark.

Each time she closed her eyes, she felt like the doctor was there, pointing the gun toward her, face red and hand shaking.

Missy did everything to escape the feeling. She even thought about letting the Others take control, but they didn't want it. They hid from the pain and trauma. They left her to live with it. Plus, even they knew she wouldn't really let them free.

There was a small part of her that was still sane, after all.

It didn't like her much.

Missy left deep, red scratches at her temples from all the times she dug her fingernails into the skin. She wanted them out. She wanted it all out. She wanted to forget, to be lost, to be somewhere else, be *someone* else.

Then Elias had his day off.

Missy tried to use other minds but they weren't the same. The agitation forced her out of bed. The phone kept ringing in Mr. Keeps' office. She unplugged it then paced the empty warehouse. Mr. Keeps had left on some errand or another. He was out delivering an item or picking one up. Missy didn't know. She didn't really care.

He didn't care about her, so why should she care about him?

She did find Madam Lo's arm. It was locked in a steel case with yellow warning tape on it. There were several sticky notes that repeatedly told anyone looking that they should not to open the case and to keep it away from flesh and bone.

It was there, in that moment, as she stood over the case and wondered how bad it could really be, that she felt Plugger's mind.

He was driving some old beat-up truck. He was both excited and agitated. He was coming to see her, not Mr. Keeps.

Missy was interested enough that she turned away from the arm and walked out into the garage. The van was gone, so the room was empty and cold as she moved across to the door.

Plugger's mind was jumbled, erratic. She kept getting pieces of what was happening but not the full picture. He was excited about something, but scared, some part of him was angry because his world was changing again. That anger sat with the anger at Mr. Keeps. They kept each other company. There was curiosity and a thin veneer of wild hope. He was trying to keep his mind on the road, but he kept failing.

The end result was that Missy couldn't get a grip on what was happening until the truck pulled up just as she pushed the button to open the garage door.

The metal trundled aside and Missy heard him yell at her with his mind.

Someone had bought the bowling alley.

Missy ran ahead and pushed herself through the gap between the door and the wall. It was cold outside. The scratches on her head and neck burned from it. She didn't care. She tried to latch on to what Plugger had thought.

"He has the pants!" Plugger yelled as he turned the truck off and jumped out. "You gave him the pants?"

Missy stilled and shivered.

Ball Return's pants. She'd forgotten all about them.

"He just rolled up with a moving van. He has supplies, people fixing things! What... How? No, Who. Who is he?" Plugger was torn between screaming in anger, panic, or joy. His mind twisted from one extreme to the other. He slammed his hand on the hood of his truck and the engine started for a moment as his power fed it the electricity it needed.

"He's..." Missy got her thoughts in order. "He deserved them."

"What?"

"I... " She realized that there was no way she could describe how she held the strange magic of stained fabric and the amplifier and just knew where they should go. "I can't explain it."

"You did your head thingy?"

Plugger had a very inaccurate idea of how it worked. Still, Missy nodded. His words were technically correct, even if the ideas behind them were flawed.

His excited energy was affecting her. She felt herself getting the same feeling.

"When?" She asked.

She read the answer as it popped into Plugger's head. Early this morning they'd shown up. The lanky, crusty man in his fifties and his moving truck. He'd watched them work for a while before spotting Plugger and wandering over.

He told Plugger about the letter, about how much it meant to him.

"He said the pants just showed up at his house!" Plugger rambled on. "Said they came with a note. A kid's note. He wanted to know who wrote it. It was you, wasn't it?"

"Yeah, I—"

"What the hell were you thinking?"

Missy reeled back at the anger. It boiled forth then retreated just as fast. She raised her hands to her burning temples, wanting to both shut it out and reach further in.

"Can…" Missy closed her eyes as her cold fingers touched her head. "Can you calm down a little? It hurts."

"What?"

"It hurts!"

Her fingernails dug into the raw skin of her scalp.

Plugger's mind shifted once more. He looked at her. He saw her fingers drawing blood.

He took her hands in his.

Missy stopped breathing. She didn't like being touched.

He gently pulled them away from her head.

There was still chaos writhing inside his mind, but now there was a focus on stopping her from hurting herself. She hated his touch, his presumption, she wanted to scream at him, to make him stop. She pulled her hands free and backed away.

"Can you, uh, make me calm down?" He asked.

Missy's rage faltered.

"You can do that, right?" Plugger said. "If it… If I'm…. Look, just do what you need to."

Missy went wide-eyed as she realized he was serious. He was willing to turn his mind over to her so she wouldn't have to hurt. All of his questions, all of his anger at things changing, at Mr. Keeps for lying to him, at his own fear...

All of it was kept under an iron weight of wanting Missy to stop hurting herself.

"No." She shook her head and stepped back. "I don't do that: not like that."

There was a flash of relief inside, but also an upwelling of unease.

They stood there for a long moment. The wind stole

away the heat of their bodies as they stared at each other. Plugger spent the time trying to calm himself and understand, Missy spent the time reading everything from the former enforcer.

He cared about her.

It wasn't an easy care, or even a deep one… but it was there.

When she'd shown up at his shop for the second time, when she almost ate the food he'd spit in… it changed how he saw her.

Missy wasn't Miss Mania in his head any longer.

It was a strange feeling to be recognized as yourself instead of who people thought you were. He still hated Miss Mania. He had nightmares about her. Now, though, he looked at Missy and he didn't see the supervillain who used to wear her face.

What he did see wasn't flattering, but it was kind. He saw a broken woman, little more than a lost child. He looked at her as if she was someone who'd never had to grow up.

He was wrong. She'd never had a chance to be young. She'd been in the minds of eighty-year-old men since she was six. She'd seen memories of murder, war, violence and hate of every imaginable interpretation.

There was a reason the Others were the way they were.

Missy forced her hands down to her side. She pulled herself out of Plugger's mind. She stopped using her power completely. In the silence she shivered and took a slow, deep breath.

Maybe this had been her real problem. If she'd never used her power, if she'd never looked within others, then maybe she wouldn't have ended up so broken. She'd seen the trauma of thousands, and created even more in her madness.

Now she sat in her own head, focusing on her breathing and not knowing what sort of panic or emotion was flowing within the man standing right in front of her.

"I'm okay." Missy looked up at him.

He had a kind face. It was beaten and worn, touched with scars and twisted a bit by broken noses of the past, but he had laugh lines near his eyes. Missy didn't usually look at people, but now she focused completely on his face.

She turned away as things got a little awkward. She looked back at the open warehouse garage.

She should stay. She was a danger to the world. She was hunted and feared and...

And she really wanted to go.

She wanted to see the bowling alley.

Missy wanted to smell the terrible shoes and bad nacho cheese. She wanted to refresh those memories with reality. She wanted to see the man who was making it real again.

"Take me there." Missy turned back. "I wanna see it."

"Alright."

"And you're gonna have to talk to me." Missy looked up into his face. "I'm not gonna, you know...read you for a while."

"O-Okay. That works, I guess." Plugger pushed the unlock button and waited for Missy to move around the truck and climb inside.

"Mr. Keeps... He's gonna be angry, isn't he?" Missy asked as she'd buckled herself in and closed the door.

"Fuck Keeps."

Missy knew that was exactly how Plugger felt, but she wasn't sure she felt the same. She watched the garage from the side-view mirror as Plugger turned the key in the ignition. She wondered what he'd think.

She wondered what he thought at all. Between Mr. Keeps and Dr. Chadwick she had too much she didn't know. All these things she didn't know in a world that should be open to her.

She thought about this a lot as they drove. She sat there thinking and watching the buildings pass through the foggy truck window, and for once she was just there looking, not reading the world for all the thoughts that clouded it.

There was a strange peace in the experience.

***

# Chapter Twenty-Eight

He wore the pants well.

He shouldn't have. Where Baller had been short and built like a melting bulldozer, this guy was unfortunately skinny. He had a plethora of tattoos that hadn't aged nearly as well as he had. They were broken, faded streaks of gray over his arms and shoulders.

He was bald, with terribly, patchy facial hair, but he wore the pants.

He stood there under the overcast sky, arms resting on hips that were too thin to let them, the purple sweatpants almost shining in the dinginess of the place. The bright stains and holes and loose threads practically glowed amidst the gray of overcast skies and cracked concrete.

Missy could feel his mind burning with passion. She didn't need to reach out to feel it. She could smell it, like a pile of dead ashes that had been reignited.

"That's him." Plugger interrupted the moment.

Missy nodded without a word, then pushed the truck door open and crossed the street.

He'd seen them drive in, of course, but now he watched her as she approached.

There was tension here. It took Missy a minute to realize that it wasn't about the meeting itself, but about how she approached it.

She could read him… or she could not.

The world itself seemed to move side to side with each step. Her hands twitched. Her eyes couldn't decide whether to look at his face or look at her feet.

He stuck his hand out and flashed a grin full of surprisingly white teeth.

"Hey there!"

Missy lifted her hand and found it grasped before she was ready for the touch.

For a moment she had a flash of panic. She remembered the feeling of the machine on her arms. She remembered being dragged away by the soldiers. The memories moved to swallow her.

"Name's Elliot. Elliot Grout." The man shook her hand once then let it drop. "How you doin'?"

"Uh, fine." Missy pulled her hand back and looked at the white teeth. "My name is... call me Missy."

A moment of silence settled between them. Missy reached out just long enough to realize she was about to open his mind and pull everything out of it.

Instead, she stopped and opened her mouth.

"I wrote the letter."

"Fuck... You?" Elliot laughed just once, "I gotta fuckin' thank you!"

He grabbed the waistband of the sweatpants with his left hand and held it out, giving Missy an unfortunately clear view of his boxer shorts. He reached in with his other hand and something turned weird in the world.

For now there was a bowling ball where there hadn't been one before. He drew it out and let the pants snap back to his stomach. The ball was blue crystal with silver flecks held in the resin. They shimmered like fresh snow.

"This is fuckin' mint!" He lifted the ball up to his face. "That shit about Baller? Took me a while to read that shit, but I got it. He was, man, he was the real shit."

Missy just nodded. Each word seemed to explode from nothing. There was so much energy behind them.

"Hell, you wanna come inside?"

The air inside Missy's lungs seemed to catch on

something.

"Yes."

Elliot grinned and almost ran to the doors, Missy right on his heels.

The darkness hit her first as she crossed the doorway. The smell of dust, stale beer, and the acrid, chemical scent of rat droppings filled her nose as she waited for her eyes to adjust.

It looked lifeless, but it was there.

She walked to the shoe counter. All the little wooden boxes stood empty. Old smells, shoe polish and sweaty socks, filtered into her mind. She ran a finger over the counter, gathering the dust and leaving a line of clean wood behind.

There was a rag. She saw it sticking out from one of the boxes. She moved around the bar and grabbed it, shaking the age and dust from the stiff cloth. It was a terrible choice, but it was good enough to scrape a couple years off the wooden counter.

"She'll really shine, you know?" Elliot said as he walked by, his eyes scanning the broken ceiling tiles above. "Used to get paid to work on old shitholes like this. Clean the fucker out, trash it, replace all the obvious shit. Landlords are always too cheap to do the good work. Never really fuckin' fix things, ya know?"

Missy blinked. She hadn't known that about him. She knew all about landlords, though. Some were awful, but most were just people squeezed too hard to do all they wanted to do.

"So tell me: why the fuck you send it to me?"

"I…" Missy tried to find a place to start her explanation.

"I don't think I know you. I figured that it had to be someone I'd recognize, right? You, though, if we've met—"

"Miss Mania." The name jumped from her mouth.

The flash of recognition lit up his face.

"I used to be her." It sounded weak even as she said it.

"I…um…"

"She can read your goddamn mind." Plugger filled the silence as he walked up from the open doors. He looked around the bowling alley and wrinkled his nose. "Can even plunk down thoughts of her own in your head if she wants. One of those types."

"Shiiiit…" Elliot looked back to Missy, "You're that bitch?"

She stepped back. The fear of what he was thinking, it crawled over her. She reached out for both of their minds. She needed to know.

"That's fuckin' awesome!"

Missy stopped, her power almost resting on his mind. It was so close to touching.

"So you did some real superpower shit to find me? Damn." Elliot clapped his hands and laughed. "Shit yeah!"

"Uh…"

"That's what fuckin' sold me, ya know?" Elliot turned his head to watch the moving crew bring in a ratty-looking couch. "You gave me magic. Fuckin' Two Town magic, the real shit! Then ya wrote all that stuff about Baller. Shiiit, I'd seen that guy. I sat right over there in the bar back when they still carded me. He was a fuckin' institution, he was."

Missy turned her head to look down to where the bar lurked behind the boxy section that had once been the store.

She couldn't see the old place, but she knew its layout. She knew how the bar stood, where the stools used to sit, where the pool tables were and how low the lights hung over them.

"I always wanted this." Elliot's voice lost its exuberance, tempered down to a lower heat. "Not like your super-shit, though. Psychic and all sounds great, but I bet it's fuckin' shit, right?"

Missy laughed. It was a low laugh, the kind that felt like it was on the edge of something else.

"Yeah." She said between gasps. "It is."

"Knew it!" Elliot leaned further over the counter. "Big power, big shit. That's how it goes, ya know?"

Missy found herself nodding along. She knew it better than anyone. She could name the terrible behind-the-scenes life of hundreds of heroes, villains, and more. Weaknesses were easy when it was all some of them thought about.

"Little shit, though." Elliot looked up, his eyes running over the rotted ceiling tiles again. "That... I can handle. For a piece of this? Fuck yeah. I'll take the loans and risk and do it. Right? Fuck it! This is Two Town, baby! Two Town needs to *be* somethin.'"

The words set off a cold light inside of Missy.

*Two Town needs to be something.*

"Yeah."

"But it's dead."

They both turned to look at Plugger. He'd been standing at the end of the counter, his mind still boiling with conflicting emotions. Missy felt it rolling off of him like the rattling lid of a tea kettle.

"It's dead!" Plugger's mouth twisted around the words. "You can't just come up here, light the sign and expect a fuckin' miracle!"

"No shit." Elliot shook his head. "Ya need some fuckin' marketing. That's the real fuckin' truth."

"What?"

Missy laughed again. Tears welled in the corners of her eyes.

She hadn't felt like this since, well, she'd never felt like this.

"You're both crazy." Plugger shook his head.

"Not me." Missy straightened up just a little. "The review board says I'm fine now."

Elliot laughed, but Plugger just glared at her. Missy let her eyes close and found herself in a moment that was filled with just her and her demons.

And the demons were mercifully quiet.

\*\*\*

# Chapter Twenty-Nine

Missy wasn't sure when the drinks came out. They'd been talking: really talking. She'd been listening with her ears instead of her powers. It was strange. She didn't know what was going to happen next. When the six-pack of beer was placed on the bar it made her jump.

They'd offered to share and she'd waved it off.

"He's just so fuckin' creepy." Plugger raised his bottle in emphasis. "He basically stalked her, bribed some dudes for reports or something, and hunted her down. What a creep."

Elliot nodded along. His own bottle was nearing empty, but he kept it upright in both hands as he leaned over the ancient shoe counter.

"But…" Missy still struggled to use words, but she'd been getting better. "He saved me."

Plugger grunted and took another drink before responding.

"I'm not sure 'saved' is the right word. He still wants to keep you locked up in his little carnival of crazy."

Missy opened her mouth then shut it. He wasn't wrong. Still, she kept thinking about how he'd removed his mask for her. Those scars told stories, and unlike Dr. Chadwick, he'd told her that story.

"I…" Missy struggled to find a way to say it. "I'm glad he does."

Both Plugger and Elliot turned to stare. The attention made her uncomfortable. Not knowing what was churning through their minds made it all so wrong in her perspective. They looked so blank! So empty!

"Here… in my head, the Others, the worst parts of me…" Missy tapped her temple with two fingers, feeling the tacky scabs from earlier. "I always worry about them. If they come out, if I become Mania again, then… then Mr. Keeps could stop me. He doesn't do these things because… he just wants, um, he wants to keep people safe."

Plugger frowned and finished his bottle. Elliot just tilted his head.

"Creeps is immune to the whole mind-reading thing." Plugger explained after a moment.

"Shit. For real?"

Missy and Plugger both nodded.

"Damn." Elliot finished his own beer and served two more to Plugger and himself. "There any others like that?"

Missy hunched her back and stared down at the uneven lines of disturbed dust on the countertop. Dr. Chadwick had always been an opposing force, but she'd always been respectful. Cruel, perhaps, but cruelty with restraint. At least until the time with the machine. The memory made the shirt on her back feel too heavy, too restrictive.

The doctor had held a gun to her head. She'd been ready to kill.

Missy reached out toward the bottles and curled her fingers inward.

If she was going to talk about Dr. Chadwick, then maybe a little drink wouldn't hurt.

One drink became two, then three, then the count became a bit more confused. Then there came larger bottles, with stuff that really burned the throat. There was also laughter, and some crying, and Missy was half-certain that there had been singing at some point.

Through it all the Others remained silent. Missy reveled in it. The joy of having her own thoughts to herself was far more intoxicating than the alcohol. A part of her swore she would never use her power again. She would just be like them: normal and human.

She knew she was lying, but it was nice to pretend.

"Ya know what I want?" Missy found that words were both easier and harder now. They were easier to find, but harder to make her mouth say them. Her lips seemed to be on a slight delay, tumbling over a letter or sound here and there.

"Wha?" Elliot was half-asleep across from her. He only had a single eye open, and it was looking glassy.

"I wanna find 'im." Missy half-mumbled.

"Who?" Elliot forced his second eye open.

"The.. the dude that did the… the taking me to the place and the stopping and— PSYCONIC!" Missy shouted it as she remembered the name. "He saved me. He's the reason I'm not 'raaarrgh' an' evil and stuff."

"I…" Plugger held a finger up from his slouch next to Missy. "I know tha' name. Was...tha' kid. Silvery whatsit."

"Right." Missy flopped herself over. "He was! Silver an'...an'… an' he did somethin'"

A moment of silence settled between them, then broke as Elliot's elbow hit one of the now-empty bottles and sent it clattering to the floor.

"Shit!" He yelped and pushed himself off the bar.

"Was gon' find 'im." Missy mumbled as she tried to straighten her own head. "Thas why I came baack."

"Back?"

"To Tootin', uh...Two Town."

She squeezed her eyes shut for a moment. They didn't seem to work right.

"Saw somethin'... in, in the mem'ries. Mine but not mine."

"T'others?"

"Right!" Missy opened her eyes again. "There's this alley here. I was gon' go there an'...an' find somethin.'"

"Somethin'?"

"Yeah, a big somethin.'" Missy found herself mumbling again. Why was everything not working all of a sudden?

"Well, let's gooo!" Elliot slapped the counter and stood up to mostly-straight. "We'll go lookie loo!"

"HA!" Plugger barked his old laugh.

Missy loved that laugh. It felt like home.

"Yeah!" She was the one who was too loud this time. She tried to slap the counter like Elliot but missed, just tipping her fingers on the dusty wood. "Let's go!"

"Field trip!"

Elliot raised an unsteady fist and led their charge toward the cold outside

\*\*\*

Missy had always been afraid.

She realized this as she charged down the crumbling streets of Two Town, her skin burning with the cold wind of night. Being here, now, with her powers off and her brain wonderfully marinated in alcohol, she saw it.

The powers gave her insight, but they also showed her the worst in everything. She'd been sitting there, thinking she knew it all… but she really only knew what people knew, and most people were just so full of fear and insecurity that—

Missy stumbled over a piece of loose concrete and cursed at the fact that Caulky was no longer around.

"The thing is..." Missy started again, then realized that the rest of her thoughts had been inside her head.

"What?" Plugger asked as he offered her a steadying arm.

"Uh…I forgot."

"Where are we going?"

Elliot ambled up on the other side of Plugger and looked like he was freezing to death in the cold. His whole body shivered from head to toe.

Missy squeezed her eyes shut and tried to pull the memory out. It was usually hard to do because of the Others, but now it was hard because it was just hard. This was a new frustration. She felt her eyebrows furrow down to point.

Then she found it: The dark, the rain, the body, the worn bricks and metal door.

She opened her eyes and looked around. She knew the place. It was nearby. It was where she had gone to get from *Meribelle's* down to the aqueduct access tunnel to the south.

She raised a finger and pointed.

"I don't know what happened." Missy told them.

Walking was really hard. It was making her split her attention, and in that split her thoughts came tumbling out of her mouth.

"He did somethin' to me!" Missy shouted hoarsely, then quieted. "He did it, and I was caught. No one caught me, but he did. I...I wanna know HOW! I want…. Did I kill him? Did th'Others…"

Missy reached out and held onto the building as they turned the corner. The old concrete felt oily under her touch.

"I miss Caulky." She blurted. Two Town just wasn't the same without the solidness of everything. To see it cracked and broken was breaking her heart.

"Me too." Plugger's voice was a reflection of her despair.

"Who's that?"

Together, they turned toward Elliot.

"She… fixed cracks." Missy answered. "An'… and she was strong."

"Really strong." Plugger added.

"Smart."

"Had… funny hair."

"Those dreads!"

"Right?!"

The three fell to giggling for a minute. It was only interrupted when Missy saw they were on the right street. The location was just a few feet away. She could see the start of the alley. She let go of the building and stumbled toward it. She saw the metal door. It was pure rust now, but it was the same position, same small step up to it.

She didn't notice if the others followed her. She was completely focused on the place.

Her heart beat in her ears as she got closer.

It had to have answers.

It had to.

She rounded the edge and looked down into the shadows of the place. The wind cut through her as she stood.

It was just an alley. It was empty and dark, marked only by the passage of time and neglect.

She wasn't sure if it was the alcohol, or the sudden silence of the place, or the lack of Other's screaming distractions, but for the first time in her life the memory was there without a fight.

She'd been there, cutting through the alley to reach a dealer she knew.

He had a lot of high-class uppers. She saw him every few weeks, using her power to make him give her whatever he had. He'd never really met her. She always wiped his mind, used him, left him confused and distraught. Miss Mania didn't care.

That's where she'd been.

Then a voice said something behind her.

She remembered the fear. It was like the first time a child touches something hot. The shock, the burning, that was what the voice was to her. Not because it was a strong voice, or a loud one, but because it came from the first mind that was invisible to her, truly invisible.

She'd reacted as she always did to threats, she reached out and took control of every mind around her, calling them to shield her, kill for her. The fear bled into rage. This was the most threatening thing she'd ever seen.

He was just a man.

He wore a costume, colored purple with silver trim. It was simple and elegant. This was Psyconic. Missy remembered.

He was older than she'd have thought. Hints of gray hair stuck out from underneath the silver band that ran around his mask. He had tired eyes that held the beginnings of bags beneath them. It looked like he saw much and slept little. Missy could empathize.

Maybe that's why she hesitated. She was blind to him, but his face…

It was so kind… and sad.

"You're her, aren't you?" That's what he'd said.

Missy had spun around in fear and panic, she'd raised her power to their height—

And then she'd stopped as she'd seen him. The sad smile, the empty hands, the complete lack of threat.

Had that been his power? Could he convince people he was no threat? It would have worked. Was that how he did it?

"Who?" Missy remembered her voice being raw and broken from disuse. She'd never needed to talk. She used others to do that for her.

"You." Psyconic had stepped into the alley after her. He bent down, like he was ducking underneath something she couldn't see. "You're Miss Mania."

The world stopped. The fear turned cold, all the hundreds of minds under her control froze with her, so many feet slowing, stopping, the scream of the Others burning within.

She'd yelled something. Missy wasn't sure if they were even words. She'd wanted him to go away, to not exist. A mind she couldn't read, a face that had nothing beneath it, she couldn't handle that.

Then he'd walked right up to her. She tried to stop him but he wasn't there. There was nothing there.

He stopped just out of arm's reach. His eyes were bloodshot. She found herself unable to look away.

"Aren't you tired?" His voice was so calm.

She was. She'd always been so tired.

He'd reached up with his hands and things got dark, blurry. She couldn't remember his face, she couldn't remember if she'd said anything, things became uncertain. She remembered the touch, though. It felt wrong.

Miss Mania didn't like to be touched.

He said something. Something in the quiet and the dark.

"There's these times, you know? These times when all you need to do to fix something is just to...give it a little push."

After that, she was lost in a mire of darkness and confusion. The next memory she could connect to was when she first woke up in the institute, shackled and under the care of Dr. Chadwick. Everything between those moments was a jumbled mess.

What had he done?

Why had he been immune?

What connected Psyconic, Dr. Chadwick, and Mr. Keeps? Why them? Out of thousands and thousands of people, why *them*?

The night sky seemed to hear the anguish within, for it chose that moment to strike a chord of thunder.

Missy opened eyes she hadn't remembered closing. The empty alley stood before her once more. There was no Psyconic, no power, no Miss Mania, just her, the cracked concrete, two men she'd decided to trust, and the burning discomfort of his last words.

Missy held it together for about five seconds, then threw up against the wall.

***

# Chapter Thirty

The walk back was slow, punctuated by Missy stopping here and there to try and spit the foul tastes from her mouth.

Retrieving the memory had left her with an awful headache. Her eyes burned, her temples throbbed. Even though she was keeping her powers off, it felt like the Others were screaming at her from behind a sound-proof door. There was pressure, and a feeling of something like anger.

"Ya had too much." Elliot was saying. "Shoulda had something to eat."

"Not that." Missy winced at the sound of her voice. "I remember it… part of it… but not enough."

"Sucks." Elliot said simply.

"It's like... " Missy reached for the words and couldn't find the right way to say it.

Words were more difficult than Missy had thought. You could never get everything you feel into them. It was so much easier with her power, when she could see what they were thinking and correct them if they were wrong.

Here, now, she wasn't going to do that. The clarity of having herself alone in her head was worth the frustration.

"It's like I was gone." Missy finally said. It wasn't what she meant, but it was close enough.

Missy knew she probably shouldn't be sharing this, not with a man who still sorta-hated her and another who she barely knew. There was just enough alcohol remaining in her system that she didn't care.

She told them everything she remembered, feeling the experience gush out in a jumble of words and re-enactments. She used her hands to show how he'd reached for her, how he'd grabbed her.

It was all wrong. Something about it was wrong. Her head ached the more she tried to focus on it.

They turned back to Second Street. The sky was a rolling sheet of darkness now. No stars to be seen and the moon was just a pale blur. The air smelled humid and sharp.

The feeling persisted, pressing down on her.

"Hey, you alright?"

Plugger's voice annoyed her. Why was it like that? It grated on her ears.

"No."

A sharp pain lanced through her head and ran down the side of her neck.

Missy doubled over.

Just as something shot past her and hit the cracked pavement.

She wasn't completely sure what happened next, but Plugger yelled something, grabbed her and almost dragged her off the street while shots rang out. Each sound was like an explosion in her head, rattling, disorienting. Something stung her on her shoulder.

She couldn't take it any longer.

Missy opened her mind.

The world stilled and laid itself out to her. There was Plugger, angry and afraid. There was Elliot, scared shitless but secretly thrilled. There were the Others, screaming and tearing at her mental defenses.

Then there were the other minds down the street. Three of them. They knew they'd missed their chance. Two were panicking. She put them to sleep.

The third was a mind she knew. She'd spent time in it before. It had a twisted, sadistic architecture that the Others admired. The mind knew it was fucked, but she was fine with it. She'd never expected to succeed, not against Missy.

Patricia.

No, she wasn't there to kill her. She was there because she had a message. Taking the shot had just been her idea of fun.

Missy withdrew when she found out there was a message in the mercenaries' mind. Missy knew it had to be a trap; she knew it because Patricia herself knew it.

"Hey, you okay?" Plugger was talking to her. He'd let her go and was debating whether he should grab her by the shoulders to get her attention.

"I'm fine." Missy's voice sounded so far away as she made herself talk. She wasn't just in her mind any longer. Her mouth was just a small part of her. "There's one left. Stay here."

Missy didn't wait for him to answer.

She felt Patricia raise her rifle and line up another shot. Two inches to the left of Missy's ear.

The shot was loud, but not nearly as bad as it had been before. She heard it from all of them at once. For some reason it was better this way. When it was just her own ears it had been like an explosion, now it was just the pop of a firecracker.

"Holy shit!" Elliot yelped from his hiding spot on the other side of the street. Missy read his amazement and fear like they were lines in a textbook.

And through it all the Others screamed at her. They wanted blood, to take all the minds and make them do horrifying things to each other while they watched and laughed.

"Patricia." Missy called out, her voice still raw and broken from emptying her stomach in the alley. "You have a message for me."

"That's right, ya bitch!"

Another shot, another purposeful miss. Missy kept moving forward, ignoring the impact and the high-pitch sounds of its ricochet.

"Ya fucked me over!" Patricia lined up her sights once more, this time aiming straight at her target, right between the eyes.

Missy paralyzed Patricia's right hand, pinching just the right cluster of neurons in her brain. It'd taken Mania years of experimentation to learn that kind of control. Now it was second nature, the precise skill of mental surgery felt natural, right.

"I thought so." Patricia laughed at her inability to pull the trigger. "You're like me, aren't you? You like to wait, watch, spend some time playing with your food."

Missy felt the idea form in Patrica's head just before she pulled her whole arm back. She was trying to pull the trigger with her paralyzed hand. Missy made a counter-adjustment, angling the pull so the shot went wide.

"I know you are!" Patricia was full of a fervent madness, knowing she had no control but pushing to see where the limits were. "You're doing it now. You could put me down, kill me, make me fucking shoot myself... but you won't. You can't. It's too easy!"

"The message," Missy yelled back. "What is it?"

"Why don't you just look?"

Another shot, another counter-move, another bullet skipping away down the abandoned streets.

"You scared?" Patricia's mind lit up with the possibility of fear within the unstoppable monster before her. "Is that it? You don't want to know?"

The sting of truth distracted Missy for a moment, slowing her reaction as Patricia snapped her sight back into place and pulled the trigger. Missy was late in her correction. The bullet cut through the top of her shoulder, filling the air with the smell of hot copper and gunpowder.

Two more shots were about to follow, but Missy was ready, deadening the nerves in the merc's entire body. Nothing below her neck would listen to her anymore.

"So that's it." Patricia's voice lost some of its fervor. "Not gonna play anymore?"

"Just tell me." Missy was close enough now that she didn't need to shout.

Only a few feet stood between them. Missy, walking in the middle of the street, and Patricia hiding just inside the second floor of an abandoned tenement. Her rifle barrel stuck out from between the boards nailed over a broken window.

"So that's the game." Patricia's laugh sent spiders down Missy's back. "I tell you and you win, but I win if you take it from me."

"This isn't a game." Missy sent the thought directly into Patricia's mind as she said it aloud.

"Oh, you know it is." Patricia whispered, knowing that Missy, and Missy alone could hear her. "Since the moment you crawled inside of my head it's been a game to you. It's life and death for people like me, but for you? No... just a game. It's always a game to the supers."

Missy stopped moving. The words were so bitter, so sour. They were woven from some place deeper than most of the twisted sadism that colored the merc's mind. Those words came from the girl she'd once been, not from the woman she was now.

"Maybe you're right." Missy whispered back.

She reached into Patricia's mind and searched through her memory, back through the setup in the building, past the drive here in an armored SUV, back to the foundry compound, back to where a woman with a burn scar above her ear gave her a message and a mission.

"Well?" Patricia's voice was like nails on a chalkboard. "What's your next move, bitch?"

Missy wanted to kill her.

She saw the message. She heard Dr. Chadwick say the words. She knew what the trap was, and knew she would walk straight into it. For the first time in a long while, maybe ever, Missy's mind screamed in concert with the Others.

She wanted to rip Patricia's apart. She wanted to fill

her mind with the agony Missy faced every moment she used her power. She wanted her to know exactly what it was like to be Miss Mania.

She wanted to, but she didn't.

Instead, Missy reached down and found the person that Patricia used to be, the one that was there before life ruined her and turned her into what she was now. Missy looked at everything within the woman for a long, quiet moment.

Then she took the recent years and she locked them away, leaving Patricia as her former self, a young woman's mind suddenly finding herself in a building with a high-powered rifle, a uniform on her body, and no idea how she'd gotten there or what she was doing.

It might not have been right, but to Missy's mind it was better than she deserved.

After all, Miss Mania had been given a second chance.

Maybe Patricia needed one too.

"You win." Missy whispered so only she could hear.

She took a long, deep breath. Dr. Chadwick's message still burning in her mind like a white-hot spike.

*"I'm going to see Lena." The doctor's voice was calm, but sharp as she spoke to Patricia. "I know she means something to Missy. You just tell her that."*

It was a trap.

Missy knew she would face everything they'd already sent after her and more. Patricia had known what was being shipped out, how much hardware and personnel had been moved upstate to the institute after the last operation.

They would be ready for her. There would be no precision, no subtlety. They would be there to destroy her.

And Missy was going to go.

She stood there in silence for a long time, struggling with the message and the screaming of the Others. She put memory-wiped Patricia to sleep just as Plugger and Elliot came running up behind her.

"What happened?"

"God, you've been shot!"

Missy blinked and looked over at her shoulder. She'd forgotten about that. Now that she was looking at it, she could feel the pain, how it burned and how the running blood was warm and uncomfortable.

Missy ignored the questions and turned around, heading straight for Plugger's shop. She felt their minds, their panic, their questions. She would answer them, she would; but she had things she needed to do first. She'd left something in the truck. Something she'd need.

Missy had to get dressed for work.

\*\*\*

# Chapter Thirty-One

"What's that?"

Elliot pointed at the circlet. Missy had removed it from her bag and placed it on the countertop inside Plugger's shop. Elliot was new to this entire affair and yet somehow, he still managed to stay calm.

"It's a psychic amplifier." She answered. "It…well…"

"It turns her from powerful into fuckin' unstoppable." Plugger stepped in from the storefront, his baseball bat sitting on his shoulder.

His mind was a roiling mass of contradictions. Missy was having trouble keeping track of it all, especially since keeping the Others in line was proving to be a full-time task. Shutting them out, even for a time, had put them into a panic. They never wanted it to happen again.

"But, like, wouldn't that make the other bastards in your head stronger?" Elliot asked.

Missy nodded.

"Sounds like bad fucking juju to me."

"It is." Missy reached out a hand, then stopped. "But I have to talk to Lena, and this is the only way."

"Can't we just drive ya?"

"No." Missy set her hand on the counter, her index finger half an inch from touching the silver metal. "Dr. Chadwick knows *everything* about me. She knows my range, my limitations, when I'm vulnerable, and even has some sort of noise that… well, it can fuck me up."

"So?"

"So she doesn't know me with this." Missy tapped her

finger near the amplifier. "It was taken away from me before we met. She has no tests on it, no metrics…. She won't know I can reach out from this far away. She doesn't know my full power at all."

A silence settled over them as Missy tapped her finger on the chipped, wooden surface. Each impact brought her closer and closer to touching the forbidden object.

"This is a bad idea." Plugger shook his head. "If—"

"I used it to find Elliot." Missy nearly spat the words. She needed them out. She wanted them to know. "It gave me range, and power… and something more. I can't use it for long, but I can use it."

Missy shut her powers away for a moment. The Other's screams fell to silence. She couldn't hear Elliot or Plugger. All she heard was herself.

Her finger moved half an inch. She touched warm metal.

She felt something, but it wasn't the explosion of awareness that she'd had before. Here, it was more like a spreading feeling of connectedness. She felt like each part of her body was more understood, more in control. She wasn't sure, but she thought she could feel things inside her body, the feelings of her organs as they moved and performed their necessary work. What she thought was her stomach seemed incredibly soured and in pain.

"Missy?"

"I'm still here." She answered. She took the circlet and placed it on her head. It fit just as well as it always had. It was like it had been made for her, sitting lightly on a line above her ears. Her hair tingled where it touched.

"I'm not… reading yet." Missy explained. "I'm just…" Words were hard.

"Breaking it in?"

"Yes!" The tension released. "That."

"Just… be careful." Plugger's face was a mask, but his

eyes held something.

Missy had an impulse.

Missy had never had an impulse before. Everything she'd ever done had come with planning, forethought, some mental expenditure of energy that allowed her to control what would happen and how. Even when events were forced upon her, like they had been in the last few days, she'd never acted without examining everything she could.

But here, now, she had an impulse to do something that had no reason or explanation.

The pure novelty of it made her want to do it even more.

She stepped forward and gave Plugger a quick hug.

She couldn't quite figure out where to put her hands and his shirt smelled of musty sweat and beer. Still, she pressed her cheek into it and breathed in, feeling Plugger stiffen into a rock of bone and muscle.

"Thank you." She finally found words that worked just right.

"Uh…"

"Both of you." Missy said as she pulled away. "I don't… I haven't…"

She tried not to laugh as she saw their expressions. Plugger looked like he'd been dipped in ice and pulled back out too fast.

"I don't have a lot of friends." She finished. "I know you still hate what I was… But I wanted you to know, whatever… when things happen, uh…"

The silence fell again and this time it was Missy who felt like things were all a bit wrong. This was being a normal human, she guessed, just an awkward shuffle of not knowing if you've done the right thing or the wrong thing and following the blind ideas that jump into your head. She wasn't sure she enjoyed it, exactly, but it was nice to feel it for herself.

"Well, I only just met ya, but dang." Elliot flashed a

worried grin. "Better friends than enemies, am I right?"

"Right." Missy returned the same kind of smile, one held on by the thinnest smear of hope. "And Lena is my oldest friend."

Elliot's smile fell. A dozen things seemed to flicker on his face for a moment, then he nodded. "I get ya."

"But…" Plugger finally moved. "Missy, you—"

"I'll be okay." Missy kept the smile on somehow. "And if I'm not, well, Mr. Keeps is good at cleaning things up."

Missy opened her power.

The voices overwhelmed. Thousands of minds poured into her. She quickly set up her filters, cutting the crowd away so she could focus. The screams of the Others became a near-deafening roar. She could hear each one individually now: all the threats and lustful wants, all the bitter angers and paralyzing fears.

She wrapped them up with the minds of other people, muffling them behind the crowd. She felt their hate, their distaste for her treatment. They'd always been a part of her, they'd always been heard, the way she shut them out sent them into a frenzy.

Plugger and Elliot were like blazing torches in her face. Their minds were open wide, every piece of their neural architecture was under her scrutiny. She felt like she was touching every layer, conscious and unconscious.

She purposefully kept herself from reading either. She would learn those things in a better way, sometime later, not like this.

Then she pushed out, expanding her reach even further. Her teeth ground together as the thousands grew in number. Minds upon minds upon minds came to her attention, sending thoughts, ideas, feelings, complaints. Over and over, a flood of mental energy.

Then she found what she wanted.

*Lena!*

Missy sent the thought before she really examined the mind. When she did, she found that Lena was asleep, but not in any natural way. She'd been drugged, probably with the same things that they'd tried to use on Missy.

There was a way that Missy could wake her up, but she would need to be closer. At this distance it was impossible.

She moved out from Lena, searching around for another mind, any mind. She found nothing. Lena was alone.

No, she wasn't.

Dr. Chadwick had to be there. She'd be waiting, waiting with drones and machines in ambush.

Missy took a different approach, turning her body around until she was facing toward Lena's sleeping mind. She searched between them, pulling back from Lena and looking for any mind that could tell her where she was.

She found a bus, and a driver, one that seemed familiar. It was the driver that had picked her up when she'd first left the institute. He'd just passed the same drop off.

Missy shut her everything out.

The sudden silence burned like hot ice on her eyes. She squeezed them shut and found herself bending over. The circlet shifted, threatening to tumble from her head onto the floor of Plugger's shop.

"Hey!" Elliot's hand touched her lightly on the arm.

Missy couldn't work her mouth enough to make words, so she held up her hand. She hoped it expressed how she was okay and herself.

Then she pulled it back to dig her nails into the sides of her head, searching for the half-healed scabs left by the last time she'd done so. Fingernails hit metal instead and she pulled back.

"It's her." Plugger sighed. "She's fine."

Missy forced her eyes open. How'd he know?

She pushed her body upright, swallowing the sick taste in her mouth and hearing nothing but the thundering pound of her own blood in her ears.

"Lena's asleep. I can't reach her from here."

"Sucks." Elliot put a lot of eloquence into the word.

"But I know where she is." Missy took a long, shuddering breath. The amplifier let her feel her stomach twist and lurch inside. "They didn't move her. Dr. Chadwick wants me to come there, to come back."

"Back where?"

"To the place they kept me in for the last six years." Missy felt a fragile smile grow on her face. It wasn't a nice smile. "She wants me to come home."

\*\*\*

# Chapter Thirty-Two

The drive north was tense.

Not just because both Plugger and Elliot had small cab trucks and neither wanted to drive separately, so all three of them were shoved into a cramped front seat. It also wasn't Missy's constant fluctuation between exhausted calm without her powers and a pitched mental fight with the Others. Nor was it because the rain had started in earnest and the roads were both dark and slick.

It was mainly because Elliot was extremely excited and wouldn't shut up about it.

"Oh man. Oh man. This is gonna be so sick!"

"You almost died today." Plugger reminded him.

"Yeah!" Elliot slowed the truck in order to take a tighter turn on the country road. "It was fuckin' intense. Never thought I'd be part of something like this. It's killer!"

Plugger just grunted and shifted in his seat. Missy sat squished between them.

She didn't mind. The physical discomfort was a pleasant distraction from the voices inside her head.

"Just shut up and watch the road." Plugger winced as the high beams of someone's Land Rover cut through the windshield and blinded him for a moment. "She'll be really pissed if you kill her before we get there."

Elliot was about to say something more, but Missy spoke for the first time in the last hour.

"Shut up."

Elliot's mouth snapped closed, but he kept the wild grin on his face.

Missy was feeling more from Lena now. They were getting closer. She couldn't wake her, not yet, but she could sense a general idea of what'd happened before she'd been put to sleep. Dr. Chadwick had returned, and enacted some sort of special protocol. It was something Lena had seen before but the details were still unclear. The result was that everyone but the doctor and Lena had been sent home.

From there things had changed. New people came in. Lena marked them as military of some kind. They had the boots for it. They'd moved some things in, worked on some of the rooms, then they'd packed up and left.

Lena knew it all had to do with Missy. She'd been worried, agitated.

Then the doctor came in, glared at her, then gave her the injection that put her to sleep.

Lena had been very, very afraid.

Missy closed her power off and relaxed as the screaming of the Other's abated. She was so thankful she had that option. She'd always thought she'd been turning off before, but she was never really doing so, even when she hadn't been reading minds, she'd kept it on high alert, waiting for a whisper of threat. It was always there, ready to give her a warning, a scrap of mental alertness.

Now, though, it was nothing. She was getting nothing from the two men she was wedged in-between. She was close enough to smell Plugger's failing deodorant and Elliot's acrid aftershave, but not a blip of what they were thinking or feeling.

She thought she'd known everything about her power, but it seemed she had a lot left to learn.

And she had to learn quickly.

"Turn right here." Missy told them as they reached the road the bus took.

Elliot slowed and took the turn with just a little more speed than she felt comfortable with in these kinds of conditions. A bolt of lightning lit up the sky, casting the forest in a stark picture of black and white. For that moment, just as the truck swerved around the corner, Missy almost thought she saw another car on the road behind them in the mirror.

She turned around to look but there was nothing there. They were alone on the road. It was too late, too dark, too much of a storm.

Not a single mind around but theirs.

She turned back and stared into the darkness as the amplifier made her hair tingle. What else could she do? What sort of power was left unexplored? Could she be even stronger than Miss Mania at her height?

*That* was terrifying to think about. Mania had been a terror who could rule entire cities if she'd felt like it. Even the idea that she could've been more was uncomfortable to consider.

Still, for all the things she'd done wrong, at least she was still here. She might be here for reasons she didn't fully understand, but she was here and her best friend needed her.

Missy opened herself up once more, hunching over as the Others swarmed, trying their best to drag her down. She fought them off, taking them on one-by-one, but the old battle was exhausting. She was getting tired and sloppy.

She reached out to Lena once again.

She could do it. She could wake her up.

"Pull over." Missy touched Elliot's arm.

The lanky retiree obeyed without question, parking the truck on the shoulder of the road with two tires in the grass and mud.

Missy took a deep breath, then pulled the triggers on wakefulness.

*Lena.*

The shock that ran through her showed Missy all her feelings. It was nearly overwhelming.

*Missy! You can't come here. Run!*

Tears welled in Missy's eyes as she felt everything that

Lena did, and how she was going to ignore every bit of it.

She'd come this far. She was not about to back down, not now.

*** 

The next hour was taken up with Lena and Missy exchanging information and analyzing what they both knew. During the exchange, Missy was aware of the mounting nervousness and fear radiating from Plugger and Elliot. They were both in over their heads.

Missy should have told them to drop her off and go but she couldn't.

Lena had made it clear that if Missy came here alone she had no chance. It was only with help that she could hope to make it through. Dr. Chadwick had prepared traps for her and whoever she might have enslaved.

The mercenary crew had brought in equipment. There were things like taser dart mini-turrets, drone parts, explosives, and webbing.

Getting through wasn't going to be easy.

Lena waited in the dining room. It was a large space with no windows and only two sets of doors. The main double doors and the door to the kitchen. She could see several traps around the main doors but she was facing the wrong way to see what was behind her near the counter and kitchen areas.

Missy shared with Lena her mental maps of the place based off of tracking where people went and what they'd seen. They figured out a few possible ways to get to her from the outside, each with their own dangers and unknowns.

Lena also pointed out something that Missy'd never noticed.

Given the shape of the building, there were at least two rooms missing from her mental map. There were two blank spots where Missy had never tracked anyone. They sat off to the side of the patient's personal rooms, just down the hall from where Missy used to sleep.

She'd never even noticed. They must have served as some sort of room for Dr. Chadwick, perhaps to monitor Missy from, or as a place to sleep. She was the only one Missy couldn't track, after all.

Lena agreed. Two weeks ago, Missy would have been terribly excited at the approval, but now it was barely a flicker. Too much to think about, too much she could lose.

The rooms were something to look at later, if they made it through. From everything the two of them knew, the traps were set to incapacitate, not kill. It was obvious that Dr. Chadwick wanted to take Missy alive. However, what she'd do to her afterwards was still in question. The last time they'd met she'd held a gun to Missy's head.

What was Dr. Chadwick's connection to all of this?

Lena was just as confused. Why treat Missy for all those years, let her loose, then come after her? None of it made sense. Why would the mere mention of Psychonic change everything?

What was it about him that twisted around Missy's life like a poisonous vine? Who was he? What had he really done?

What was she missing?

She wished she could save those questions for later, but they were important now. What would the doctor do if she got the answers she wanted? What would Missy do if she remembered?

Too many questions for the blank spots in her mind.

Missy took a deep breath and squeezed her eyes shut. She cut her powers off and fell into the blissful silence of her own mind.

"Hey, um…" She winced as her own voice came out raw and pitched higher than normal. "I've talked to her."

"Well? What's the plan?" Elliot's hands twisted around the truck's steering wheel.

"Uh…."

"Lemme guess, you haven't got one." Plugger mumbled.

"Not yet." Missy shrugged her shoulders, rubbing them against the others. "We know the place is covered in traps, uh, but not...um, the killing kind...uh."

"Non-lethal."

"Yeah, that."

Why were words so hard?

"What kind?"

Missy explained everything she'd learned, slowly, with several false starts and corrections as she said things in the wrong way somehow. She was sorely tempted to use her power and just drop information into their minds, but she knew enough about Plugger now that she didn't even suggest it.

"So you know the layout, but not where the traps are." Elliot summarized after Missy had run out of words.

"Yeah."

"Is there a basement?"

Missy shook her head. She'd never tracked anyone going below the first floor.

"Weird."

"What is?"

Elliot let go of the steering wheel and scratched the thin strips of hair around his bald spot, "Well, commercial buildings with medical areas like this one usually have some sort of underground area, something with backups for power and utilities and a biohazard disposal area. I had jobs that kept me working down there."

Missy shrugged once again.

"How would that even help us?" Plugger rumbled.

"Well… Sometimes the older hospitals and the like would have delivery tunnels in the underground. It allowed them to move things in and out without the patients seeing it and getting panicked and stuff." Elliot put his hands back on the wheel.

"Things like what?"

"Bodies, mostly."

"Oh."

Missy considered the mystery rooms that Lena had mentioned. What if there was something below? It seemed impossible.

"Where would it lead?" Plugger asked.

"Somewhere near a parking lot or road, usually paved. It needed to be somewhere a heavy truck could sit."

Missy realized that that was nearly useless to her. She knew almost nothing about what the institute looked like from the outside. The only time she'd even had a look was on the day she left… and she hadn't even taken the time to do so.

"Well…." She tried her best to straighten up in her spot between the two men. "It doesn't hurt to look."

***

# Chapter Thirty-Three

The institute was a squat and ugly thing, built more like a factory than a place of healing. The forest around it made it look even worse by contrast. Beautiful trees and lush foliage cut off at some arbitrary line around the grounds. They followed an overgrown driveway through the open gates and around the back of the building. The whole structure was dull and uninspired, built from flat concrete with no color or distinction. Once around the back of the lot, Elliot spotted an electrical shed. It was locked tight, but Plugger had a way with locks. It was amazing what a baseball bat could do in the right hands.

"Well, good news is that there is a tunnel." Elliot's voice echoed back from inside the shed.

Plugger leaned inside to yell back. "And the bad?"

"It's full of stuff." Elliot climbed around a rusted tool chest and wiped his hands on the tail of his shirt. "Looks like some sort of outside gas supply, extra electrical work, some sort of heating system…"

"Sleeping gas." Missy said. "I… forgot about it. They used it on the whole place when I… when Mania started riots."

"Ah." Elliot's face blanked for a little. "Well, we're not getting in that way."

"We should disable it." Plugger said.

"Ohhhh… right. If she turns on the gas while we're inside, then we're done, ain't we?" Elliot punched Plugger in the shoulder. "I got this, be back in a shake!"

They watched him crawl back inside and listened for a few moments as the sounds of pipes clanged and rattled back up to them.

"This is stupid." Plugger's voice was low, meant only for Missy. "You're gonna get him killed."

"He wants to be here."

"And millions of people want drugs that are killing them." Plugger's scowled, "People are idiots."

Missy couldn't argue with that.

"Make him stay here. We'll be the ones to go inside."

"All the traps are—"

"He's in his fifties, Missy. He's retired. You think he can take a dozen taser darts? Do you think he can get through there with no experience, no prep? This is stupid and you know it. He's *not* Baller." Plugger grabbed Missy by the shoulder and turned her around to face him. "He's not."

She hated the touch.

"I know you want Two Town to magically come back to life. Hell, you can probably make it happen… but it won't be real. You can't change the past. Baller is dead, and the place we knew is gone."

Missy shook her head. She didn't have time for any of this right now.

"Elliot is not some badass like *he* was." Plugger's voice was now a mere whisper. "Don't do this to him."

The Others would have killed him, struck him, gotten angry… but they weren't here. It was just Missy. She felt the urge, felt it strong enough to say he was wrong. She needed Elliot. She needed both of them! If they didn't come then… then…

"You don't understand!" Missy's voice cracked on the words. "If you don't come… she'll… put me in the machine. She'll make me…"

Plugger waited for Missy to finish, but the words dried up in her throat. She stood there, looking up into his face, into eyes she'd never noticed were a dark, muddy green. They held no answers, just further questions. She didn't know what was happening inside of him. She didn't know anything.

"I don't want to be like that." The words undammed and burst forth. "I don't!"

"What machi—"

"All done!" Elliot's chipper voice broke the moment.

Missy turned away as Plugger pulled his hands back.

Elliot climbed around the tool chest and began to wipe even-grimier hands on the grass and his clothing.

"Closed a safety valve and unplugged the control unit." Elliot beamed. "Anything she does won't matter until she comes out here herself!"

"Elliot…" Missy took a deep, slow breath. She knew Plugger was right. "Good work, but…"

"It's gonna be dangerous once we get inside." Plugger said.

Missy thought about turning her power on, just for a moment. Plugger seemed to be shaking with some strange energy she'd never seen in him before.

"You're gonna have to stay far behind us, alright?" He went on. "Stay low and don't go anywhere we don't, got it?"

Elliot saluted almost-correctly.

"And if you see us go down…" Plugger glanced back at Missy. "You run and get anyone you can to help. Hell, we should have called the cops or—"

"No." Missy was firm. "There's more here than Dr. Chadwick could arrange alone. Those mercs, the plans in her office, all this money spent just… just for me?"

"Ah." Elliot nodded. "Government crap."

"Yeah."

"That's fine." Elliot flashed a wild grin. "I know some guys."

Once again Missy was tempted to have a peek inside of Elliot's head, but she couldn't risk it. She couldn't do that while the amplifier was on her head, not with all the strain she'd already put herself through. She was going to be careful this time, she needed to show Dr. Chadwick something she'd never seen from Missy before: focus.

"We should go in through the laundry." Missy straightened up. "It has counters for cover and its only hallway leads to right to Lena."

The two of them nodded.

"And…." Missy looked from Elliot's balding head to Plugger's oft-broken nose and scarred cheeks. "Thank you… both of you. You don't have to be here."

"You kiddin'?" Elliot reached into his sweatpants and pulled out a glittering, golden bowling ball. "This is awesome!"

There were so many new things Missy was feeling at that moment that made it impossible not to smile.

***

# Chapter Thirty-Four

The door had been left unlocked.

Dr. Chadwick wanted them here.

She would be watching the cameras, seeing every movement the group made from start to finish. The doctor could be activating the sleeping gas right now and finding it nonfunctional.

Missy didn't know.

What she did know is that it was time to power up.

Missy opened her mind and crushed her teeth together at the onslaught from the Others. They were pissed. They hated the dark, they hated not being heard, they hated the weakness, the refusal to cause pain. They used the power of the amplifier to rake pain and misery into Missy's mind.

It took a long time to get them under control, but she managed it.

Then she reached out to Lena.

Now she had eyes and ears in the cafeteria. Lena was stuck facing one direction, but she was doing her best to check reflections in the glass and to listen to everything around her.

She was terrified, but like Missy, she was trying to keep focused.

She'd always been helpless. This was nothing new, but being betrayed by the person who was supposed to care for her?

That shook her.

She hadn't even seen it coming, despite all they'd found in Missy's previous visit.

Lena's self-recrimination and worry increase tenfold. She wasn't worried for herself, she was worried for Missy and her friends. That was Lena, through and through.

Missy crept through the laundry room. She could hear something down the hall that was motorized and mechanical: micro-turrets probably.

Plugger thought about using something in the room as a shield.

"Good idea." Missy told him.

"Damn, I hate that." Plugger moved off to the right to grab a cart and pull it closer. "Big enough?"

Missy examined it. It was big enough for her, but Plugger was a lot to hide.

"Anything else?"

Whatever else she'd been about to say was quickly forgotten as a terrible, yet familiar sound began to play around them.

Missy felt the mind-echoes immediately. Only this time, it wasn't just copies of her mind. There were copies of Plugger and Elliot as well. A dozen at first, then it multiplied until it felt like there was a small town around her, all shouting at her with her own thoughts.

"It's a drone." She heard the thought hundreds of times from each of them.

Missy doubled over as the Others screamed and shared their pain. She was only slightly aware of anything beyond the echoes and agony. She knew Plugger and Elliot were doing something, but the thoughts blurred and crashed into each other so many times she couldn't make sense of them all.

Missy felt tears well as she squeezed her eyes shut.

The amplifier fell off, clattering to the floor.

She had a moment, just a brief moment as the sound fuzzed from the change in her power. She had one moment of clarity, and she used it to shut everything out.

The screams vanished: all minds, all sounds, all the hundreds of echoed thoughts. Missy gasped for air at the sudden freedom.

Yet there was still the sound.

It was strange, more like the high-pitch squeal you'd hear when your ears were ringing or from a speaker system that was going bad. It made the skin on the back of her arms crawl and shiver. It made her itch.

It also forced her power to switch on. She'd have moments, feeling snippets of thoughts and feelings.

"What... is that?" Elliot whispered as he crawled up toward her. "Were you... I wasn't thinking about speakers, and then I was."

"What?" Missy turned her head toward the lanky contractor. "What about speakers?"

"I thought the sound... was like them, but it didn't feel like it was a me-thought."

Missy's mouth opened and closed. She'd been thinking that, hadn't she? Had she been pushing thoughts out to them as a way to compensate? Was that the real reason she could block it out now, because she was just shifting the assault?

"No, you're not." Plugger answered her unspoken question.

Missy turned to find him crouching beside her, his hand frozen in the motion of grabbing her amplifier off of the concrete floor. His eyes were as wide as saucers and his arms were covered in goosebumps.

"It's... another amplifier." Plugger's voice came out hoarse and terrified.

He sounded almost like Missy did.

"Lena... she says it's activating psychic powers... forcefully." Plugger's face twitched, his lips curling up to bare his teeth. "God, I can feel her. I can hear... I can see..."

Missy kicked the circlet out of his hand. She had a momentary flash of insanity as her foot touched the device, then it skittered over the ground and left Plugger to collapse onto the floor.

"That was..."

"Yeah, it sucks." Missy finished for him. She grabbed his arm in an effort to help him up. It only took her a second to realize that she had neither the weight nor strength to offer any kind of assistance to someone his size.

"An entire lifetime there, all the pain, agony, worries, regrets, all the discomfort and self-loathing." Missy had no trouble with the words now as she felt Plugger get his feet beneath him. "Diving into the misery of others can take you out, can't it?"

The former bouncer nodded mutely.

"Uh… guys?"

"What?" Plugger snapped. His words came out short and fierce, with a strangely feminine undertone.

"Look."

They both turned. Down the hallway from the laundry room a shadow was moving over the floor. It was roughly cross-shaped and it carried with it the sound of spinning rotors.

"Oh, I got this one." Plugger grabbed his bat off of the ground and launched himself forward.

Missy remembered what he was like in his prime. She remembered the tank tops Plugger used to wear, the way he'd carry around a television on his shoulders, and the way he walked like the world was meant to follow behind him and snap their fingers. He'd been quick, sudden. Where most people would get ready to move, Plugger just did it.

This wasn't the same.

He'd spent too much time in his little shop. He'd spent too many years nursing that deep well of regret. He was slower, more awkward. He held the bat more like an old enemy than the friend it should have been.

All the while the drone came bearing down on him. Something shot forth.

A pair of taser wires bounced off the side of a laundry cart and rattled along the tile floor.

Plugger hopped the wires and pressed closer as Missy

held her breath. He was just a few feet away now.

The drone paused and pulled back down the narrow hallway, forcing Plugger to follow at close range. There was little room to dodge.

He saw the next attack coming, moving aside just as another pair of taser darts shot out. He pressed his back against the wall beside the hallway entrance. There was barely enough room for him there as the rest of the wall was taken up by two industrial-sized washing machines. They were the kind that stood as tall as a person and were bolted to the floor.

He stood there, bat held up and ready, eyes closed as he listened for the drone.

Missy wanted nothing more than for the drone to creep forward. The sound was grating into her skull. Even with her powers off, the added amplification was bringing it back to life. She was getting flashes of her multiple minds. A hundred of her own selves would blink in around her, then vanish.

Missy squeezed her eyes shut against another one of those moments.

She heard the drone move.

She opened her eyes again to look.

The drone had moved up toward the ceiling, far out of Plugger's reach. It was slowly moving down the hall. She wanted to send Plugger the image, let him know, but she couldn't with the noise still hammering her.

He just stood there with his eyes closed and his chest heaving.

The drone crept closer, turning to line itself up with where its prey was hiding.

Missy opened her mouth to say something, anything.

Then Plugger reached up and grabbed the top corner of the industrial washing machine. Old muscles tensed as he crouched.

Missy realized what he was doing just a moment before it happened.

Plugger bolted forward just as the drone turned the corner, using his handhold to lever himself upward in something like a terribly awkward half-jump, half-vault. The dart shots missed him, flying beneath his legs as they swung up to kick.

Every part of him seemed to be sweating or shaking. His face was beet red.

The kick hit the edge of one of the rotors, sending the drone into the ceiling, where it bounced and slewed off to the right until it hit the far wall. Now it was turned the wrong way, its weapon pointed at an unoffending wall.

And Plugger wasn't done yet. As he came down from his jump he spun his body around, launching his bat upward.

If it had hit the rotors, it would have been perfect.

It would have been elegant if the bat had sailed through the blades and tore them up, sending the drone careening down the hall to crash as the imbalance took it down.

However, Plugger had spent too much.

He faltered on the throw, fingers let loose too soon and the bat's arc was shallow. The weapon banged off of the wall and tumbled away.

Plugger landed on his back, unarmed, unbalanced, and exhausted.

In a brief flash of her powers, Missy felt the air get knocked out of him.

Then a silver and red bowling ball sailed up in a lazy arc. It flew to the ceiling, just barely grazing it and leaving a trail of plaster dust in its wake. It smacked right into the drone's left rotor casing.

The impact sent the drone into the wall once again, twisting it even further sideways.

Even as the first projectile slammed heavily into the ground there was another coming. The second was bright green and had the word 'Yikes' written in gold along its side. It found the spot between the rotor covers and smacked the drone body itself. There was a crunch as something broke off and pieces of plastic rained down with the ball as it fell.

Plugger didn't yell or scream this time. He got to his feet and charged, legs stepping awkwardly to avoid the bowling balls rolling around the hallway.

He jumped up as the drone wobbled lower. His hands reached up and grabbed the main body of the machine.

There was a loud, crackling pop, and then the sound ceased. Missy gasped for air as her mind stopped sparking with reflections of herself. She was alone again, just her and her thoughts.

The air filled with the smell of baking electronics as Plugger threw the drone down to the floor. The machine sat there, blocking a good section of the hall as its rotors slowed and thin streams of blue smoke curled out from its body.

"Shit." Plugger bent down and held himself up with his hands on his knees. "Shit."

Missy looked behind her. Elliot was standing in the doorway to the outside, the storm of the night raging behind him. He was in a perfect bowler's pose: feet together, eyes focused forward. A brand-new bowling ball supported in his left hand with his right hand steading it.

The stained, ragged purple sweatpants somehow shone like gold amidst the darkness.

"Hell!" Plugger's cursing broke the magic of the moment.

Missy turned back and moved to the old bouncer. She didn't know what she could do, but she would be close enough to do it at least.

"Are..." She tried to say something.

"Fine," Plugger's voice wheezed, "Just give me a minute."

Well, Missy could do that.

She turned her power on again.

The Others were pissed and scared. They wanted

control. They wanted to burn down the building with everyone in it. No one here could be allowed to live. Everyone here knew her body had a weakness now. They had to die. The body must be protected for the Others to—

Missy mentally stabbed them.

They recoiled as she gave them pure mental pain, striking them with all of her own suffering.

She was tired of just pushing them back

It was time to make them afraid.

Missy gave them her panic and her suffering as the sound had dug into her skull. She gave them her terrible anguish as she sat in Mr. Keeps' little room. She gave them the pain of her body as she fought against the machine that Dr. Chadwick had put her in. She shoved it all at the horde inside of her. She gave them all the pain they'd forced her to endure for them.

They wailed and shrieked, running for the dark corners of her mind.

All except the one.

That one mind was different. She knew it. It had taken the assault with barely a shudder. It sat there in the darkness of her inner thoughts: watching and considering.

Then it too pulled away, leaving Missy in her own mind, with her own powers, and no distractions.

She felt all of Plugger's exhaustion and all of Elliot's fierce exultation. She felt Lena's fear and anxiety. Lena had heard the battle, she wanted to know what had happened. Missy even heard the faintest whisper of the mind inside the sweat pants. It felt something like pride.

"Okay." Plugger gave one last heavy breath, then he straightened up. "Ready."

"Same!" Elliot piped up.

Missy didn't say anything. She just moved toward the hallway.

The other two fell into step behind her. She heard heavy

breathing from one and excited muttering from the other. She knew she could hear even more from inside them, but she chose to mute that as much as possible.

They were almost to the common room when she felt it.

She had a half second of warning. The skin on the back of Plugger's shoulders started to itch. The hair on Elliot's arms rose up. Missy felt her scalp go dry, and the half-sentient mind of the summoning sweatpants screamed at her.

Missy looked up and the ceiling tiles exploded.

*\*\**

# Chapter Thirty-Five

Missy's eyes burned. She couldn't hear hardly anything beyond a high-pitch whine. She tried to look around but the only thing she saw was smoke and the purple afterimage of an explosion.

It took her a moment to realize that she was lying on the floor, rolled onto her side. She felt the cheap plaster shrapnel all over her head and chest.

Then there was one sound that was louder than the ringing in her ears.

It came twice in rapid succession. It was like the distant pop of two soda cans being opened.

Missy got an arm under her and tried to push herself upright. The world swam sideways at the effort.

The purple splotch before her eyes grew darker and something grabbed her arm.

There was a moment of hot pain in her shoulder then the world went blurry and dark.

She remembered only pieces of what happened next. She was grabbed by someone, lifted into a gurney.

Missy imagined that Patricia had somehow come back to get her, but the deeper part of her knew who it was. The one person who truly scared her. Her eyes cleared once, just long enough to look up to see the long, white lab coat and the scar above the ear.

Then the world blurred away again. There were lights, and a voice, and the sound of a door locking. There was more pain in her arm, whispers from the Others, fear, great amounts of fear, and cold metal on her arms.

Things took time to connect inside of her.

She tried to scratch the scabs on her head but her arm wouldn't move.

She tried again and failed.

Missy looked down as she waited for the world to stop swirling.

Her arm was locked into something. She knew the shape of it. It was something she was afraid of, wasn't it? Something from nightmares.

Ice-like lightning shot through her.

She was in the machine.

Missy screamed.

She tried to kick or punch or reach for other minds, but metal locked her body rigid and all the minds she could touch had been heavily sedated.

Then her arms and legs moved by themselves. The machine pushed her with the sound of motors and the faint clicking of the controller that ordered it.

"You used to be more of a challenge."

Missy stopped fighting.

Her eyes turned to the source of the words, trying their hardest to blink away the blurs and splotches.

"When you first came here, you didn't have any weakness."

Dr. Chadwick was there, sitting down on the bench side of one of the many cafeteria tables. Missy's sight was still marred by the aftereffects of the explosion. She couldn't see the doctor's face yet, but her hands were clear. They held the kludgework controller to the machine. The hands were shaking. The nails had been chewed on. Missy focused on one of them. It was red with infection.

"Afraid of nothing." Dr. Chadwick's voice was raw, dry, unsteady. "A power unmatched, unchallenged. You played with the world like it was a toy you wanted to break."

The sound of her own heart thundered in Missy's ears.

She screamed at Plugger and Elliot to wake up.

She couldn't do this. Not this.

"It took me two years."

The machine made Missy stand. Her body turned to face the doctor. Missy fought against it. Her muscles found nothing but cold metal and pain for her all her resistance.

"Two years to find a way to break you."

Dr. Chadwick stood up and walked closer.

The blur cleared to the point that Missy could see the face.

She looked into eyes that were bloodshot, framed by flesh that was circled with darkness.

"That's what they wanted from me." The words came as a whisper. "They wanted you broken... so they could learn how you do it. They wanted all your little secrets."

Dr. Chadwick put the controller down somewhere out of sight.

"Do you even know?" The doctor laughed. It was a hollow sound. "Do you know how you work? What gives you the power to pull people apart? To make them cut their own throats?"

Tears leaked from Missy's eyes as she gave herself more bruises and pain.

"Do you know why I'm different? Do you know why you can't touch me, why I had to be the one here... in this awful place, this place I hate? Watching as day after day you tore people up and destroyed them? Do you know *why*?"

Missy tried to shake her head but she couldn't. The cage that was locked onto her skull just rattled.

"No, you don't."

Dr. Chadwick reached up and grabbed a part of Missy's hair. She pulled on it, forcing Missy's skull to press into the metal frame even more. Tears that were welling now fell across the ceiling plaster on Missy's cheeks.

"Even we don't know." The hand let go. "Apparently

your brain has something... extra, something that can process and broadcast strange things on strange wavelengths. Apparently, everyone alive broadcasts it. It's how we sometimes know when someone's about to call... why our skin prickles when someone's watching. You hear it all, and more... you can make it work for you. You can shout so loud that it even rewrites perception."

"I..."

"SHUT UP!" Dr. Chadwick slammed her hand on the table, causing the controller to jump and move Missy's arms slightly to the left.

"You should be able to read me." The doctor pointed an unsteady finger at Missy's face. The chewed fingernail seemed to blur as it shook. "There's nothing different about me, nothing special. They tested it, over and over. Same energy, same wavelength... they thought you were just playing with me. Even I thought so, until I tested it... with this."

Dr. Chadwick reached down and picked the controller up.

Missy tried her hardest to wake Plugger from his drugged sleep. It was no use without the amplifier. He was under too deep. She needed him. She needed the man she'd seen in Two Town all those years ago, the one who knew he was going to be better.

"I thought I'd won, you know." Dr. Chadwick was saying.

The machine forced Missy to turn and reach for something on the table. Missy couldn't see what it was, but she knew what it had to be.

Her fears were brought to life as her hand was raised to her face, holding the scalpel in between encased fingers.

"I thought the worst was over." Dr. Chadwick's voice shook. "I thought I could go home. I thought that maybe, just maybe, I could learn enough that I might get some insight into... into what happened..."

The words trailed off. Missy found it hard to breathe. She kept staring at the scalpel. There wasn't enough air. There wasn't enough to breathe. She squeezed her eyes shut.

"I thought I was done." Dr. Chadwick whispered. "Then you said his name."

Missy opened her eyes.

She could see more clearly now.

She was in the cafeteria, somewhere near the middle. Lena had to be nearby. Missy looked for her and found the sleeping mind a few feet away. She was so close…

"You told *her*."

Dr. Chadwick moved the controller and Missy spun around.

Lena was sitting in her wheelchair a few feet away. She was leaning to the side as she always did but her pillows had been taken away. She needed those. Without them the pain in her ribs and her neck would be unbearable.

Missy needed to fix it. She needed to get the pillows back.

"You said you wanted to thank him."

Missy's arms and legs moved again. She was forced to walk forward, the scalpel held before her.

"No!" Missy screamed as she realized what was happening.

"I thought I'd broken you." Dr. Chadwick went on. "I was wrong. You were just afraid. Normal, everyday fear, the kind everyone has. I didn't break you… I just made you human."

"You can't… you can't make me—"

"To really break someone, they have to love something first. That's how it works." Dr. Chadwick's words were drawn out slowly, like a straw scraping through the lid of a paper cup. "When you love someone… and then some, some MONSTER takes them away from you! When they take your family… when they take everything…. THAT is what breaks you."

"Family?" Missy latched onto the word. She tried to look at the doctor but all she could see was the metal casing holding her head. She didn't want to look forward. She didn't want to see the blade as it got closer and closer to Lena's neck.

The Others screamed deep in the depths of her mind. They didn't want to be here. They could see that Missy was about to break.

"You left him there."

Dr. Chadwick turned Missy's head to look toward her. The doctor's lips peeled up to show teeth. "You left him there in the garbage. This whole time I was looking for the person who took him from me... and it was you."

"I'm sorry." The words fell from Missy's mouth like water from a bursting pipe. "I don't... I don't know what happened."

"I DON'T CARE." Dr. Chadwick dropped the controller and grabbed Missy's face in both hands, pushing fingernails into her jaw until she felt them pressing on her teeth. "You left him there. My brother... all he ever wanted was to help people, and you left him there."

Tears ran down Missy's face and hit the shaking fingers that pressed into her skin. Her brother? The picture in her office. Is that what Missy had done? Is that what this was all about? Wait, she'd said in an alley... she said—

"My... my *job*... was to break you." Dr. Chadwick let go and took a step back. "I didn't do it right the first time. You're not like me, not yet."

A low whine escaped from Missy as she watched the doctor bend down and pick the controller back up.

"But you will be." Dr. Chadwick whispered the words as she lifted her head, hands falling into a comfortable grip on the black plastic. "She's not empty, but you're gonna make it so she is. Then, when she's empty, you'll know what it's like."

"Please..."

"How many of them said that?" Dr. Chadwick smiled,

a crooked smile that twitched. "Do you remember? Do you? Did my brother say it?"

Missy rattled her head against the machine. It hadn't been like that. Psyconic had come for her. He'd hunted *her* down.

Then she heard it.

It was a small noise, something that Dr. Chadwick might not even notice. It was something that seemed normal in a place like this. It was a sound that Missy would have ignored on any other day in any other circumstances.

It was the sound of a wheelchair rolling.

Only Lena was here. She wasn't moving.

Missy didn't have the time or focus to reach out and find out who was out there. She could barely control her own breathing. Still, she knew she could do one thing, just one thing to buy some time.

"I'll tell you!"

"What?"

"I'll tell you... what I did." Missy's mind raced. She had to think of something to tell her. What would the Others have done?

The Others latched on to the idea and surged forward, offering up monstrous fantasies and desires so fast that they overwhelmed Missy, showing her an endless parade of blood and pain and screams.

"I burned... no, I cut, No! I—" Missy's neck muscles twisted beneath her skin as she tried to fight the machine. "Stop! It's too much."

"WHAT DID YOU DO?"

*"WE DID NOTHING!"* The Others screamed the words through her. Two dozen voices speaking together. All of them except the strange one. It was the one left alone in the back as she lost her grip and the Others took control.

Missy turned to the mind and sent a question to it.

She wanted to know what it was. It didn't feel like the

rest of her.

"Stop it."

The words snapped Missy back to reality. She was breathing so hard. Her throat burned from the Other's screams. Her arms and legs were bruised and cut from thrashing about.

"I've had enough!" Dr. Chadwick moved Missy's arm, the scalpel swiveled back up to Missy's eye like it'd done so many years ago. It hovered just millimeters from her skin.

"If you don't know, then I don't want you here." Dr. Chadwick's expression fell, tension and anger bleeding out to a countenance full of weariness. "I hate the sight of you."

Hands tensed on the controller and the weapon in Missy's hand drew back to strike.

Then the door opened.

It wasn't kicked open like in some action hero story. It also didn't creak open with dramatic tension like in a horror movie.

No, it opened smoothly, artificially. The way a door opens when someone presses the big silver button meant for people with their hands full with things like a gurney...

Or a wheelchair.

It came through first, revealing a blanket over a pair of atrophied legs, a thin body, a straight back.

Missy knew the face.

Her breath stopped.

It was him: Psyconic.

And behind the chair, pushing him forward with black gloves, a strangely formal suit, and the heavy gas-mask on his face, was Mr. Keeps.

"Oh, I wouldn't do that." He said in his curiously light tone.

Dr. Chadwick spun around. A strangled cry escaped her throat.

"After all," Mr. Keeps pushed the wheelchair further

into the room. "If you kill the girl… then I believe you kill your brother."

"You… you wouldn't."

"Oh no, not me. I'm not presenting a threat." Mr. Keeps paused mid-step, "I mean it quite literally. If you kill Miss Mania, you'll be killing your brother. You see—"

Mr. Keeps held his hand up, bending his index finger ever-so-slightly toward Missy.

"—I don't think she is *who* she thinks she is."

\*\*\*

# Chapter Thirty-Six

For a long moment nothing happened.

Dr. Chadwick stood like a statue. Only her hands moved: shaking and twitching. Her left hand was clasped over her mouth, while her right held the controller in a tenuous, unsteady grip. Missy's initial relief hadn't lasted long. Her attention was torn between the shaking controller and the scalpel poised to cut out her eye.

"What... Who are you?" Dr. Chadwick's neck joined in the twitching.

Mr. Keeps didn't answer at first. Instead, he spent the silence pushing the wheelchair forward until it was next to Lena's. Only about a foot of space stood between them.

"This has been quite confusing, for many of us." Mr. Keeps said as he adjusted the chair so that its wheels lined up with the one next to it, so neat and correct, "Tell me, doctor, what was your brother's power?"

"Get away from him!"

Dr. Chadwick held the controller up before her like it was a shield. Her shaking fingers hovered over the sticks that controlled the arms. Missy couldn't break her eyes away from them.

"Please, now. I am trying to provide a solution." Mr. Keeps' looked straight at the doctor. "But I do require some cooperation."

"Who *are* you?!"

"My name is Mister Keeps."

"How...?"

"I followed her."

Missy blinked. There had been someone behind them.

"I was able to ferret out quite a lot about you, this facility, its patients, even the PMC that funded it," Mr. Keeps moved around from behind the wheelchairs to stand between the two invalids. "Its location, however, was kept out of all documentation. Now, tell me, what is his power?"

"Why does it matter?" Dr. Chadwick practically wailed. "He can't do *anything* now."

"Because you want to know what happened." Mr. Keeps clasped his hands before him like a bodyguard at a state funeral. "And it's the last thing I need to know in order to tell you."

Silence settled over the room.

Missy stared at Mr. Keeps with pleading eyes. If he was bluffing, then he had to have a plan. He always seemed to have a plan. She hoped he wasn't counting on her to do anything, because she was truly stuck. She had no power here. Even Psyconic's body was empty to her. How did they do it?

They were all here: the three people she couldn't influence. All of them were here, right now, in this place... and she still didn't even understand why.

"He could invoke people." The words dropped like stones from the doctor's lips. "Tell them to do things.... and they would."

Mr. Keeps sighed. His shoulders relaxed, his masked face lifted up as if to thank some god above, then he looked back down.

"Perfect. Absolutely perfect. He had the perfect power. Can I assume that once he used this 'invocation' that the subject remained bound by it?"

Dr. Chadwick nodded.

"Then I can now explain everything, but first... I ask that you put that down."

"No."

"I insist." Mr. Keeps unclasped his hands and lightly touched Psyconic's armrest with his fingertips. "I won't require you to hand it over, but it does seem to me that you are having a... difficult... time holding on to it."

Dr. Chadwick looked down to witness the shaking of her own hands.

"Please."

"How many people…" Dr. Chadwick murmured, then she shook herself.

She moved to the cafeteria table and put it down. It rattled against the cheap plastic until she let go.

"Thank you." Mr. Keeps re-clasped his hands. "Now, I wish to begin by telling you that this was not Missy's fault, not exactly. Your anger toward her, while understandable in light of her horrific past, is actually unwarranted in this particular instance. You see..."

Mr. Keeps turned to look down at Psyconic's comatose body.

"...This was exactly what your brother wanted."

"What are you talking about?"

"You should know him better than anyone." Mr. Keeps continued. "Psyconic was a hero, not the front-page, mall-opening, television-commercial hero that everyone knows about. No, he was the real kind, the kind that helped people just to help them. It was quite difficult to track him down and learn of his activities. Due to the nature of his powers, he was able to work with great precision and subtlety. He was only noticed when there were a crowd of witnesses, too many for him to easily 'invoke.' In fact, if Missy herself had not told me he was an element of her story, then I would have been just as confused as you are."

Mr. Keeps took two steps forward toward Missy and the doctor.

"Miss Mania drew his attention at some point. Perhaps he had a close call with her, or she hurt someone important to him, or perhaps he just felt that he had a connection with her. Regardless of the reason, he became focused on stopping her: specifically."

Dr. Chadwick reached up and touched the burn scar over her ear but said nothing.

"And demonstrating once again his incredible capacity for forethought and planning, he cast an 'invocation' on you, the person he cared about the most. He wanted to make sure that if things went wrong—"

"What? No, he never did that to me."

"Yes, he did." Mr. Keeps raised his voice just enough to speak over her. "He ordered you to keep your thoughts confined. His powers must function similarly to Miss Mania's. He knew enough about the way it worked to assume that an intervention using his powers would make you immune to hers."

Missy turned her eyes to the body of Psyconic. He looked older than he'd been in her memory. His face didn't have that interest. It was empty, void of everything. Yet, she remembered the look in his eyes that day.

"It was never an accident that a well-educated therapist ended up being immune to Miss Mania's power. He planned it that way, from the very beginning. He informed someone with the right connections and the right personnel that you would be the one who could treat her once he was done."

Missy looked back at Dr. Chadwick. Her bloodshot eyes were wide, seeing something in her own mind and not sharing the secret.

Mr. Keeps took another step forward.

"I think he knew that he would only get a single use of his power. He had one chance, and he made it the boldest, most desperate plan he could consider. The kind of thing that even a paranoid, seemingly-schizophrenic telepath like her wouldn't be able to anticipate."

He turned to Missy.

"Missy, when were you born?"

"Uh…" Missy tried to follow the jump in topic but failed.

"I don't mean your body, I mean the consciousness, you're one of many, correct? You told me back on that rooftop that your mind was full of 'Others.' I know this may be a difficult concept to consider, but do you think that, perhaps, *you* are the Other?"

Ice crawled into Missy's spine.

When was she born?

She was born… was she? Was that her memory? Or was it one of the Others? Was she there that day in the alley? Was that her? What about before… The one who hid… the one who snuck around Two Town, was that her?

It felt like her.

"I…" Missy focused as hard as she could at pulling apart what memories were hers and what weren't. The Others milled about in confusion as she sifted through her mind. They all hated this. It felt wrong.

Except the one.

The one Other crept closer to the surface. Missy was about to push it back when she felt it give her something. A piece of a memory, the barest scrap of a moment where the mind was standing in an alleyway, full of fear and desperate hope.

Looking at a rain-soaked girl with black hair and eyes full of panic.

"*Fuck.*" Missy realized what she was looking at.

"The Others… they may seem like schizophrenia, but they aren't, are they?" Mr. Keeps pressed on. "No, it's not multiple personalities. It's multiple *minds*, minds that Miss Mania absorbed: strong, angry minds. The kind that a traumatized little girl might take on as protectors. Perhaps it started with the very one that tortured her. That little girl… she didn't just stop her tormentor with her power, she took the entire mind and made it a part of her. She kept doing it. When someone scared her, she didn't fight them off, she absorbed them. She made sure that she was always angrier, scarier than anyone else by stealing the minds that scared her."

"Nonononono…no!"

Missy fought the machine once more. She wanted out, she needed to get out. She was going to suffocate. She was going to die. The Others screamed inside. They'd known the truth. They'd kept it from her.

The special Other protected her, keeping itself between Missy and the surge of hate.

"Psyconic knew somehow." Mr. Keeps walked closer, nearly standing next to Dr. Chadwick as he looked down at Missy. "He might have even been able to do the same kind of transfer. Perhaps that's *how* he figured it out. He used his knowledge, his ability, he used them both to do the one thing that only he could do."

"No." The word slipped from Dr. Chadwick.

"He ordered Miss Mania… to take *his* mind."

Both Missy and the doctor screamed together.

"That's why his body lies empty!" Mr. Keeps raised his voice to be heard. Gone was the light and airy way his speech normally sounded, now there was a heaviness to his tone, a richness to it as he turned around.

He picked up the controller and pressed the release button.

The clamps loosened and Missy clawed herself free. She wanted to run, to never look at Mr. Keeps or Dr. Chadwick, or Plugger, or Elliot, or anyone else. She never wanted to hear their names. She wanted him to stop. She wanted it all to *stop!*

"Psyconic is still here." Mr. Keeps tossed the controller away. "Isn't that right, Missy?"

"No." Missy grabbed her head in her hands. The battle within her mind raged louder and stronger than ever. "He… isn't… me."

"Missy…"

"He isn't!" Missy screamed the words. "But he's here."

Silence fell as she dug her nails into her scalp. She felt the scabs break and blood flow. The screaming within was consuming, deafening. They wanted her to break. They wanted to destroy everything.

Only Psyconic's mind kept them back. He fought them off alone.

This entire time he'd been there… inside her.

He'd been the one that gave her the power back.

Missy hadn't been alone.

Her advantage, her sudden power over the Others… it hadn't been her: it had been him.

"Oh." Mr. Keeps' voice fell. "Well, I was close."

Missy whimpered as her mind burned. She doubled over and felt like tearing her skull open to release the chaos.

No. This wasn't it.

She wasn't the sad one any longer.

Missy forced herself to stand up straight. She dropped her bloody hands and pushed them to her sides. She glared at the dark glass circles of Mr. Keeps' mask. She stared into the darkness and the darkness stabbed back into her.

She pulled all of her pain together. She took all of her fear, her anger, her focus.

Every bit of torture from the last six years she took and crushed it together into a weapon.

Missy pushed Psyconic's mind out of the way and went to town.

She bludgeoned them with her rage.

Her body dripped with sweat. Blood ran from her hair, then from her nose, then a touch leaked from her eyes. She could almost feel the capillaries burst from the strain.

The Others rallied just once, and she fed them such pain and anguish that they broke like a glass pitcher, fleeing down the darkest parts of her mind.

But she wasn't done.

Missy turned and charged down between the cafeteria tables, hands leaving trails of red behind her as she locked her eyes on Psyconic's empty body.

Dr. Chadwick screamed, and made to run after her, but Mr. Keeps grabbed both of her arms as she rushed past.

Missy reached the wheelchair. Red hands latched onto each side of Psyconic's head. Her blood squeezed from between her palms and his temple.

Missy closed her eyes.

She felt him there. For the first time since she'd noticed the strange Other, she felt fear.

It was too late. She was in full-force. Missy grabbed the mind with her own. It writhed and fought against her, but it had expended too much while protecting her.

If she could absorb a mind… then she could cast one out.

Missy took Psyconic's mind and pushed it back to the emptiness she held between her hands.

The pain was blinding. So much of her power burned all at once. It was like trying to read the minds of an entire city, hundreds of millions of memories and feelings and thoughts came screaming through her. Psyconic's entire existence was held for a moment in her thoughts, every piece of her was consumed with it.

Then it was gone.

Missy's body failed.

She fell backwards and lay still on the ground, heart and lungs laboring to work as her eyes stared at the dirty crumbs on the tile floor. She couldn't move her hands, or legs, or anything. She couldn't blink. She wasn't meant to do something like that. Or was she? Who was she?

Then she felt something move against her back. At least she had feeling. That was something.

It pushed against her.

Missy realized it was a foot; Psyconic's foot. She was lying on the ground right before his wheelchair.

Then more. Missy wished she could move, look, anything.

Then it didn't matter.

"Sis…" A voice croaked out.

There was a sound of someone sobbing. Dr. Chadwick, it had to be.

"Sorry…" The voice above Missy rasped. "Should have… told you."

"Micah..."

"Yeah." Psyconic answered her, from his own body, using his own voice. "Been… a while."

Mr. Keeps must have let the doctor go, for she rushed to her brother, hands and arms reaching for each other as tears and wails took the place of words, leaving Mr. Keeps to pull Missy out of the way before she was stepped on or rolled over. He spent a moment propping her up against a bench seat so she could watch as the two siblings mumbled half-sentences at each other in between sobs.

"Quite impressive." Mr. Keeps said it just loud enough for Missy to hear. "I had no idea you could do that."

Missy felt her hand twitch. She seemed to be getting some of her body back under her control.

"I'm guessing you were unaware as well." He hummed a little tune to himself. "You're too impulsive, Miss Missy. You could have waited at least a little bit longer. I didn't even get to explain all the work I had to do to put the pieces together. Ah, well."

Missy moved her eyes. She could look over now. She stared up at Mr. Keeps.

"Not the way I would have done things," He reached up and undid the straps on his mask, pulling them loose and lifting the edge of it to show his twisted visage. "But I believe the world would be a terrible, awful place if everyone was just like me."

He turned to look down and meet Missy's eyes.

"Or like you."

Missy felt her lips twitch up toward something like a smile.

\*\*\*

# Chapter Thirty-Seven

It took something like an hour for Missy to regain control.

Dr. Chadwick had taken her brother and left. Mr. Keeps had let them. There were villains aplenty in the world and he said he had no desire to make any more. He'd stayed with Missy until she could lift herself up to the actual bench and sit at the table under her own power.

Then he left, but he said he'd be back.

Missy enjoyed the peace and quiet for a few minutes, but too much had happened, too many questions filled her, too many dangers still lingered.

She could feel the Others stirring. They were wounded, but now they knew Missy's hidden ally was no longer among them. They were creeping up from the dark recesses of her mind. The longer Missy sat there alone with her thoughts, the bolder they got.

It took her three tries to get to her feet. Her muscles and mind were still sending the wrong signals to each other. Still, a lingering fury and a half-felt panic of pursuit were great motivators.

Missy's head was killing her and her hands and hair were caked in blood. She stumbled to the washroom.

Her hands made a mess of the white porcelain of the sink as she braced herself and stared at her ragged reflection in the mirror. She looked like a monster from a horror novel. Her black hair was stuck to her head in an uneven mess, red grime streaked down her jaw and cheeks.

Her entire body shook, and the look in her eyes….

Missy punched the cold water handle and began to scrub.

The water turned dark.

He'd messed with her head.

Her hands shook under the cold.

That's how he'd done it.

Fingers raked against the lingering stains.

He'd been in her head for years.

Her balance shifted and she fell forward, her left elbow taking her weight as she leaned against the sink. Her head bent forward. The Others clawed their way upward inside of her, closer and closer.

He'd been there.

Every time she'd invaded someone else's mind, every time she'd changed them, twisted their memories. It had never once occurred to her that someone might have done the same to her.

Now she knew how it felt.

Awful.

Bile surged in her throat and she accepted it, spitting the foul taste down into the water as her head swam.

Who was she?

That was the real question.

What part of it had been her, and what part had been him?

Missy pushed herself upright. She stared at the dark eyes in the mirror.

She wasn't sure she liked what she saw. She didn't trust it.

She looked away and began the process of washing her hair as best she could in a bathroom sink.

\*\*\*

After she was sufficiently recovered, Missy went looking for everyone else.

She found Mr. Keeps loading Elliot onto a gurney.

Missy watched him. He'd put his mask back on and his breath seemed louder from wearing it. He lifted the unconscious retiree up in a fireman's carry before he noticed Missy was there.

He didn't even stop. He just nodded once, then placed Elliot on the gurney and adjusted the man's arms and legs until it looked like he would be comfortable.

"You've done that before." Missy said it as she realized it herself. The way he'd moved, he'd done it carefully, making sure to do no harm.

"Yes."

"Did you work in a hospital?"

"No." Mr. Keeps looked down at Plugger. The man was much larger and heavier than Elliot. "I'm just used to… taking care of things."

Missy felt that there were a hundred things she could ask in the silence that followed.

All but one of them could wait until later.

"Need another gurney?"

"Yes, that would be helpful."

"I'll get one."

Missy knew where they were. She knew where everything was in the hospital. She was halfway there before she realized that the thought wasn't completely true.

She found herself looking down the hallway to where the missing room was: the room that Lena had noticed. The one that no one had ever been in.

Missy turned and made her way down to it. It had been broken into. A crowbar sat discarded on the floor nearby. Missy pushed the broken door open and looked inside.

It was a patient's room.

Only this one wasn't stark white. It wasn't some sterile place without life. It was a bedroom, a place to be lived within. The walls had been painted a misty blue, with posters and pictures hung around.

Missy moved inside, being careful to step over the wooden splinters from the broken door. There were marks on the tile from a set of wheels. There'd been a wheelchair here. It must have been used quite a lot based on the scuffs and scratches.

The posters were for heroes, ones the Missy remembered. She saw Terra Cotta posing on the steps of a city hall in one of them.

Miss Mania fought him once. She'd forced him to jump off the roof of a building with his sidekick.

Missy looked at the next item in turn.

It was a picture. A tall, awkward-looking kid stood smiling next to an older, more-serious teenage girl. The girl had a clump of hair missing on one side of her head. Dr. Chadwick had grown up since the picture was taken, but her frown had remained the same.

Missy stared at it for a long time.

Six years… and all this had been hidden from her.

Fingers moved up to touch the spots on her head as she felt them bleeding again. She'd just cleaned them up.

All that time, and she'd been living a part of a lie.

The Others heard her uncertainty and crept closer.

Missy moved on, finding a door that led to a small bathroom and closet. Her eyes scanned over the clothes and toiletries, lingering for just a moment on a pair of yellow bunny slippers.

There was something so un-special about them.

He'd been here the entire time.

At least his body had.

Two halves… sitting a few meters from each other and Missy hadn't even guessed.

She used to pride herself on knowing everything.

It was clear now that she hadn't known shit.

"Fuck you." She whispered at the picture on the wall. She stared into the grainy, printed eyes of the smiling kid. "Fuck you!"

Missy closed her eyes as the Others tried to ensnare her with their little tendrils of hate. She poured her pain out onto them. They shied back, running for the dark corners.

She opened her eyes again and touched the picture with her fingers that were clean of blood.

"...and thanks."

She left.

She found the gurney and returned to Mr. Keeps. He'd removed most of the debris and dirt from Plugger's face and chest. He said nothing as she arrived, opting instead to just pick up the old bouncer and drop him heavily onto the gurney.

The tranquilizer dart was still sticking out from between Plugger's ribs. Missy reached out and pulled it free, trying her hardest to keep from dropping it.

"How did you know?" Missy asked as they both stopped to catch their breath. "He was here. How….?"

"Because she didn't fit."

"What?"

He turned away from the unconscious body and looked down at Missy. The dark plastic of the mask was as blank as ever, yet Missy could almost feel the look beneath it. Under the plastic and rubber and the scars that disfigured him… she could almost see the hesitation.

"I read her reports over and over. All of it made sense, everything lined up… except for her." Mr. Keeps took hold of one of the gurneys and gestured toward the other with a questioning tilt of his head.

Missy nodded and took hold of Elliot's gurney. Her muscles were still misbehaving, but Mr. Keeps set a slow pace as he pushed the other one down the hall. She would manage.

"She was a blind spot to you." Mr. Keeps continued.

"So are you."

"Ah, true," He stopped for a second, straightening up and turning his entire body toward Missy, "But my immunity is decidedly… artificial."

"What?"

He answered by reaching up and undoing the top buttons of his suit, pulling enough of the fabric away to show the sparkle of something metal around his neck.

"Psychic dampener." Mr. Keeps said simply. "I…"

Missy stared at the metal. It had spines on it, like some sort of inverted version of her own circlet.

Mr. Keeps cleared his throat. "I found it on Psyconic, when I recovered him from the alley."

Two feelings vied for control of Missy's emotions. One was a breath-stealing shock, the other was a terrifying rage. Unlike previous times, this wasn't a gift from the Others, it wasn't a trick to make her lose control, it was hers, held close and focused.

"I told you." The words hissed forth from her lips. "I told you his name."

Mr. Keeps said nothing in response, only tilting his head further down.

"You could have told me!" Missy pushed the gurney out of her way, closing the gap between them and reaching for the metal around his neck. She wasn't certain if she wanted to rip it off or strangle him with it.

"You could have… you had…. You *knew!*"

"Not enough."

"ENOUGH FOR ME!"

Missy's entire body shook as her fingers squeezed the metal of the collar. The cold metal bit into both her skin and her mind, quieting the voices internal and external.

Mr. Keeps didn't even struggle. "I was… waiting."

"For WHAT?"

Missy jerked the metal, pulling his head down.

"For when I had everything." His voice was strained by the pressure on his throat. "That is why I wished to keep you close. It is why I left. The last pieces were found in-"

"I don't care!" Missy's hands shook. "You should have told me."

"Why?"

"Because… I…"

"What were you? Terrifying? Unstable? Under the care of a system that had every reason to lie to you, to leverage you against others?" Mr. Keeps grabbed her wrists. Missy felt the leather of his gloves press into her skin. "I am sorry, but I couldn't trust you… not until…"

Missy let him pry her hands free of the metal.

The rage dried up.

"You were there, weren't you?" She asked. "You found him in the alley."

"I did."

Missy pulled back, fighting the urge to dig her nails into her head once again.

"But not until you were long gone." He continued. "Back then I had many informants in Two Town. It was where things were heard. They said there was a dead hero. I came to clean it up."

"But he wasn't dead."

"No. He wasn't." Mr. Keeps rubbed his neck with his gloved hand. "He was still breathing. I don't often find myself in such a situation. I called the emergency line, but…"

"You took his equipment."

"Yes."

"To keep it from being abused."

"Yes."

"To protect people."

Missy looked down at the sleeping faces of her friends. She'd watched him take such care with their bodies, spending the extra energy and attention to make sure they would be comfortable when they woke up.

"You're always so careful." Missy said it out loud. "Everything you do… it has to be done just right, doesn't it?"

He stopped rubbing his neck and let his arm drop.

"It's why you wanted me to stay." She followed the logic, as foreign as it was to her. "You wanted me there when you learned everything."

He nodded.

"Fuck you…" She breathed, then finished with, "…and thanks."

Mr. Keeps tilted his head but remained silent.

"Not the way I would have done things." Missy's lip twitched as she threw the words back at him.

The laugh was short, hoarse, and ended quickly. Still, Missy was glad to hear it.

"Fair enough." Mr. Keeps gave her a mocking bow. "For what it's worth, I believe I was wrong."

Missy shook her head. She'd spent enough time in the heads of others to understand the way perspective could destroy reason. No one ever had all the information.

Even Missy could be blind to reality.

Psyconic had given her that lesson in full.

"I think…" Missy stared down at Plugger's face. "I think I'm the wrong person."

"For what?"

"For this life." Missy looked back up. "Mr. Keeps?"

"Yes?"

"Will you take your mask off?"

He was silent for a moment, then he did as he was asked. He went through the complicated process of undoing straps and peeling the rubber and plastic from his skin. He pulled it away, showing his clipped ear, shrouded eye, bald head, and the expression that sat beneath it all.

"Thank you." Missy looked into the one eye she could see clearly. It was dark, like hers. "Can you do something for me?"

"I would be glad to."

Missy looked down at Plugger, then Elliot, then back up into his dark eyes.

"Tell them... to be her friend."

"I'm not sure I understand."

"Don't worry." She said as she reached up and adjusted the collar of the shirt that she'd mangled just moments before. "You will."

\*\*\*

# Chapter Thirty-Eight

When Lena woke up, she was immediately engulfed in the mental equivalent of a crushing hug.

Missy poured everything she had into the feeling, and her weariness washed away as she received an equal amount in return.

Lena was still sitting in the cafeteria. Missy had moved her chair up next to one of the tables, close enough that Missy could sit on the bench beside her. Missy had also gathered her things from the hallway and brought them here. Her old backpack looked deflated as all of its assorted contents lay spilled out before her. All of it was ignored as she let Lena's head rest on Missy's own.

She was probably gonna get some blood in Lena's hair, but at the moment she didn't give a shit.

*I was so worried.*

"I know." Missy curled into the comfort of Lena's mind. "You want me to fill you in?"

*I can feel it.* Lena answered, showing Missy a fuzzy reflection of her own thoughts. *It's amazing.*

"That's one way to say it."

*There's something more, though.*

Missy nodded, rubbing the sore spots of her head against Lena's.

*Something you're keeping from me.*

"Lena…" Missy paused to wet her lips. "What would you do if you could walk again?"

*Everything!*

Missy laughed at the raw exuberance in the answer.

"What if it wasn't perfect?" Her smile faded to something lesser.

*Missy, nothing's perfect.*

Missy closed her eyes.

"Lena…" She reached up with her right hand and pressed it into Lena's cheek. The skin was dry and scaly. "I'm gonna need you to trust me."

*…Okay.*

Missy used her other hand to reach up to the table and grab the psionic amplifier.

Her full power erupted within her. She opened it up to its fullest, pulling all of her potential, more than she'd ever dared use before. The Others surged with it, but this time Missy didn't care. She reached for every scrap of power. She felt thousands of minds, then the number doubled, then tripled.

She ignored it all to focus on her own mind… and Lena's

For a moment there was no barrier between them. She felt the electric, paralyzing shock as Lena read her plans.

Missy reached out.

Lena crossed into Missy.

Unlike with Psyconic, there was no pain. The amplification, the willingness, the understanding: it all worked together to ease the transfer. It might have helped that there was a space open, a place left empty by the loss of an Other

Lena fell into Missy's mind and the joy spread so strong and so fast that Missy felt tears leaking from her eyes.

But she wasn't done.

She bound herself to Lena. They knew each other. Lena knew what was going on. She knew what had to be done.

The Others screamed as they came after them.

One by one they cornered the minds, herded them, biting at them with pain, fear, anguish, all the things they loved to inflict but hated to face themselves. They corralled and pushed, tearing into the horde with weapons built from years of suffering.

The Others surged in retaliation, sensing that this was the end. They gambled everything on one last desperate rush to take control, to become the Miss Mania they'd once been.

Lena and Missy stepped aside. They fell back as the Others grabbed control. Missy's gentle hand suddenly turned to a claw that dug into Lena's cheek.

Flesh tore, blood spilled.

Then Missy and Lena *pushed*.

They pushed the Others out.

The anger was overwhelming. The Others fought with everything they had as they felt themselves slipping from one mind to the other. The door had been left open, so open that they had partially crossed over into Lena's mind in their headlong rush to dominate.

Parts of them were already there.

It took one surge, one bludgeoning blow with two minds working together in perfect concert. There was no discord, no infighting, none of the weaknesses that plagued the riotous mass of the Others.

It was pure, perfectly-connected grace.

Missy surged ahead, taking every attack head-on, her soul suffering, but never yielding. Lena came after, focused, calculating. She made all the right moves at the right time and in just the right way.

Missy gasped when the final Other was exorcized. She shoved herself away from Lena's body. Her reaction was so violent that the wheelchair tipped over, throwing the body it held onto the floor.

It twitched, eyes and lips shaking as dozens of angry minds fought to do something, anything from within their prison.

Then Missy let go. She let go of the pain, of the fear. She let go of arms and legs and a power that had been more crutch than blessing. She let go of the sounds and sights that confused and scared her.

And Lena lifted a hand that wasn't hers. She moved her legs, stretched her mouth open as wide as she could, and rolled her neck. She laughed and cried and doubled over as it all overwhelmed her.

"Missy…" Lena said with Missy's voice, Missy's lips. "This…. It's…"

Missy sent her love.

Lena stood up. She let go of the amplifier, gasping at the strange sensation as the telepathy weakened. She searched through the new muscles, touching on the minds of Plugger and Elliot as they slept nearby. Feeling them about to wake, feeling their gathering awareness of Mr. Keeps watching over them.

Tears of one body and two minds came free and heavy.

"I didn't think you… you're *amazing*." Lena choked the words out.

She reached up to wipe her face, then laughed at the fact that she could do so.

"So we'll… share?"

Missy sent her answer.

"No. No! You can't."

Missy shared the depth of her tiredness, of how she wasn't comfortable, pieces of all the things she'd seen and heard and read in thousands of minds.

"But…"

Missy showed her how much she wanted it to end.

Lena fell back down onto the bench, hands clenching and unclenching her lap. She let her head tilt to the side like she had when she was in her own body.

"You can't leave me."

Missy let her know how much she'd lost in the battle with the Others, how much had been torn out of her.

"No…."

The only response was the last piece of her: her trust in Lena, an all-encompassing knowledge that Lena would do it better. She would be the best.

"But Missy, I... I love you."

Then Missy let go. What was left of her drifted apart like a dandelion in the wind, fading away until it was a mere whisper of a memory.

\*\*\*

# Epilogue

The bowling alley was looking good.

Elliot was still riding the high from their adventure. It didn't matter that it had ended with a tranq dart in his neck, or that he still didn't understand half of what it was all about.

All he knew was that he'd been a part of something.

He'd spent the whole week telling everyone all about it. He called every friend and relative he knew. He used a handsaw to make drone noises for his Aunt Kathy while he built a set of drawers for the shoe rental counter. He'd rattled crates of beer to demonstrate the epic crash of the drone when he told the story to his former roommate.

He told them about Missy, and Two Town, and the crazy, purple pants that he had to fill.

And they all came to see it.

It had only been a week since everything had happened, but there was already a small, but steady, stream of customers coming in to drink and bowl and tell their friends and family about the crazy times they'd had in this place. They told them all about Two Town, back when it was the place to be if you were looking to cause a bit of trouble.

Plugger ended up closing his shop to work at the bar inside. When word got around that he was part of the original crew, even more people came. Old faces and older names dropped in to buy a bottle from their old friend, to catch up on what was and what wasn't.

Some even asked if he still had their old stuff in his shop and if he'd consider selling it back.

It was at the end of one of these days that the doors

opened and the small woman with the dark hair and scabs on the side of her head walked in.

"Missy!" Elliot shouted from behind the shoe counter. He'd been sorting the shoes to clean for tomorrow.

Plugger turned from his seat to watch her walk in. The outside light wasn't that bright, but it was enough to outline her body, to show how she moved.

"That's not Missy." He said with a finality that made Elliot turn to him with a questioning look.

"Missy told me you were sharp." Lena grabbed the chair beside Plugger and leaned over the counter. She flashed a wicked grin at Elliot, then turned and raised her eyebrows at the old bouncer in a way that might have made a younger man's heart stop for a second.

The two of them stared at her for a long moment

A moment which broke when she stuck her hand out toward Elliot.

"I'm Lena." She said as he slowly took the offered palm. "Missy kinda left me in charge, for now."

"Fucking hell." Plugger shook his head, "It never ends with you."

Lena gave an elaborate shrug, then nodded toward one of the beers sitting on the counter. "Got another?"

Elliot reached down to one of his newly-crafted drawers and pulled it open to reveal that there was a cooler hidden inside. He tossed her something from its contents.

Lena popped the cap and drained half of it one go, smacking her lips loudly after.

"Everything!" She exclaimed to the air above.

"What?"

"Nothin'" Lena smiled and waved it off. "Just something I said I'd do."

"Uh-huh."

"God, you're grumpy." Lena tilted her bottle up for another sip. "Fit, though. Missy had good taste."

Beer left Plugger's mouth in a plume and landed on the counter.

"You, though!" Lena spun on Elliot, "You seem fun. I'm getting good feelings off ya."

"I'll drink to that." Elliot lifted his beer, and they drank together as Plugger tried to stop choking.

"So…" Lena held the empty bottle by its still-wet top, she spun it so it rolled along on its bottom edge in circle after circle. "I know I have a lot to explain. It's been a crazy, crazy time."

Plugger grunted his agreement with that.

"But first… there's something I want to know." Lena's smile dropped from a high beam to a low simmer. "I figured you two would be the best source."

"Oh?"

"Yeah." Lena rubbed the healing scabs on the side of her head, "I want to know about Two Town."

Another bottle was passed her way and she left the scars behind to grab it.

"Tell me *everything*."

# THE END

# ABOUT THE AUTHOR

William D. Cornwell III has been writing for more than thirty years. He has a degree in Creative Writing from Ashland University and a degree in Psychology from the University of Dayton. His first story, The Bone Lord, was published in 2011. He lives in Dayton, Ohio with his parents and four spoiled cats.

# <u>MEDIA LINKS</u>

https://xacktar.wixsite.com/william-d--cornwell

https://www.goodreads.com/user/show/165661136-william-cornwell-iii

https://www.youtube.com/@xackwrites4635/